WAR FROM A DISTANT SUN

SAVAGE STARS BOOK 1

ANTHONY JAMES

CHAPTER ONE

IT SEEMED LIKE A CHANCE ENCOUNTER, out in the middle of nowhere.

The moment the *Finality*'s sensor officer reported the appearance of ternium particles two hundred thousand kilometres above planet Sarus-Q, Captain Carl Recker knew he was in trouble.

"Full alert," he ordered, slamming the control bars to the end of their runners.

The spaceship's immense propulsion grumbled with the strain of acceleration and Recker banked the *Finality* hard towards the only source of cover available - the planet a few thousand kilometres ahead.

"What've we got?" he snarled, already sure he wasn't going to like the answer. His gaze swept over the screens, status displays, touchpads and switches on the wrap-around command console in front of him. Numbers and text rolled upwards in an endless stream and his brain absorbed it all like second nature.

"Something bigger than we are," said Lieutenant Adam Burner. "Waiting on the sensor data analysis."

"Maybe we got lucky and it's an ore carrier," said Commander Daisy Aston from her station adjacent to Recker.

"Zero chance of that," grunted Lieutenant Ken Eastwood, not looking up from the engine panel. The bridge lighting was muted, and his face was illuminated in green from the console displays.

Recker knew it too and he gritted his teeth.

"Magnitude of the cloud suggests we've got an enemy destroyer inbound, sir," said Burner.

"Should've kept my mouth shut about that ore carrier," said Aston dryly.

"Dammit," said Recker. "It'll take fifteen minutes to load up our ternium drive, so we'll have to play the hand we've been dealt."

He kept one eye on the forward sensor feed. Sarus-Q was close to its sun and comparatively small, with a surface of molten iron and erupting gases. It was just the sort of place that might contain worthwhile quantities of ternium ore and numerous other metals the Human Planetary Alliance needed for its weapons factories. Not that it was a good time to call in a low-orbit dredger.

"We're not going to make it around the Sarus-Q curvature before that vessel enters local space," said Recker.

"Why do we always get the shit?" asked Burner.

"A question for later," snapped Recker. "Did you send the FTL comm?"

"Yes, sir. Six hours and it'll bounce off the closest relay. Another ten after that and it'll reach someone capable of making a decision. In two days, we might have backup."

The intel team on deep space monitoring station Quad 1 had picked up something out here. *Low probability of hostiles*, Recker remembered from the mission briefing. *Worth checking out*, Admiral Telar had said in the short meeting before departure. *Not enough of a lead to send anything other than a single riot class.*

The particle cloud reached its peak diameter and began to fade. At the same time, the inbound spaceship emerged from lightspeed, drifting slowly like always happened at the end of a jump.

"We've got a Daklan destroyer at 195 thousand klicks," confirmed Burner. "Looks new."

Recker swore under his breath and felt the sweat beading on his forehead. The moment you gave an old ship like the *Finality* anything like full power, the life support ran out of juice for the basics like crew comfort and hot air pumped in through the aft bulkhead vents, making the tiny bridge feel like a metal-lined sauna.

He breathed in the familiar scent of overstressed tech. "Put it up on the screen."

"Sensors locked. On the forward, sir."

The bridge forward bulkhead was a single curved screen, which could simultaneously display any combination of feeds from the warship's external or internal sensors. The central section updated to show a faintly shimmering outline of the Daklan spaceship.

Recker had seen plenty of ravager class destroyers and this one was noticeably different, with an aggressively tapered nose and a lower profile. The spaceship didn't exactly gleam in the normal sense of the word – hull alloys weren't reflective – but it seemed fresh and unmarked. The feed wasn't sharp enough for Recker to distinguish the destroyer's external armaments, but he could imagine them well enough: missile launchers and plenty of countermeasures.

"Nine hundred metres end to end and a billion-ton displacement," said Burner. "And as far as the Daklan fleet goes, it's a baby."

The *Finality* was totally outclassed - the riot class spaceships were the smallest lightspeed capable vessels in the navy. A bunch of them could handle a Daklan destroyer. Alone, they stood no chance. Or so it said in the rulebook.

If there was one thing Recker had learned in his eighteen years' service, it was that surprise could change anything.

He scanned the available data and took a gamble. "Commander Aston – target and fire the rear missile clusters."

"That's going to tell them exactly where we are, sir."

"Launch the missiles. We'll be around the planet's cusp before they obtain a lock."

"Yes, sir. Firing rear clusters one and two."

The *Finality*'s rear launchers were 250 metres back from the bridge, with most of the intervening distance being solid ternium. Even so, Recker heard – or sensed - the boom of detonating missile propulsions along with the faintest of vibrations through the alloy of the spaceship's control bars. The Ilstrom-5 missiles were more engine than anything else. A small payload but designed to reach their target quickly.

"Time to impact: 30 seconds. Missile clusters reloading," said Aston, her voice tight.

"Sixteen direct hits might not be enough," said Eastwood. He was the oldest of the crew, with grey hair and a gravel voice. "Not that we're going to land a quarter of that number."

Recker could feel the maddening prickle of day-old stubble, but he couldn't take his hands off the controls. "What's that destroyer doing, Lieutenant Burner?"

"Nothing yet, sir. Let's hope our sensor deflection keeps them guessing."

The velocity gauge climbed, and Sarus-Q occupied the entire forward feed. Recker did his best not to be distracted by the hostility of the planet and the sense he got that most of its surface was moving slowly, like an ocean of sullen red magma.

Burner gave the bad news. "They're coming for us, sir."

"Damn, that's a high output from their engines," said Eastwood. "Must be packing something bigger and better than what we're used to."

"Just our luck to run into a warship fresh out of the dock." Recker swore under his breath and watched the sixteen Ilstrom-5s racing across the tactical. "Come on, come on."

"We're not going to make around the curvature before they lock and fire," said Burner.

"Rear clusters reloaded, sir."

"Fire."

A second wave of missiles burst from their launch clusters – another sixteen green dots on the tactical display.

Light flashed on the bulkhead feed, telling Recker that the enemy ship had launched shock-pulse bombs to knock out the Ilstrom-5s. The single flash was followed by dozens more, laid out in a computer-determined pattern to maximise the chance of destroying the missiles. Amongst the shock-pulse bursts, Recker saw elongated streaks of hardened ternium slugs rip across the darkness of space, as the Daklan aimed their Graler turrets at the Ilstrom-5s.

One-by-one, the *Finality*'s missiles were pulverised, and they disappeared from the tactical until only a handful of the first wave remained in flight.

"Enemy missiles inbound," said Aston. "Twenty total. ETA, 40 seconds."

Recker had misjudged both the skill of the Daklan crew and the effectiveness of their hardware. Now he had to deal with his failing.

"Launch disruptors."

"Disruptors away."

A hundred tiny drones spilled from the *Finality*'s rear deployment tubes and their tiny single-burst engines hurled them towards the Daklan missiles. The drones emitted heat, light and ternium particles. Sometimes it was enough to fool the enemy guidance systems.

The *Finality* was travelling fast and – at an altitude of five hundred kilometres - Sarus-Q seemed close enough to touch. Overlays and projections from the spaceship's mainframe cluttered the tactical and Recker's mind combined them into a picture of the engagement. In a few seconds, the planet's curvature would break the enemy weapons lock, leaving only twenty Feilar homing missiles to deal with.

"The final two Ilstroms stopped transmitting right on top of the enemy vessel," said Aston. "I can't confirm impacts."

The second wave wasn't faring any better than the first and half were knocked out by enemy countermeasures before the missile transmissions were blocked by Sarus-Q. They dropped off the tactical along with the enemy destroyer.

"We're out of enemy sensor sight," said Recker. "Shame about those Feilars."

The enemy missiles maintained a lock on the *Finality* and they hurtled across the planet's surface.

"Disruptors away," said Aston. "Five Feilars taken out by our first drone deployment."

The Daklan fleet was armed with several types of missiles. The Feilars were the slowest and carried the smallest payload. Even so, Recker didn't want them testing the *Finality*'s armour.

"Railer chain gun hunting for a lock," said Aston.

"Spray and pray," muttered Burner.

Recker took the *Finality* lower. Sarus-Q didn't have much of an atmosphere, but the heat began to accumulate on the spaceship's nose. The underside feed was like a vision of hell – a grey-black ocean of semiliquid rock with areas of red and orange.

"Hull temps rising," said Eastwood.

"I know it, Lieutenant."

"The disruptors took out another four inbound missiles," said Aston. "Eleven to go."

A second later, the Railer got a target lock and a green light appeared on the weapons panel. The chain gun started up with a roar of pure savagery – like the perfection of metallurgy given its own voice.

Recker had once seen a recording in which the captain of a Teron class cruiser directed his vessel's Railers at the surface of an uninhabited vacuum world. The four underside weapons had smashed a vast, unbelievable hole in the side of a mountain. It was a brutal example of what could be achieved with a large calibre, an enormous rate of fire and a muzzle velocity of five thousand kilometres per second.

The *Finality* only had one Railer and it was smaller than the equivalent on a Teron class. That didn't mean it was inefficient. The weapon fired an extended burst and one of the Feilars vanished from the tactical. A split second for retargeting and the Railer discharged again.

"Nine left," said Aston. "Third wave of disruptors out."

"Nose temperature at two thousand degrees Centigrade," said Eastwood.

"That gives us another two thousand to play with, Lieutenant."

The *Finality*'s nose burned a fierce orange, but Recker didn't let up on the controls. He watched the Feilars closing on the tactical. They'd burn up before the spaceship in the atmospheric friction, but Recker didn't think he was going to have it that easy.

"Drones took out another three," said Aston.

She didn't need to remind anyone that the disruptors weren't so effective at short range. That left the Railer to do the cleaning up and the chain gun fired continuously, its motor and barrel temperatures climbing rapidly towards their design maximum.

With four Feilars still inbound, the Railer's in-built safety mechanisms shut the weapon down, leaving the bridge in a peculiar silence.

"Shit," said Burner.

The *Finality* was an agile craft, but evading missiles was an exercise in futility even if you timed it right. At the last moment, Recker threw the spaceship hard to port and he imagined the life support module fighting against the lateral forces. The muscles in his forearms strained and even the walls around him groaned under the stresses.

For a second, he thought he'd pulled off the improbable and made the Feilars overshoot. A glimpse of silver on the rear sensor feed told him he was wrong. Then, missiles struck the *Finality*.

CHAPTER TWO

TWIN DETONATIONS SENT a wave of vibration through the spaceship. On the bridge, the results of the missile strikes seemed muted, like a gentle collision heard from a place of safety.

Recker knew the reality. "Damage reports!" he barked. Several amber warnings and a couple of reds appeared on his command console, but he had to fly the damn spaceship and couldn't spare a moment to check the alerts out in detail.

"Two successful Feilar strikes on our rear plating," said Eastwood. "We've suffered engine damage and I'm checking the extent. No breach into the interior."

That last part at least was a relief. Like all warships, the *Finality* was mostly propulsion and weapons systems, with a limited central area given over to the crew. If a missile opened a hole into the interior, it usually meant the damage was terminal.

"An amber appeared on rear Ilstrom cluster #2," said Aston.

"Out of action?" asked Recker sharply. He didn't look up – the *Finality* wasn't responding like normal and it was taking all his focus to keep it steady.

Aston's expression was one of angry uncertainty. "I don't know."

"The monitoring tools don't tell you?"

"There's a fault on them too, sir."

"Do what you can to find out." Recker raised his voice. "Lieutenant Burner?"

"All sensor arrays operational, sir. I sent an FTL comm to base informing them of our engagement with a new Daklan warship."

"Hull temps at 2500 Centigrade," said Eastwood. "It might be time to pull up or slow down, sir."

Recker didn't want to do either. The Daklan were persistent and they didn't like to lose a target. The alien bastard piloting that destroyer would come looking for the *Finality* – that was not in doubt.

"I screwed up once and I'm not going to risk another engagement," he said. "Not yet anyway."

Already Recker's mind was working out the possibilities. The *Finality* had taken a couple of missile strikes, but the riot class was tougher than the sum of its parts. That's why the hull specifications hadn't been changed for about fifty years. At a few trillion feds each, riots were cheap to build, reliable and with a design that could be easily fitted out with new weaponry. They were a good way to increase fleet numbers and the best place for a newly promoted captain to prove his or her worth.

Or somewhere for Recker's enemies to show him that the past wasn't forgotten.

He shook away the distraction of memories and concentrated on the here and now. It was likely the Daklan vessel had suffered some damage from the *Finality*'s missiles, though Recker wasn't ready to push for a second confrontation. The mission documentation didn't require him to sacrifice his ship or his crew – he was meant to hunt for signs of the enemy and report in.

Clearly the intel team on DS-Quad1 hadn't expected him to run into a Daklan destroyer, else they'd have sent something with more firepower than the *Finality*. Maybe.

"I just had Sergeant Vance on the internal comms," said Burner. "He reports no casualties. I told him to hunker down and keep everything crossed."

The *Finality* wasn't a dedicated troop carrier, but it had a squad of soldiers stationed onboard in case they were required for any one of a hundred different reasons. Staff Sergeant James Vance and his fourteen soldiers were cooped up in their quarters aft. The internal alarms would make it clear the *Finality* was engaged, but they wouldn't know anything more.

Soldiers on a fleet spaceship generally had it rough and the smaller the spaceship, the rougher it got. Vance and his squad had been assigned to the *Finality* a couple of months ago and they were probably still cursing their luck. Recker knew from first-hand experience how it was, but he couldn't waste time on sympathy.

"Any news on the engines, Lieutenant Eastwood?" Recker asked.

"I've just finished querying the status monitors, sir. We've got a forty-metre hole, right through the plating."

"What's it done to the propulsion?"

"Some of our ternium drive got burned out." Eastwood blew air through his teeth. "Our maximum output is down six percent."

Recker picked up on Eastwood's concern. "We're leaving a particle trail?"

"Yes, sir. It's not a big trail – only a few hundred klicks long."

"Enough."

Eastwood nodded. "It'll make it easier for that destroyer to locate us."

"Can you stop the leak?"

"On anything bigger than the *Finality* I'd shut down the engine module."

"A riot class only has two."

"Yes, sir. Front and back. If I shut down one, we'll lose fifty percent of our sub-light capability and we won't be able to enter lightspeed at all."

Recker knew the score. "And once you shut down the module it might not come back online again."

"The odds of getting it restarted aren't good. Not until we return to the shipyard."

"We could shut down the aft module and lay low, sir," said Burner. "Four days and we could see some backup."

Aston wasn't buying it. "That's a long time to play cat and mouse."

"Sarus-Q is the nearest planet to the Virar-12 star," mused Recker. "The second planet is 160 million klicks from here."

"A hard run in the circumstances," said Aston.

"And if they're watching out, they'll detect the particles in plenty of time to come find us," said Eastwood. "Unless we shut down the aft module."

Recker called for silence. "I'm aware of the options," he said, watching the hull temperature creep past 2800 Centigrade. The outer plating had a melting point of 4300C, but the Daklan missile strikes had exposed some of the solid state ternium drive and that wasn't so resistant to high temperatures. Not only that, the *Finality* was travelling fast enough that it would soon complete a circuit of the planet. The Daklan captain might well have stayed put to see if Recker would save him the effort of giving chase.

"Sarus-Q is between the Daklan vessel and the second planet," he said. "Lucky for us – that should make it harder for them to see where we're going."

"According to the database, someone named the place Rilar," said Burner.

"Should I shut down the aft module?" asked Eastwood.

"We either get seen because we're going too slow or we get seen because of our particle trail." Recker wanted to ease the tension in his muscles but he couldn't release the controls for even a moment. "If it's going to happen, I don't want to be waiting for it."

"In that case, I'll leave the aft module online, sir."

"I've added a course overlay for Rilar," said Burner. "I've made it a slightly divergent route so that we aren't too predictable."

Burner didn't take many things seriously but underneath the veneer, he was one of the best sensor operators in the fleet – wasted on the *Finality*. There again, anyone associated with Recker tended to find their careers stalled.

"Thank you, Lieutenant." Recker took a deep breath and waited for the right moment. "Here we go."

He turned the controls and drew them towards him. The spaceship lifted away from Sarus-Q and, the moment it was free of the atmosphere, Recker fed in the power. The *Finality* was responding differently after the missile impacts, though he'd flown long enough that it was simple to adjust.

The engines grumbled at first and their note gradually increased in pitch, becoming something closer to a harsh growl. Recker closed his eyes, losing himself in the sound for the briefest of moments. For twenty or thirty seconds, Sarus-Q was the only thing visible on the rear feeds. Then the edges became visible and the planet dwindled in the *Finality*'s wake.

"No sign of the enemy," said Burner.

"They've got plenty of time," said Eastwood. "That particle trail will bring them straight to us, assuming they know how to run a basic wide-area sweep."

"Maybe we blew a hole in them and they're heading in the other direction," said Aston. Her expression was neutral, but her eyes were full of cynical humour.

Recker didn't reply and wiped his forehead, leaving a gleaming patch of sweat on the back of his hand. "What I wouldn't give for a cold beer."

"Still clear on the sensors," said Burner.

The *Finality*'s velocity gauge kept on climbing and the spaceship approached its maximum sub-light speed. Recker's eyes darted from place to place, making sure he kept the vessel glued to the route line on the navigational screen. The course projection had the *Finality* heading for a waypoint positioned on a direct line between Sarus-Q and the Virar-12 star, to throw off the Daklan spaceship if it was following. After the waypoint, Recker would adjust onto an intercept course with Rilar as the planet sped along its orbital track.

"We could still shut off the engine module, sir," said Aston. "Coast through the vacuum for the rest of the journey."

Recker was torn. The destroyer was faster than the *Finality* and if it detected the fleeing vessel, could overhaul it before Rilar. If that happened, Recker would much prefer to have the additional flexibility which came from having both propulsion modules operational. He drummed his fingers in thought.

"Sir?" It was Burner and he sounded agitated.

"What is it?" asked Recker, expecting to hear that the enemy ship was confirmed in pursuit. It was something different.

"I've received a comm message direct from Admiral Telar, sir. He must have sent it hours ago and it just reached us."

Recker's intuition was being put through its paces today and it set alarm bells ringing in his head. "Tell me."

"Seems like the guys on DS-Quad1 didn't stop looking after we started our trip out here. They've located an anomaly on the fifth planet – a place called Etrol."

"What kind of anomaly?"

"They have no further data. We're instructed to complete a full scan and report back. Priority 1."

"Priority 1 and they don't have any data?" Recker felt his calmness eroding.

"No, sir."

"Admiral Telar doesn't know what we've run into," said Recker. He swore.

"They can't order suicide," said Aston quietly.

She was only half-right and if Recker decided to ignore the Priority 1 in favour of his crew's safety, he'd be dragged upside down and backwards over the coals once the *Finality* returned to base – whatever justification he presented. Not that the threat would stop him from doing the right thing.

"We're losing this war, Commander," he said.

The words were enough for Aston and she shrugged in resignation. "They reckon the Daklan will find one of our planets within the next twelve months," she said. "The odds went past fifty percent."

"Which means the frontline can't take the easy way out every time," said Recker.

Aston smiled. "Not any time."

"Let's check out that anomaly."

"Want me to calculate a new course, sir?" asked Burner. "Or are we sticking with Plan A and taking cover behind Rilar for a while?"

Recker called up the planetary data on the Virar-12 system. The HPA deep space monitoring stations had mapped the planets and their orbital tracks, which gave enough information to plot a course without the *Finality* having to undertake extensive scanning of the solar system.

"Etrol is 900 million klicks from our current position," he said.

"That's 13600 minutes sub-light travel at our maximum velocity," said Eastwood. "A little more with our reduced engine power."

"More than nine days," said Aston. "Admiral Telar might have something to say if we keep him waiting that long. He could have a fleet out here in two days if he wanted."

"A Priority 1 with no backup data," said Recker. "There's more to this than we're being told." He grimaced. It was an old joke that high command acted without logic, but this was different. Telar had wind of something and, given the war situation, he'd be desperate for answers.

"If the enemy destroyer stayed looking for us on Sarus-Q, we'll be out of detection range by now," said Recker. "Do you agree, Lieutenant Eastwood?"

"Yes, sir. Unless they happen to be looking directly at us. I guess you're thinking of a lightspeed jump. The particle cloud from that will be more visible than the trail we're leaving now."

"Except the propulsion doesn't throw out the extra particles until we enter lightspeed. We'll be gone by the time the enemy detect it."

"Assuming they find it at all," said Eastwood.

Recker felt the weight of the inevitable pressing against him. "The game's changed. This isn't about escaping anymore – now we've got to find out what kind of intel was enough for Admiral Telar to issue a Priority 1."

"Is that an order to warm up the lightspeed drive, sir?" asked Eastwood. "We can't accurately target the arrival place when we're already moving."

Entering lightspeed took everything from the ternium drive, meaning it couldn't be under stress while the navigational computer worked on the maths. Since the *Finality* was already coasting, the engines could be cut and it would continue drifting through space. Unfortunately, that made it impossible for the mainframe to target an exact destination. The further the jump, the less accurately a coasting spaceship's hardware could predict where it would exit lightspeed.

The computer was programmed to work around the issue using *fuzzy algorithmic compensation* as they called it in the research labs. Someone had once tried to explain the basics to Recker and he'd got lost after about five seconds.

"I don't want to slow down and I don't want to arrive too close to Etrol. Aim for a place three million klicks out. That should keep us safe from immediate detection and give us an opportunity to build up a picture of what we're facing."

"Roger that, sir," said Eastwood. "Aiming for three million klicks above Etrol. Estimated margin of error over that distance at our current speed is ten percent."

Eastwood put in the coordinates and the warmup routine automatically reduced engine power to a fraction above zero. The comforting background hum fell away, leaving Recker with a strange sense of loss.

He flexed his shoulders, though the tension in his muscles remained. With the engine modules at idle, the air conditioning blew cold again and a waft of overchilled air played across his short hair, drying the sweat on his scalp and face.

"Ten minutes until departure," said Eastwood.

Recker tried to get comfortable but his brain was working overtime. The Priority 1 might be the result of a bad call from the team on DS-Quad1. It might turn out to be nothing at all. Somehow, he didn't think so.

The comm from Admiral Telar also made him wonder if the encounter with the Daklan destroyer was the result of more than chance. Maybe the enemy was busy in this solar system. Recker accessed the star charts. The *Finality* was at the extremes of HPA Quadrant 1. No-one knew the location of the Daklan home worlds, the same way as the aliens didn't know how to find humanity's population centres.

Out on the fringes it was tough, and every mission was potentially deadly. Both species wanted the same resources and the Daklan were ruthless whenever they came across a human spaceship or outpost. The HPA navy was badly stretched, while the enemy seemed to keep coming with bigger numbers.

Something was going to give and soon.

"Five minutes on the ternium drive warmup," said Eastwood.

"I've located the destroyer," said Burner. "Heading straight for us."

"Time to intercept?"

"Five minutes."

"For a scouting mission this is turning into real big steaming mound of crap," said Eastwood.

"Don't I know it," Recker replied sourly. "Commander Aston, have you finished the calcs on their launch range and missile travel time?"

"Yes, sir. At our current velocities, the enemy will have a single launch window."

"Twenty missiles."

"No, sir. Sixty missiles. They've got time to swing around and show us their flank."

"Way too many for a single Railer and a few waves of disruptors. Will those missiles reach us before we enter lightspeed?"

"Too close to call, sir. As you know, there's a chance for variation in the lightspeed calcs."

"And all we can do is wait and watch it happen."

"Yes, sir. The Daklan missiles will lock at a greater range than our Ilstroms. We won't even get a shot at them."

Nobody said anything to that. Space combat was defined by moments like these. Some people beat the odds dozens of times, but for every one of those, another thousand or more personnel got vaporised by Daklan explosives.

"Why are we always one step behind?" said Burner. His voice sounded calm, though Recker could detect the undercurrents bordering on fear.

"Steady, Lieutenant."

"I'm steady, sir. Here's the bastard on the rear feed."

The Daklan warship was so far away that it showed as little more than a grey blob against the darkness. Burner did what he could to improve the image, though Recker suspected the gradually increasing clarity was more a result of the speed at which the destroyer closed the gap.

"Faster than I thought," said Eastwood. "Twenty percent up on any other destroyer we've encountered."

It was sobering to hear. The Daklan weren't only building warships in greater numbers than the Human Planetary Alliance, their war tech was also advancing at a greater rate. Add the two together and it was storing up some bad news for the near future.

Worse yet, the Representation hadn't called total war and military funding was still under restraint. It was easy to pretend there wasn't a problem when most of the conflict happened a few thousand light years away from your marble-walled house and manicured lawns.

Recker normally swallowed the anger which inevitably came when he thought about politics. This time, he embraced it as a distraction from the coming enemy.

"Enemy launch window coming up," said Aston.

"They're swinging around," said Burner.

The feed was clear enough for Recker to see it happen. In a few seconds, the destroyer turned so that its flank was visible.

"Missile launch detected. Sixty warheads coming our way."

"Screw them," said Burner.

"Deploy the disruptors," said Recker. "For all the good they'll do."

"First disruptors gone, sir."

The ammunition readout on one of Recker's screen updated to show the remaining quantity of disruptor drones.

"Down to sixty percent of capacity," he said.

"The *Finality* wasn't built for an extended engagement," said Aston. "I can hold the next launch and hope we enter lightspeed before those missiles arrive."

"I'd rather die with an empty magazine than a half-full one."

"You and me both, sir. Next wave of disruptors gone."

Seconds passed and the Feilar missiles came after the *Finality*. A few were destroyed by the first wave of disruptors and more by the second wave. It wasn't enough.

Lieutenant Eastwood began a countdown at thirty seconds to lightspeed. At fifteen seconds, the Railer locked and fired, the weapons discharge the loudest sound on the bridge. Eastwood raised his voice to be heard over it.

"Ten seconds."

"Disruptors away."

All Recker could do was await the outcome, his influence reduced to zero. Without power from the engines, he couldn't even try a last-second evasive manoeuvre.

"Five seconds."

"Forty-one missiles remaining."

"Three..."

The red dots on the tactical were so close to the central green dot representing the *Finality* that Recker couldn't see how they'd fail to impact.

"Two..."

"Shit."

The lightspeed calculations finished half a second early and the *Finality* launched into its jump.

CHAPTER THREE

THE TRANSITION MADE Recker feel like he'd been beaten with a dozen rubber hoses. He didn't have time to welcome the pain. Less than a second after entering light-speed, the *Finality*'s ternium drive cut out, dumping the spaceship once again into local space and subjecting the crew to a second round of agony long before the first had faded.

In-out jumps were always the worst and Recker clenched his jaw to stop himself from groaning. The other crew members weren't so restrained and Burner unleashed a stream of obscenities aimed at the Daklan and the universe in general.

"Status report!" shouted Recker, more angrily than he meant.

The harshness in his voice did the trick and the complaints dried up.

"Scans commencing," said Burner.

Recker's half-blurred vision cleared and he stared at

his console. The instrumentation hadn't settled yet and the readouts were all over the place. He looked up just as the sensor arrays recalibrated after their time at lightspeed. The bulkhead screen was covered in darkness and stars, just like he expected.

"No additional damage to our hull, so those Feilars didn't hit us," said Eastwood. "We got lucky."

"We'd be dead if they hit us," said Aston. She had her face close to her console and her expression still held an echo of pain from the lightspeed jump. "Twenty klicks," she said. "Our sensors stopped tracking the Feilars at twenty klicks."

"Damn," said Eastwood. He sounded stunned by the hair-thin margin. "That's the closest yet."

"Let's not talk about it," said Recker. "We've got a job to do."

"Near scan finished," said Burner. "I've got Etrol on the underside array, at three-point-two million klicks."

"Let's see it."

"Not much to look at."

The central section of the bulkhead screen filled with a sphere of mixed greys. One half of the planet was in darkness and the image intensifiers turned that side into a different shade to the other. It was too soon to tell what imperfections were represented by the other varying hues – usually on a rock like this Recker expected to find craters, mountains and other signs of billion-year-old catastrophic upheaval. The universe was hard on its children.

"Diameter, sixteen thousand klicks," said Aston. "Cold and old."

"Lieutenant Burner's going to have his hands full," said Eastwood.

"I can help out," said Aston. "I worked sensors for three years."

"And then someone offered you a promotion. Only trouble being it was on the *Finality*," laughed Recker.

"No regrets, sir."

"I've expanded the local area scan sweep and still nothing," said Burner.

The further out you looked, the exponentially harder it became to locate and identify objects or spaceships. The *Finality* wasn't exactly packing old hardware, but neither was it the newest kit. It also wasn't fitted with as many sensor arrays as a larger warship and the mainframe which processed the data wasn't a fraction as quick as the cores they were installing on the most recent cruisers and battleships.

"Commander Aston will take over the area sweeps. Lieutenant Burner, concentrate on the planet. If there's something on the visible side, I want to find it."

"Yes, sir. I recommend we approach to an altitude of one hundred thousand klicks. If the surface isn't too broken and what we're looking for isn't small or hidden, I should be able to locate it in one or two circuits."

If the Daklan had installed any halfway sophisticated detection tech on the ground, the *Finality* would be vulnerable at that distance. It was a matter of balancing speed and thoroughness against safety.

"A hundred thousand klicks it is, Lieutenant," said Recker, after giving it some consideration. "Let's aim for one sweep."

"And not too fast, sir."

Recker knew the routine, though he didn't much like it. "Not too fast," he confirmed. "Commander Aston, you'll need to juggle weapons and local area sweeps once we get closer."

"Yes, sir."

"Let's get on with it."

With a deep breath, Recker fed power into the ternium drive and the *Finality* sped towards the planet. The nav comp indicated it was a fifty-five-minute journey once acceleration and deceleration were taken into account. In the scheme of things, it wasn't long, but Recker was tight like a spring and his mouth was dry from the alternating hot and cold air on the bridge. He found himself suddenly desperate for a drink.

Before he could deal with the physical requirements of his body, Recker had another duty to perform. He was feeling shitty that he'd kept Sergeant Vance in the dark for so long. The internal comms indicated the soldier was in one of the spaceship's two small bunk rooms and Recker opened a channel.

"Sergeant Vance," he said.

"Sir," growled Vance. The man was built like a wrought-iron Daklan shithouse and had a voice that suggested he chewed live rounds for pleasure.

"We're on the run from a Daklan destroyer and we're spilling ternium particles," said Recker. "And our mission's not over yet."

Vance gave a rumbling laugh. "It's never over until the landing feet touch solid ground, sir."

"We're on a Priority 1 now, Sergeant." Recker didn't

need to disclose the details of the mission, though there was nothing preventing him doing so if that's what he decided. He'd encountered plenty of COs who took pleasure in keeping everything under lock and key, and Recker wasn't going to be one of them. "Deep Space Quad1 found something that's got high command interested and we're the only warship close enough to find out what it is."

"Sounds easy." Another laugh.

"Like you said, Sergeant. Once the landing feet hit solid, that's when we can congratulate ourselves."

Recker cut the channel and briefly checked his console. Everything was holding stable after the Daklan missile strikes and if it wasn't for the cone of ternium particles they were leaving behind, he'd have felt comfortable with the operational status of the warship.

"Commander Aston, watch the controls for me."

"Yes, sir."

He handed off to Aston and got to his feet, stretching and feeling his joints crackle.

The food replicator was installed in the rear-left corner and Recker stepped between Burner and Eastwood's identical consoles. The two men performed entirely different functions, but the HPA tech was made to be flexible. Almost everything ran on the same back-end software which had been developed to such a state of reliability that Recker couldn't recall having to deal with a failure in the last five or more years.

Eastwood met his eye and nodded when Recker walked past. Meanwhile, Lieutenant Burner was too engrossed in the sensor data to look up. A half-empty cup of cold black coffee balanced precariously on the edge of his console. The tech was purportedly sealed against liquid ingress, though Recker didn't want to put it to the test. He picked up the hard-plastic cup.

"Thank you, sir," said Burner absently.

It was tight on most warship bridges and a riot class was the worst of all. Six paces from his foam-padded seat, Recker was at the square blast door which kept this area sealed off from the rest of the warship's interior. Four paces left from there and he was at the replicator.

Once he'd dropped Burner's cup into the waste tube, Recker studied the device. A single touchscreen with green text allowed hungry or thirsty personnel to select from variety of nutritionally balanced meals and drinks. It was an ongoing joke that it didn't matter what you chose, the result would look and taste like every other option. As with most legends, this one contained an element of truth.

Recker wasn't hungry and he stabbed his finger at the *water* button. The replicator whirred softly and a cup of cool water appeared, which he drained in one. Temptation got the better of restraint and Recker ordered a coffee, no milk and no sugar. The HPA's standard caffeine-shaming banner appeared on the screen warning him of the dangers of elevated blood pressure and low-level addiction, alongside a number he could call if he needed help with either.

The nannying pissed Recker off every time he saw it. "This is a damned warship," he swore, pushing the on-screen cross to close the banner. The message disappeared and his drink appeared. A scent that was partially reminiscent of real coffee came to his nostrils.

"Not even worth getting angry over," he muttered,

wrapping his fingers around the cup. Recker turned from the machine. "How're the scans, Lieutenant Burner?"

"Nothing so far, sir. Etrol's just a place like a gazillion others. Thin atmosphere, freezing by day and colder at night. Surface rocks and formations that have almost zero percent chance of yielding any usable ores. We're too far for me to give you anything more specific at the moment."

"A shit from the asshole of the universe," said Eastwood with real feeling.

"I thought you'd been taking positivity classes," said Aston, keeping her face straight.

"Chance would be a fine thing, Commander. If I didn't carry a photograph, I'd forget what my wife and children look like. You think I have time between flights for anything else?"

The missions had been coming nonstop lately. Usually a spaceship crew would spend a month on patrol, followed by a couple of weeks on the ground. Lately, the *Finality* had been landing for a re-arm and a maintenance once-over before being ordered somewhere else. The spaceship was long overdue a thorough strip-down.

For a time, Recker had thought his crew had been singled out for extra duty and he'd made some enquiries. It turned out every ship in the fleet was being served the same crap and it had him worried. Fleet personnel talked and most knew that the war situation was bad. Recker was beginning to wonder if it was worse than high command was letting on.

He made a mental note to wring some answers out of Admiral Telar next time he saw the man. For now, the mission wasn't going to complete itself and Recker returned to his seat. A sip of the coffee made him wonder why he'd bothered, and he grimaced at the taste. The knowing grin on Aston's face didn't help his mood and he put the cup to one side.

"I've got the controls, Commander."

"Sir."

With the *Finality* approaching Etrol, Recker prepared himself. It was easy to succumb to wandering attention when travelling from place to place. The engine note and the way the vastness of space distorted the visual clues of movement somehow conspired to lull the brain into a state of relaxation – assuming you were inexperienced enough to let it happen.

"Half a million klicks to Etrol," said Burner.

"Plenty of time," said Recker. "Have you detected anything on the approach?"

"Negative, sir. We're only just coming into range where the sensors will have a reliable chance of finding anything useful to us."

"What are the conditions like for the search?"

"No better or worse than any other place, sir. Mountains, canyons, that kind of crap. If the Daklan have an installation on the visible side of the planet I might pick it up from here, but if we aren't about to rely on chance then it's going to require a full scan."

"Keep on it."

"Yes, sir."

"What if the enemy have camouflaged their presence?" asked Eastwood.

"I don't think it's likely, Lieutenant," said Recker. "If

there's an enemy base here, I doubt the Daklan have gone to the trouble of concealing it."

"Yeah, with a few hundred million planets to hide on, you rely on numerical improbability to keep you safe," said Aston.

"Even so, here we are," said Recker. "Our deep space monitoring stations make the universe a little smaller each time the tech guys come up with a new sensor array design."

"One way or the other our ships keep meeting their ships," said Burner.

"We're chasing the same resources," said Recker impatiently. It was old news and he didn't want to listen to another discussion on the background of the war. "What's done is done," he said.

"LIKE YOU SAY," agreed Burner with a shrug. "Anyway, I've sent two new vectors to the nav comp, sir. Either one will take us around the planet and allow me to scan the entire surface. Take your pick."

Recker spent a moment studying the options. The first course would take the *Finality* over the planet's geographic north pole, while the second headed in the opposite direction. Recker chose north and altered the spaceship's course onto the new trajectory. At the same time, he hauled back on the control bars. They slid towards him with just the right amount of resistance and the *Finality*'s velocity gauge tumbled.

"Two hundred thousand klicks," announced Burner.

"Get ready, folks," said Recker. "If there's anything

down there, it's likely to be fitted with military grade sensor tech. If that destroyer issued a warning, they'll know we're coming."

At an altitude of a hundred thousand kilometres, Recker levelled out and stuck to the vector. The *Finality* was travelling at what felt like a crawl and his instincts urged him to go faster and get this done as soon as possible. He ignored the whispering voice – surface scanning required patience and care, assuming you valued accuracy.

A glance at the underside sensor feed told him the expected story – Etrol was a bleak, harsh world, cracked and torn by five billion years of unkind history.

"I've updated the vector," said Burner.

"Seventy thousand klicks altitude?" asked Recker sharply.

"Either that or we reduce speed further. This place is like a patchwork quilt of the tricky stuff they throw at rookies in training."

Recker bit his tongue and reduced altitude. His skin felt tight, like his body was pumping adrenaline or the replicator had fired a quadruple shot of espresso into his coffee.

For the next ten minutes, he held course. Every few seconds, Lieutenant Burner would provide an update, though all he turned up was rocks. The tension built on the bridge and Recker wasn't blinkered enough to deny that he was feeling it too. This was how war could be sometimes and handling the threat of the unknown was a test of mental strength.

"Can you estimate a time to completion, Lieutenant?" Recker asked after another ten minutes.

"Three hours, sir."

Admiral Telar was probably expecting results yesterday, but Recker had a duty to keep his crew and soldiers alive, and to let them do their jobs without him yelling at them every few minutes.

For a while, nobody spoke. Aston and Burner kept their eyes on the sensors, hunting for danger or for clues as to what had got the operators on DS-Quad1 so interested. For once, Recker was more of a spectator and he watched the sensor feeds, hoping they would give him a feel for what lay ahead. For once, his intuition was keeping its head down and the adrenaline chill subsided.

Gradually, the *Finality*'s path revealed more of the planet. The altitude of seventy thousand klicks was enough for Burner to scan with confidence, or at least he didn't say otherwise. So far, the results weren't inspiring.

"Rocks and more rocks," Burner said, as the *Finality* crossed over the planet's north pole.

"That's the best description you've got?" asked Eastwood.

"Okay, lots of big rocks and a huge mountain range," Burner replied. "Canyons that make anything on Earth look like a pencil line on a piece of paper."

Recker was watching the same thing and could only agree with the assessment. With the sensors on maximum zoom, the mountains looked jagged and angry like a badly healed scar. One side of the range was in stark, bright sunlight, while the other was in near darkness, with long shadows that extended for dozens of kilometres.

In one area, a vast fissure ran crossways to the range, splitting several of the largest peaks right across the middle and making Recker stare in wonder.

"Like someone took an axe to the place," he said.

"Hell of a big axe," Aston agreed.

"We've got no records of the Daklan building anything in terrain like this," said Recker. He checked one of the other feeds - the mountain range continued over the planet's curvature and out of sight.

"It's all got to be scanned, sir," said Burner. "You know I'm a perfectionist."

Eastwood cleared his throat loudly but said nothing.

"I'll maintain course, Lieutenant," said Recker.

"If there's something in these mountains, we might need a second sweep," Burner admitted a few seconds later.

Recker twisted in his seat. "You told me seventy thousand klicks altitude would be enough."

"I'm sure Admiral Telar is expecting to find Daklan, sir. If so, they won't be in these mountains – just like you said. If they're out in the open, one sweep will do it."

The flight continued without Burner locating anything unusual on the surface. Recker didn't much like boredom, but on balance it was preferable to being shot at by a superior foe. His agitation returned – Priority 1s weren't thrown about like confetti and Telar would have been obliged to notify other members of high command when he generated the mission briefing for this one.

Of course, if high command thought the Daklan were out here on Etrol there was an excellent chance that numerous fleet warships were already inbound. It was a shame the comm from Telar hadn't given Recker any details. He gritted his teeth at being left in the dark, though it was entirely possible that the admiral hadn't been in possession of any more information at the time of transmission.

"Ternium particles detected on the far side of Etrol," said Burner, cool as you like. "Something's about to join us in orbit."

The sensors couldn't see through solid objects, but ternium had different properties to every other known substance. Even so, it was an excellent spot.

"What does the cloud modelling say?" asked Recker. It didn't take a genius to know the answer.

"It's the Daklan destroyer, sir. Either that or an identical model come from somewhere else."

"Bad news but good work, Lieutenant."

"Any other day and I'd have missed it, sir."

It wasn't the kind of development Recker wanted. Already it seemed like the enemy ship was determined to show up everywhere it wasn't wanted, like the proverbial bad penny. He slowed the *Finality* even further, to buy himself some time to think.

"Are you able to pinpoint its location and manually add it to the tactical?"

"It's not going to be accurate, sir, but here you go."

On the tactical, the planet was represented by a semi-transparent rotating sphere and the red dot of the Daklan spaceship was at a similar altitude to the *Finality* and a few thousand klicks ahead. Additional overlays indicated the positional margin of error. On its existing course, the *Finality* would have come perilously near to the enemy ship and Recker didn't want to imagine the outcome of an unexpected engagement.

"We haven't scanned that area of Etrol yet," said Aston.

Recker understood the implication. "Maybe they targeted their arrival at the location of their facility. Or whatever the hell it is we're looking for."

"And now our chances of taking a look without being blown to pieces are significantly lower."

"What next, sir?" asked Burner. "We have no data to create a predictive model of that destroyer's movements."

"I know, Lieutenant."

Recker tapped his fingertips on the edge of his console as he considered the situation. If the enemy captain had decided that the *Finality* was gone from the Virar-12 system, the destroyer would probably remain stationary over Etrol. Maybe. Or the unproven Daklan surface facilities might have pulled off a thousand-to-one chance and detected the *Finality*'s exit from lightspeed, in which case the destroyer would come hunting. This time it might not be alone, if the Daklan had other warships stationed here.

The possibilities whirled around in his head and Recker caught Aston watching him expectantly.

"Too much to guess, Commander," he said with a short laugh. "If you fear the fog of war, it'll kill you every time."

"So I'm told, sir." Aston's stare didn't waver.

"I've got a plan."

Now she smiled. "What're the orders?"

He returned a smile of his own. "We've lost control,

through no fault of our own. Let's finish this and get out of here."

Aston understood at once what he meant and she nodded. "Death or victory."

"No death, only victory," he corrected her.

CHAPTER FOUR

RECKER'S PLAN wasn't elaborate, but he hoped it would be effective. The arrival of the enemy destroyer meant the slow and steady approach was no longer viable and, in such circumstances, the only answer was to go to the opposite extreme.

"I'm taking a gamble, folks," Recker said. Time was tight and he talked quickly. "If the captain of that destroyer believes we came to Etrol, he'll have taken his spaceship straight to the place he doesn't want us to find."

"Giving the game away," said Aston.

"And if he doesn't think we're here, he'll have gone to the same place anyway," said Eastwood.

"That's how I look at it," Recker agreed. "What we're going to do is fly in low and fast along the edge of the mountain range. Lieutenant Burner reckons the destroyer arrived at a ninety thousand klick altitude, so it's going to see us if the sensor crew are on their toes. What we're hoping is that they're looking upwards, rather than towards the surface. If this works, we'll fly straight underneath without being spotted, scan their facility and get the hell away."

"If it fails, we're dodging missiles," said Burner.

"We'll handle whatever comes our way, Lieutenant." Recker called up one of the sensor feeds, which showed the edge of the mountain range directly beneath the spaceship. "If we find something, you'll need to get the word out to base before we're turned into a fireball by enemy warheads."

"Any chance we're getting some help at any time?" asked Eastwood.

"I don't know," Recker admitted.

"Admiral Telar wouldn't hold back useful intel just to screw with you?" said Aston.

Recker hesitated. "Not Admiral Telar. Even if it was someone else pulling the strings of this mission, it wouldn't happen. Not here. Not on a Priority 1."

"So why the lack of comms from base?"

The most likely answer didn't bear thinking about. "Maybe every warship is committed elsewhere," said Recker. "Maybe we've only got scraps left that can come to Etrol. Warships that take hours to reach with an FTL comm."

"Are you aware of any big plans that might leave our fleet with nothing available, sir?" asked Aston.

Recker had some connections. "I get to hear things once in a while, that's all. And I didn't hear anything about this."

"In that case it's not happening," Aston said firmly.

"Which means that backup's either a long way off or it's not coming."

"It doesn't matter much either way," said Recker. "We're not waiting to find out. Does everyone know what's expected?"

When the crew had spoken their agreement, he readied himself. The course overlay was a green line across his navigational screen and he hardly needed to glance at it.

With steady hands, he slid the control bars to the end of their runners and the *Finality* entered a steep dive. The forward feed showed nothing but greys which soon resolved into the jagged lines of the central mountain range as the spaceship gathered speed. Seconds passed and Recker didn't let up. The howling propulsion filled the bridge and a vibration from the controls entered his palms.

"Atmospheric friction, sir," Aston reminded him.

"And mountains," said Burner.

"I know. Find that destroyer."

"On it, sir."

At the last moment, Recker hauled the controls towards him and the *Finality* levelled out. Etrol's atmosphere wasn't dense and only extended to an altitude of eighty kilometres. With the engines grumbling and the hull shaking under deceleration, the spaceship skimmed the upper reaches of the atmosphere and the temperature of the armour plates increased.

At this height there was little worry about burning up, but Recker reduced altitude further and the altimeter fell to fifty klicks and then thirty. Here, the atmosphere was denser, and the heat accumulated, clinging to the nose section and setting off high level alerts on the instrumentation.

"Some of those peaks are pretty high," said Burner. "Average height, seventeen thousand metres."

"I'm not planning to hit them, Lieutenant. Where's that destroyer?"

"Still looking, sir. It could have moved on."

"I'm not convinced."

"Me either. If it's there, I'll find it."

At an altitude of twenty-five thousand metres, Recker held the spaceship level. Incredibly, some of the mountaintops were higher still – vast broad-bladed spears of rock - and he was required to bank left and right to avoid them. Still the hull temperature climbed, and the forward sensor feed's dedicated processor was nailed on a hundred percent as it filtered out the visual distortion from the burning heat.

Nobody spoke and Recker felt the muscles in his forearms beginning to ache. He was holding too tightly, and it took an effort to lessen his grip on the controls. Information from a dozen or more sources vied for his attention, while the rough terrain raced by in a blur. Another of the colossal peaks came up ahead, this one towering almost thirty thousand metres.

With fast reflexes, Recker guided the *Finality* around the peak and found another one directly ahead. He banked again and lifted the nose, reluctant to reduce the spaceship's velocity by even a fraction. Rock and alloy almost met and Recker gritted his teeth at the margins.

"Missed that one by an easy two hundred metres," said Burner.

"Watch the skies, Lieutenant," snapped Recker. "I'll deal with this."

"Yes, sir. Eight hundred klicks and then we're directly under the most likely arrival position of the enemy destroyer."

The distance counter flew downwards and Recker wondered what the hell they were going to find here on Etrol. He asked himself if the lenses on DS-Quad1 had picked up a false positive, or maybe there was some dense metal ore which had flagged up as a Daklan base. Errors happened, though not often enough for him to believe this was one of them. The presence of the destroyer was solid evidence that the Daklan were up to something out here.

"Five hundred klicks."

"Where's that damned destroyer?"

"Still no sensor lock, sir."

Recker didn't like the unexplained. In theory, it should have been straightforward to locate a spaceship at ninety thousand klicks and Burner didn't usually make mistakes.

He swore in realization. "What if it set down behind these mountains?"

"That would do it," said Burner, his voice indicating his horror at overlooking the possibility.

"If that's the case, we won't be able to see them, but they'll sure as hell be able to detect those ternium particles we're leaving behind," said Eastwood.

It was like the enemy had been waiting for light to dawn in Recker's head before they acted.

"Oh shit," said Burner. "Daklan warship at six

hundred klicks, rising straight up from behind the mountains."

Aston acted with incredible speed. "Ilstroms locked. Firing."

The thumping sound of sixteen missiles launching from the forward tubes momentarily overcame everything else. Orange specks of their propulsion appeared on the feed and then vanished over the horizon. Recker wasn't watching. His brain evaluated the available data and his hands threw the *Finality* lower into the mountains.

Sheer rock faces rose on both sides and the spaceship entered a craggy, boulder-strewn canyon that twisted between the peaks. At the current speed it was hard for Recker to maintain control and he was forced to back off to give his reactions a few extra milliseconds.

The enemy warship was at such a low altitude that its firing angle was cut out and he hoped he'd been in time to prevent it obtaining a weapons lock.

No such luck.

"They got off a salvo," said Aston. "Twenty coming our way. Disruptors out."

Drones ejected from the upper tubes and into Etrol's dark sky. Recker didn't see them go, such was his focus on piloting the spaceship. The canyon turned and narrowed, and it took everything to keep from colliding with the sides.

The Daklan missiles didn't appear on the tactical, leaving Recker guessing as to their position. Six hundred klicks wasn't much distance for a Feilar to travel and it seemed like ten of them struck the same place in the canyon wall ahead of the *Finality*. White hot plasma blossomed starkly against the image intensified darkness of Etrol. Rock erupted from the impact points, jetting outwards like the planet's lifeblood.

With neither time nor room to avoid the showering rock, and with the noise of the Railer's sudden activation drowning out his thoughts, Recker did his best to avoid impacting with the canyon walls. The spaceship crashed through a few thousand tons of stone like it was nothing. He heard the distant thudding against the armour plating and ignored its irrelevance to his fight for survival.

Ahead, at two thousand metres, the canyon split. The left branch would take the *Finality* further from the approaching destroyer and an idea slotted itself neatly into Recker's brain. He acted without thought and banked left.

"Prepare the aft missile tubes," he instructed.

To her credit, Aston didn't ask questions. "Still got an amber on cluster #2," was all she said.

As soon as the *Finality* was inside the left branch of the canyon, Recker increased altitude. A ternium drive didn't only provide thrust from the rear and an experienced pilot could make a spaceship perform all kinds of tricks. Without lifting the nose or losing speed, Recker brought the *Finality* vertically out of the canyon. He heard the quiet beeping of a weapons lock from Aston's console and at the same time, the destroyer appeared on the rear sensor feed – a speck of grey climbing high and approaching fast.

"Rear clusters #1 and #2 launched," said Aston. "Failures on three tubes."

The moment he heard the words, Recker dropped the *Finality* back into the canyon. "Have they launched?" He knew the destroyer's initial attack had come from its forward launch tubes and he was relying on their reload being incomplete.

"Negative launch, sir."

"Ready forward clusters."

As he said the words, Recker twisted the control bars and cut power to one half of the propulsion. With a violent lurch, the *Finality* flipped front to back and the sensor view spun crazily. The spaceship's nose came within a hair of the canyon wall and then Recker got it under control. He immediately increased altitude and the bridge walls shook and groaned under the conflicting stresses.

"Weapons lock on the enemy destroyer," said Aston. "Forward clusters #1 and #2 launched."

Recker's heart jumped at the sight of the Daklan warship. The *Finality*'s first missile attack must have taken the enemy crew completely by surprise and the vessel was ablaze, trailing a white smear of plasma light as it continued climbing. It was no longer hunting Recker and his crew. Now, the destroyer was banking hard as it sought an escape.

The destroyer's altitude was such that the canyon would no longer cut out its firing angle, so Recker made no effort to take cover again. Instead, he accelerated towards the enemy and watched the orange propulsion trails of sixteen Ilstroms flying to meet the stricken craft.

Seconds later, the next wave of the *Finality*'s missiles crashed into the Daklan ship. For a moment, it was completely lost in the flash and Recker narrowed his eyes, trying to gauge if the damage was fatal.

"Yes!" said Aston. "It's breaking up!"

The destroyer's burning aft section separated from the rest of the ship. Its propulsion module was still operational and three hundred million tons of alloy and ternium accelerated into the sky. Without guidance, it began spinning and soon it was turning so fast that Recker could no longer distinguish the shape of the damaged section.

Meanwhile, the forward section's upward momentum ran out and it hung in the sky in apparent defiance of gravity, like a dying sun. Then, physics took over and it started the long tumble towards the ground.

It wasn't unheard of for an apparently defeated warship to fire a last, defiant salvo from its weapons clusters. Recker was certain the destroyer had nothing left, but he gave Aston the nod to launch again once the Ilstroms were reloaded.

"Five seconds until we can launch, sir."

Recker didn't want to hang around even for that long, and he aimed the *Finality* in the direction of what he hoped would be the Daklan installation. The acceleration pushed him into his seat and the missile reload finished. Aston fired at once, dividing the salvo between the two main sections of the Daklan warship. A series of new detonations added to the still-burning flames and the forward section split again, scattering armour plates and unrecognizable chunks of wreckage in every direction.

It was an old truism that if you stared too long at the death of your enemy, his replacement would happily take advantage. With that in mind, Recker kept his focus on guiding the *Finality* towards its destination. He increased

47

altitude to thirty klicks and the mountains once more raced by as the spaceship gathered speed.

At this altitude, the range of his view ahead was increased, and he saw that the faraway mountains diminished in both height and ferocity.

"Four hundred klicks to target," said Burner. "The destroyer's rear section just left orbit."

"Don't waste time on it, Lieutenant."

The destruction of the enemy ship was a great result, but Recker's agitation didn't subside. If anything, it grew, and he was starting to wonder if his instinct had gone into overdrive.

He turned an eye to the forward sensor feed. Far in the distance, the mountain range vanished completely and the surface became an undulating plain of monotonous grey with few variations.

"Three hundred klicks," said Burner. "If the Daklan have anything significant out here, we should see it from this altitude." He went quiet for a second. "There! Oh shit."

Recker opened his mouth to ask for details and then he saw it on the feed as well. The Daklan did have a fixed presence on the planet. Not only that, they had a second warship and this one was far more threatening than a ravager class destroyer. The moment Recker realized what they faced, he knew the destruction of his spaceship was unavoidable.

CHAPTER FIVE

THE DAKLAN HAD BEEN busy on Etrol. A massive cylinder made from a dark material jutted from the ground. The sensors estimated the cylinder to have a diameter of two thousand metres and a height of eight thousand. Recker didn't have time to stare and the feed wasn't clear enough to reveal anything else about the object.

He had bigger things to worry about.

Parked on the bare ground a thousand metres beyond the cylinder, a desolator class heavy cruiser promised death to anything smaller than an HPA battleship. The Daklan spaceship's shape was unmistakeable even when it was partially obscured. The rounded nose, broad midsection and cut-off rear weren't unusual, but the pair of double-barrelled Terrus cannons on top gave the game away.

"What the hell is that doing here?" asked Aston in shock.

"Fire the damn missiles!" shouted Recker, his mind trying to process everything.

"Target?"

"The cylinder!"

"Firing!"

The missiles burst from their tubes and Recker brought the *Finality* around in the tightest of turns. At the same time, he aimed for the ground and the altimeter dropped like a stone. The combined stresses made the hull groan like a deathbed soldier and a pair of new amber lights appeared on Recker's console.

He ignored the ambers and concentrated on getting the hell away from the heavy cruiser. Somehow, they'd caught the enemy crew off-guard, which was the only reason he could imagine they were still on the ground and the *Finality* still in the air. Luck was a wave you could only ride so far before it dumped you headfirst into the crap and Recker clenched his jaw, hoping beyond hope that his ship and his crew would be granted a few seconds to get beyond visual range across the planet's curvature.

A flash appeared on the rear sensor feed.

"Sixteen successful Ilstrom detonations," said Aston.

"What's the assessment of the damage?"

"The cylinder hasn't fallen over," said Burner. "I don't know if I'll be able to provide a reliable damage estimation on the enemy structure."

"We'll have the feed recordings for later. Have you transmitted our findings to base?"

"Yes, sir. Now I'm watching for that heavy cruiser and nothing else."

Recker kept his attention on flying. He brought the

spaceship as low as two thousand metres and gave it everything. The propulsion gauge showed a reading of 94% and the hull temperature climbed fast. He gave the briefest of glances at the rear feed and saw that the cylinder was no longer visible.

"They've got no line of sight on us," he said.

"That might not keep us safe," said Aston.

"I know."

"What's the plan, sir?"

Recker didn't have one yet. "We're going to put as much distance as we can between us and them."

"Mountain range ahead," said Burner.

"I see it."

The land rose and Recker was forced to increase altitude to avoid impacting with unyielding stone. Every couple of seconds, his eyes went to the rear feed, knowing that a response was inevitable.

An orange line streaked into the sky with an origin point near to the cylinder.

"Shit," said Burner. It seemed to be the only word coming from his mouth. "What the hell is that?"

"I don't know," said Recker. He'd seen plenty of Daklan heavy cruisers, but this was something new.

The sensors tracked the line, which kept climbing until it escaped the planet's atmosphere. As it gained altitude, the colour intensified and turned to white. Then, the line split, becoming five, ten, a hundred, then a thousand or more separate traces. Each formed its own arc and the trails headed for the surface.

"They're going to incinerate half the planet," Eastwood said.

The words echoed what Recker was thinking. He was sure the Daklan had launched a massive surface-scouring weapon and he didn't want to be nearby when any of the explosives went off. A feeling a helplessness gripped him. The *Finality* was at maximum thrust and at any second, he'd need to back off in order to prevent the spaceship burning up. Already the nose temperature exceeded two thousand Centigrade and the thick forward plating glowed fiercely.

"They're coming down in a semi-random pattern, sir," said Aston.

The *Finality*'s mainframe estimated the landing positions of the inbound missiles, based on sensor data. Either the weapons team on the heavy cruiser was good or exceptionally lucky and the warheads were going to land all around, whatever Recker did to try and avoid them. He stared at the pattern on the tactical, hunting for a gap into which he might guide the spaceship. There was nothing.

"Launching disruptors," said Aston. "Setting Railer on auto."

"Hold the Railer," said Recker.

"Sir?"

Recker didn't answer immediately, and he scanned the incoming weapons. The randomness introduced gaps where there were fewer warheads projected to land.

"Manually assign the Railer to targets Xo-19 through Xo-22," he said. "Beginning at the lowest."

"On it."

The Railer started up within a couple of seconds and combined with the propulsion to fill the bridge with layers of sound that assailed Recker's eardrums made it hard for him to think straight. Part of him wanted to aim the *Finality* towards the dark canvas above and head for the stars. A different voice told him to stay low. Once the heavy cruiser lifted off, Recker knew that every millisecond would be important. As soon as the Daklan obtained line of sight, the *Finality* would be pulverised by a molten ball of alloy travelling at twenty thousand klicks per second. It seemed better to risk the explosives.

A clarity of thought settled upon Recker – the kind that only ever came when the fighting was at its toughest. He worked the controls and the *Finality* twisted through the air, over the mountains and towards his chosen place.

"Xo-19 destroyed," said Aston. "The inbound warheads aren't deviating towards the disruptors."

"Dumb weapons," said Eastwood. "Sometimes they're all you need."

"Second incendiary launch detected," said Aston.

Burner swore loudly. "Trying to get you something on the tactical, sir."

"Railer heating up," said Aston. "Xo-20 taken out. Xo-21 taken out. Impact in five seconds."

By now, the summits of the mountain range were at their highest. Rather than climb above them, Recker risked everything by flying as low as he dared. The peaks rose before him and he guided the spaceship around them, his breathing even and his eyes unblinking.

"Xo-22 taken out. Impact."

From his periphery, Recker saw one of the warheads come down a few kilometres to starboard and he knew there were others. He braced himself and narrowed his eyes, just as one of the larger peaks appeared ahead. Every one of the feeds turned abruptly white and the bridge was starkly illuminated, turning the dull metals into a sickly corpselike grey.

Knowing that an impact with the mountain was imminent, Recker hauled the controls to one side. The Railer stopped firing and the engines rose once more to prominence. An infinitely deep thud of impact told him he'd misjudged, and the flight instruments jumped around, refusing to settle.

"Hull temps at three thousand Centigrade," said Eastwood. "And heading the wrong way."

The feeds attenuated and the outside become visible once again, just in time for Recker to discover that the *Finality* had been knocked completely off course and was heading directly for the sheer side of another mountain. Aside from that, the entire planet seemed to be alight. Amber lights became red and Recker knew that his spaceship was on the brink of destruction.

"Come on!" he roared, hoping his anger would channel into the technology around him and somehow hold it together.

With an effort, Recker turned the spaceship onto a new heading and another peak loomed. The impact had completely fooled his spatial sense and he took the only available option which was to increase altitude until he knew where the hell he was going.

The flames of the Daklan incendiary withered from their full height of ten thousand metres and died on the rocks. The hull temperature stabilised at 3700C, though the alarms didn't fall quiet. Recker wondered if the chaos would mask the ternium particles spilling from the aft breach. Maybe it didn't matter – the heavy cruiser wasn't going to forget about the *Finality*. The Daklan would keep hunting until Recker and his crew were reduced to carbon. And those ternium particles were going to make it easy for them.

Anger turned to fury and his body shook with it. His breathing deepened, his vision sharpened, and his body felt the chill of pumping adrenaline, making him shiver despite the blistering, metal-scented air coming through the bridge vents. Burner had managed to get the detonation patterns of the coming incendiaries onto the tactical. They were falling directly ahead.

Recker knew what he had to do. The huge fissure he'd noticed earlier was only a few hundred kilometres away. Unfortunately, an ocean of plasma incendiary was going to blanket the intervening space in a few seconds. Smiling in defiance, Recker aimed the spaceship right for the middle.

"Sir, the incendiaries."

"I know. Lieutenant Eastwood, shut down the aft engine module."

"Sir?"

"Now!"

"I've got to enter some overrides. Ten seconds."

Recker chose his target from the hundreds on the tactical. "Commander Aston, fire the Railer at X1-72, 73 and 74."

Her expression indicated she was desperate to know what he planned, but she didn't ask questions. "Yes, sir."

Those warheads were coming down at the exact place Recker was aiming the *Finality*. If the Railer didn't take

ANTHONY JAMES

out the three incendiaries, it was all over. Success was no
guarantee of survival either. For what seemed like many
seconds, the Railer thundered, taking out X1-72 and 73,
while X1-74 remained stubbornly on the tactical.

The countermeasures did their job.

"X1-74 destroyed!" said Aston loudly.

"Aft engine module offline, sir," shouted Burner, just
as the Railer shut off.

Recker knew it already – the spaceship became slug-
gish and unbalanced. He compensated automatically and
got the *Finality* under control at the same time as the portside, starboard, and forward feeds turned white with the
detonation of Daklan incendiaries.

The margins were tight, but the destruction of the
three warheads created a pocket within the flames. Recker
hauled on the controls and the *Finality* slowed to a crawl.
In every direction, accelerated plasma turned the billion-
year old rock into molten rivers.

Without fuel, the fires died quickly and Recker accelerated again towards the horizon. The once-grey rocks
were blackened and mottled with patches of red and
orange. Whatever the Daklan called their incendiary
weapon, it was utterly savage and Recker was terrified
what the aliens would do to an HPA populated world if
they ever found one.

"Watch out for that cruiser," he ordered. "If we're
lucky, they've lost our trail. Or they think we're dead."

"Yes, sir." Burner sounded shocked that he wasn't
dead.

"Where are we heading, sir?" said Aston.

"You remember that fissure?"

"Like someone took an axe to the place," she said, repeating his words from earlier.

"That's where we're going."

"The Daklan will know we didn't leave, sir."

"Not quite, Commander. They'll know we didn't go to lightspeed. If they can't find us on Etrol, they'll believe we went into space."

"Shouldn't we do that anyway, sir?" asked Burner.

"We're using the planet to keep us hidden, Lieutenant. The moment we head for the skies, the enemy will have a far greater chance of detecting us."

"We're glowing pretty brightly. If they sweep for heat, we'll stick out like a sore thumb," said Eastwood. "The plating will cool down a whole lot quicker up in space."

"I know. We're going for the fissure."

"Yes, sir."

In truth, Recker was tempted to leave orbit and take his chances. He knew from experience how tenacious the Daklan could be and they'd keep on searching. Out in space, a crippled riot class would be an easy find for the enemy. In Recker's best judgement, the survival of his ship and his crew was best served by taking cover on Etrol and hoping that Admiral Telar had a fleet of warships inbound.

The *Finality* gathered speed and the distance counter to the fissure decreased. Watching the digits fall away was agonizing and Recker refused to torment himself by staring too long. The other sights weren't any better and when he turned his attention briefly to the rear feed, he saw a square, orange-glowing object drop away from the hull and vanish in the *Finality*'s wake.

"There goes ten thousand tons of armour plating," said Eastwood.

Another slab detached itself from the hull, this time on the portside and Recker thought he heard a distant screeching wrench as it tore free. Two more warning lights appeared on his console and soon he'd be looking at more reds and ambers than greens. The *Finality* had been Recker's ship for several years and he knew this was its last mission.

"No sign of the cruiser," said Burner.

Recker wasn't reassured. It seemed like the enemy weapons team had been ready, which meant that the cruiser was operational and the only reason he could think for the spaceship remaining on the ground was because its commanding officer was elsewhere – maybe inside that massive cylinder.

"Two hundred klicks and we're at the fissure," said Burner. "Nothing in the sky."

With his eyes flicking across the terrain ahead, Recker guided the spaceship between the peaks, doing his best to balance outright speed with the requirement to keep the hull temperature from climbing any higher.

"One hundred klicks."

A bead of sweat ran down Recker's left temple and he brushed it away with his cuff. The Daklan would come, he thought. Right at the last moment to destroy his hopes of escape.

"Fifty klicks."

The *Finality* was at a low altitude, but not so much that it hid the view of the opening in the ground. Recker saw it – a yawning darkness that started between two mountains and then cut others in half further along its length, widening until it seemed like the planet itself was ready to split in two. He banked the spaceship towards it and came lower towards the floor of the canyon in which the fissure started.

"I've got the enemy cruiser on the sensors, sir," said Burner. He no longer sounded shellshocked, just empty.

Recker couldn't spare the time to look, but his eyes jumped to the rear feed of their own accord. Burner had a visual zoom lock on the enemy spaceship and it climbed like it had no requirement to obey any physical laws. The only positive was that they hadn't yet seen the *Finality* and the reason Recker knew it was true was because he wasn't dead.

The fissure yawned wide and with rock-solid hands, Recker dumped the *Finality* into the darkness at the highest speed he dared. So far apart were the sides that the light from the glowing hull hardly touched the sheer walls.

Deeper went the spaceship, heading into damnation or salvation.

CHAPTER SIX

THE CHASM DIDN'T narrow until the *Finality* was two thousand metres below the surface. Even then, Recker had plenty of room. Here and there, outcroppings extruded from the walls, but they were easily avoided.

At a depth of 2500 metres, a vast, snaking crack in one wall provided the cover Recker was looking for. Getting the spaceship inside should have been a difficult manoeuvre, but he managed it almost without conscious thought. All he could think about was the Daklan cruiser sending fifty missiles down here to find them.

With his teeth grinding, Recker finished positioning the *Finality* lengthways in the crack, midway between the floor and the ceiling. Heat continued to spill from the spaceship's hull and he hoped the rapid change in air temperature wouldn't cause the stone to shatter and come tumbling down upon them.

Once he was satisfied with the position, Recker activated the autopilot to keep the warship in place. He removed his hands from the controls and his fingers ached from the tightness of his grip.

With a loud expulsion of breath, Recker sat back in his seat. He turned and met Aston's gaze.

"Piece of cake."

"Yeah, easy," she said. "Just another day in the military."

"I'm going to turn off the audible alarms," said Recker, realizing how much the background chorus had been irritating him. A quick input of his override codes and they fell silent. He closed his eyes for a moment.

"That's better," said Eastwood. "I can just about hear myself think again."

"We've got plenty to do," said Recker. He flexed his fingers and the stiffness subsided.

"Every second we aren't dead is a bonus," laughed Eastwood.

"Let's take stock," said Recker. "Lieutenant Burner, while I'm thinking, you let those soldiers down below know where we've taken them."

"Yes, sir."

While Burner passed on the details, Recker pursed his lips in thought. His console told a sorry tale and it didn't require training to understand that the quantity of red lights on the panel was bad news. "Plenty of redundancy," he muttered, checking each light in turn.

Most of the *Finality*'s backup systems had kicked in, which meant the spaceship was able to remain airborne – assuming the backups didn't fail. Of course, there wasn't a backup hull and no backup propulsion modules. Last of all, Recker checked the magazine readouts, which informed him the *Finality*'s ammunition reserves were below thirty percent.

"Well, folks, we're in the shit."

"I'm glad you said it first, sir," said Burner.

Recker stood and stretched his back muscles. Then, he leaned forward and rested his knuckles on the hard surface of his console while he stared at the bulkhead feeds like there were answers to be found in the external view of orange-lit rock.

We'll get out of here, he promised silently. *One step at a time.*

"Lieutenant Eastwood, report," he said.

"We're in bad shape, sir, but then again you knew that already. The aft propulsion module is offline so we're no longer spilling ternium particles. Lieutenant Burner will be better placed to tell you whether or not we went undetected coming in here."

"You said earlier there was no guarantee we'd get the module restarted without shipyard facilities."

Eastwood took on a pained expression, producing fine lines across his forehead. "I did say that, sir."

"We don't have a shipyard and without that module we're not getting home."

"Not unless there's an extraction."

"Let's not pin our hopes on that," said Recker.

"The military doesn't abandon its own, sir," said Aston. "Even the..." she hesitated, "...*unfashionable* members."

"Unfashionable?" said Recker, raising an eyebrow. "I guess that's one way to describe it." He sighed. "You're right – we got out a comm and they'll send someone."

"You still look worried, sir."

"I don't know that whatever comes will be able to face that heavy cruiser. And if the rest of the fleet is elsewhere then we might be waiting a long time until there's enough muscle available."

"And there comes a time when enough is enough," said Eastwood. "I wouldn't expect the military to send so many resources here that they leave an opening for the Daklan elsewhere."

Recker thought the same, though he hadn't wanted to come right out and say it.

"Anyway, we might need – eventually - to get that engine module online."

"Assuming for a moment I can use the forward module to kickstart the aft one, we'll start leaking ternium again."

"I know. I thought you might be able to do some advance preparations. Whatever happens, I want to give the crew on that cruiser time to get bored of hunting for us and stand down."

Eastwood ran fingers through his short-cropped hair. "I'll do what I can, sir. I think this is going to be one of those times when you have to try something to find out if it's going to work."

"Lieutenant Burner, your turn," said Recker, pointing at his comms officer.

Burner had a cup of his usual super-strength coffee in his hand, though Recker hadn't seen the man go to the replicator.

"If the enemy ship saw us come down here, we'd be dead already," he began. "Since we aren't dead, and what with the Daklan being alien bastards and all, they'll probably begin a sweep of this area of the planet." He took a sip of the steaming drink.

"And?"

"The heat from our hull is enough to produce detectable traces in the atmosphere, sir. If they pass the fissure at an angle, there's a chance they'll miss it."

"What if they go straight overhead?"

"If their sensor team is incompetent, hungover and blind, they might not see us."

"Not much we can do to influence that."

"No, sir. It gets worse."

"Always does before it gets better."

"Our FTL comms booster isn't functioning. It's only showing an amber, but it won't let me put anything in the transmission queue. The hardware protrudes through the hull in six places and best guess is it all got burned out by the high temperatures."

"So we're cut off from base?"

"Effectively. I can send a sub-light comm, though we'll all be long dead from old age before it gets anywhere near its destination. If the cruiser doesn't kill us first."

The options list was getting progressively shorter and losing the FTL comms was a kick in the balls that Recker wasn't ready for. He took a deep breath and insisted to himself that only a fool got hung up on the immutable.

"See what you can do."

Burner gave a tight-lipped smile. He didn't say the words, but it was clear he wasn't expecting the FTL comms to work again. Recker didn't press him on it.

"What did you find out about that cylinder?" he asked

instead, raising a hand to forestall the objections. "I'm not expecting a detailed report."

"The outer casing was a metal alloy of some kind, sir, of a type unknown to us. It was also extremely dense, but I was able to direct a lightspeed ping through the middle. The area the ping hit was partially hollow."

"That's still a lot of material to bring out here," said Aston.

"What purpose does the cylinder serve?" wondered Recker. "It's not likely to be benign."

"I gathered a whole lot of raw data, sir," said Burner. "I just haven't had time to analyse it."

"And now we can't transmit to base."

"If it's any consolation, there's too much data to go in an FTL comm, sir, given the limitations of riot class hardware."

"Start looking at what we've got anyway. If you uncover something, it might save time later."

"Yes, sir." Burner looked like he had something more to say.

"Tell me, Lieutenant. I don't care if it ends up incorrect."

Burner took a fevered swig from his coffee and placed the empty cup on the floor. "Well, sir. I think most of that cylinder is there to generate power for something else."

"There wasn't anything else, Lieutenant. Except that cruiser."

"No, sir, I mean that the cylinder performs more than one function. It generates power for something else also contained within the casing."

"Any guesses as to what?"

"Not yet. It may be in the raw data."

"Check it out."

Burner still wasn't finished. "There's more, sir. I ran the composition of the alloy through our database and it's completely new. We've been fighting the Daklan for years and this is the first time we've encountered that material."

Recker was sure this was significant, though how exactly, he couldn't be sure. He turned to Commander Aston.

"How much damage did our missiles inflict on the cylinder?"

"I can only confirm sixteen detonations on target, sir. You saw how big that thing was. A riot class is designed to knock out armoured vehicles and cargo vessels. Against anything else we're little more than a nuisance."

"That's not what the captain of that destroyer was thinking when our missiles took him down."

"Thank you, Lieutenant Burner," said Recker. "Sometimes we can punch above our weight, but however you look at it, we're lacking firepower. Let's assume the cylinder didn't fall over."

"If Lieutenant Burner is correct and it's hollow, then a bunch of missiles into the operational section would give the Daklan something to think about. That's if the armour isn't two hundred metres thick."

It was food for thought, even if the *Finality* wasn't in a position to launch a second attack and likely never would be.

"Let's see what progress we make on our other priorities before we think about anything else, Commander."

"Yes, sir. What do you want me to do?"

"Watch out for our fleet coming in so that Lieutenants Burner and Eastwood can work without interruptions."

"Yes, sir. I'll back them up."

The crew were professionals and Recker left them to it. He knew himself well enough to recognize that the coming minutes, hours or however long it took for the next development, would be difficult. They were in a situation that wasn't all-out combat - where reflexes and adrenaline took over - nor was it a time that allowed for any form of relaxation. It was an in-between place that took the worst aspects of an engagement, whilst removing any possibility of influencing events.

A couple of hours passed and the hull slowly cooled. The air outside was sub-zero, but each of the *Finality's* armour plates was a big slab of alloy and it would be many more hours before they reached anything near ambient. Still, it was a positive sign that the cruiser hadn't found them yet.

As time went by, Recker experienced a creeping fatigue – it had been a long shift even without the stress of the twin engagements. Sleep wasn't an option, but he didn't want to make an error because he was tired. The pocket on his spacesuit held pills that would help, though he was reluctant to take them so soon. Once he was running on boost, every decision would seem too easy and he didn't want to surrender to drug-induced overconfidence.

Plan B – caffeine - was tried and tested, and Recker ordered a coffee from the replicator. The taste was bad enough that he was tempted to pour it away and take the boosters anyway, but he forced himself to drink it quickly.

In other circumstances, Recker would have left the bridge and spoken directly to the soldiers. Ten years ago, he'd been one of them and could well recall the nervous tension of waiting in cramped quarters, exchanging terse, unfunny wisecracks with the other troops and hoping there wasn't a swarm of Daklan missiles heading your way.

Right now, Recker couldn't go anywhere. Even so, with no immediate requirement to fly the spaceship, he spoke regularly to his crew to see if he could help.

"What've we got, folks?" he eventually asked, after a total of four hours underground.

"Still working on it, sir," said Eastwood. "We took a beating and I'm having to audit some of the backup support systems before I can concentrate on the engines."

"Lieutenant Burner?"

"I've got some preliminary ideas, sir."

"Let's have them."

Burner didn't get an opportunity to discuss those ideas. He spotted something on his console which made him jump in surprise. "Sir, I've detected a fission cloud near Etrol!" he said. "The magnitude and pattern indicate it's another riot class."

In two steps, Recker was at his console and he dropped into his seat. Aston had the information on the tactical already and he stared in dismay.

"Two hundred thousand klicks and straight over the top of the cylinder. Shit, get them on the comms!"

"I'm trying, sir," said Burner. "It'll take a few minutes for their sensors and comms to recalibrate after they exit lightspeed."

"What're they doing coming in so close in the first

place?" said Recker angrily. "If the lightspeed calcs were even a fraction out, they could have appeared in the centre of the planet."

"They must have been ordered to take the risk, sir," said Aston. She swore under her breath. "Here's a second fission cloud, right on top of the first. Another riot class."

"Get that comms channel!" yelled Recker.

"I'm trying, sir. Still nothing."

Against the Daklan cruiser in a normal engagement, two riots were utterly outmatched. Add to that their vulnerability when emerging from lightspeed and this would be over in moments if the enemy were quick to react.

"Got a channel to the *Sunder*," said Burner. "I've broadcast an emergency *get the hell away* message. Now the *Brimstone* has joined the channel."

The two spaceships were out of the *Finality*'s sensor sight, but they broadcast their positional and tactical data automatically, which appeared on Recker's console. Like Aston said, they were low and overhead.

A red dot appeared on the shared tactical, travelling fast.

"Shit, no," said Recker.

"Both the *Sunder* and the *Brimstone* report an engagement with a superior opponent, sir."

Smaller green and red dots, representing missiles, raced across the tactical. The *Sunder* vanished from the screen before the heavy cruiser's first salvo was halfway there.

"Terrus cannon," said Aston.

A moment later, the *Brimstone* also vanished.

The one-sided conflict was over almost before it had started. As soon as the HPA ships stopped broadcasting, the desolator disappeared from the *Finality*'s tactical, leaving the screen empty once again.

Recker closed his eyes and tried to control his fury.

CHAPTER SEVEN

FOR TEN MINUTES, the crew of the *Finality* said little as they watched and waited to discover if any more HPA ships were inbound. None came.

"What's done is done," Recker said eventually.

The crew looked at him and he knew they were waiting for him to offer some hope. Recker didn't know what to tell them and stayed quiet while he thought.

"That's our backup gone," he said at last. "If we're getting out of here, we'll be doing it alone."

"Maybe there are others coming our way, sir," said Burner. "If Admiral Telar diverted warships from different places, they wouldn't arrive at the same time."

"It's possible," said Recker. "But I'm not pinning anything on it happening."

"That means we're escaping," said Aston.

"I don't plan to die on Etrol," said Recker.

"Nor me, sir."

"Escape just became a whole lot more important," said Burner, his face draining of colour.

"You found something in the data?" asked Recker striding to the comms station.

"Not in the data, sir. It's been staring me in the face all along, but I only just realised."

Burner was studying a screen filled with apparently random letters and numbers – the raw data from the sensors – and he'd plotted a series of charts on an adjacent screen.

"You said it wasn't in the data," said Recker.

Burner tapped the side of his head to show where the idea came from. "Sometimes you have to look away from the details and see the bigger picture. I asked myself what requires a power source the size of the one housed in that cylinder and there are only two possibilities."

"Weapons and propulsion," said Recker.

"Yes, sir. But that cylinder must be anchored at least a thousand metres underground in order to stay upright."

"Which means it's not about to fly anywhere."

Burner nodded vigorously like a converted zealot. "It's got to be a weapon."

"That doesn't necessarily follow," said Aston, though her expression told its own story.

"How come?" asked Recker.

"The Daklan could be working on all kinds of experimental kit that we don't know about. Not everything they create is intended to kill."

"Isn't it? They live for war, Commander. All I ever see is examples of how they're trying to get better at it. More efficient."

"I know, sir. We should consider everything."

Recker sighed. "While we're out here and until I see evidence to the contrary, I'm assuming that cylinder is a weapon. For all the difference it'll make."

Aston let it drop, confirming that she agreed with Recker and Burner's assessment. If she disagreed strongly enough about something, she had no fear about making her views plain. Some commanders thought that saying yes to everything was a good way to advance their careers. Aston wasn't one of them.

"Our backup is gone," Recker repeated. "The HPA military has lost some good personnel. We're not going to be next, which means we've got to escape from Etrol and make it back home to let high command know what we've found. Maybe they'll send more warships out here, whatever happens to us. If they don't, the HPA will be missing out on some vital intel."

"I'll do what I can to prepare the aft module for restart, sir," said Eastwood. "Are you hoping to fire it up while we hide in this canyon?"

"I don't know," Recker confessed. "If we limp out on one module, there's a greater chance the desolator will find us. If we head out on both modules, they might detect our ternium trail."

"Either way, we're hoping the dice will roll in our favour," said Eastwood. He grinned. "Don't you love it?"

"Not much." Recker smiled anyway. "You're suddenly the most important member of the crew. If you need assistance, ask."

"Will do."

Recker got himself another coffee and his growling

ANTHONY JAMES

stomach prompted him to request a cheeseburger from the replicator menu. A banner advising him to limit his saturated fats intake appeared on the screen and the effects of seeing it elevated his blood pressure more than any fifty burgers would have done.

When the machine was finished vending, Recker found his coffee in the slot, but his cheeseburger was nothing more than a pile of grey sludge which smelled like warm mince. He swore and re-entered his cheeseburger order with the same outcome.

"Now the damn replicator's faulty," he said.

"Try ordering something else," Aston suggested.

Recker requested something easy – one of the nutrition blocks that formed part of a soldier's emergency rations. A brownish object appeared, which he withdrew and studied.

"Looks like we're stuck with the basics." He bit into the block and found it bland with undertones of fermented vegetables.

"I thought you ground pounders couldn't get enough of the grunt fuel," said Aston with a grin.

Coming from most other people it would have been an insult or a bad attempt at humour, but Recker wasn't offended.

"It's like chewing cardboard," he laughed. "You'll have to get used to it, Commander, since I think it's the only food this machine is going to produce."

"I'm not hungry, sir."

"You'll crack."

"Never."

Recker took another bite from the block and

concluded the nutritionists hadn't done anything to improve on the taste in the last eighteen years. "How's it going, Lieutenant Eastwood?" he asked.

"I'm making progress, sir."

Recker leaned closer to have a look. The screens on Eastwood's consoles were covered in data tables, routing diagrams and schematics.

"What kind of progress?"

Eastwood tapped a thick finger on a side-by-side representation of the spaceship's two engine modules. "Normally when you shut down a ternium module, it requires a huge charged burst from another power source in order to align the molecules, at which point they become agitated and..."

"I know the background, Lieutenant."

"Well, our forward propulsion module doesn't *theoretically* have enough grunt to fire up the aft module."

Eastwood was getting animated as he usually did when talking about this kind of stuff and Recker felt it rubbing off on him.

"You've found a way to overcome the limitation?"

"Yes. Maybe. I think so."

Recker stared. "So which is it?"

"When they create these ternium blocks, the fabrication plant subjects them to a one-off overstress test where they create a semi-stable alignment within the structure and they hold it there for a couple of hours with the module at three hundred percent of its operational maximum. If the block passes the test, then it's signed off for installation."

"Aren't those the tests they do inside heavily armoured

ANTHONY JAMES

underground facilities?" asked Burner, looking up from his station.

"That's right," said Eastwood. "As soon as they detect anomalies in the block, they shut it down and the whole thing gets sent back to the reprocessing plant, where it's recreated from scratch."

Recker guessed where this was heading. "You're planning to overstress the forward engine module and use it to kickstart the aft one?"

"Yes, sir. Even if the kickstart fails, with the forward module in a semi-stable condition, we'll have enough grunt to get out of here and at a greater maximum speed than if we had both modules functioning in their normal state."

"Will that allow us to reach lightspeed?" said Recker.

Eastwood shook his head. "No such luck. The *Finality*'s mainframe works out the calculations and balances them evenly across both propulsion modules. We need both working in order to reach lightspeed."

"Can we alter the programming?"

"If I'm honest, sir, I can probably do that. Eventually." Eastwood scratched his head and looked pained. "It's a big job – they have dedicated teams of software experts for this kind of work. I can't guarantee I won't break something."

"How long can we safely hold the module semi-stable?"

"We can't safely hold it semi-stable for any time whatsoever, sir." Eastwood gave a gravel laugh. "That's the answer I *should* give you. In reality, the module might run for a long time and still return to its normal state. Or it might become totally unstable, in which case we're screwed."

"Define *screwed*," said Burner.

"Results of past failures are mostly non-explosive," said Eastwood. "Usually the ternium heats to a few million degrees and destroys itself."

"What about the other failures?"

"The HPA has experienced several more dramatic outcomes. Luckily, ternium only generates power when all the atomic ducks are in a row. Once things fall out of shape, it can no longer generate energy. It effectively kills itself before it can cause a catastrophic outcome."

"Atomic ducks?" said Aston with a raised eyebrow. "You'll have to trademark that one."

"I'll think about it. In the meantime, I can overstress the forward module and then it's down to Captain Recker to decide what happens next."

"Can you guarantee the forward module will restart the aft?" asked Recker.

"I can't guarantee it, sir. I can only tell you that in theory it should work."

Recker wasn't a man who settled for the easy way out and his mind was working. "If the *Finality* was operating with a single overstressed propulsion module, it wouldn't be enough to outrun that desolator."

"No, sir. Not even close."

"With one overstressed module and one module operating within normal bounds, we'd match the desolator for speed."

Eastwood looked at Recker closely. "Want me to simulate the outcome?"

"No. And if we ran both modules overstressed, we'd hit eighteen hundred klicks per second. A desolator tops out at sixteen hundred."

"You worked that out in your head?"

Recker shrugged. "They tell me I have the gift of understanding tech."

"I don't think we should rely on an outcome that requires both engine modules to be overstressed."

"We might need the extra velocity."

"What are you thinking, sir?" said Aston. She clicked her fingers. "You're going to take another shot at that cylinder."

"I'm considering it."

"Those Terrus cannons will reduce us to scrap," said Burner. "And the desolators carry more than just Feilars."

"Odan warheads," said Recker.

"We won't escape them easily," said Aston. "They lock at half a million klicks."

"If we fire at the cylinder from our max range of 210,000 klicks, we'll need to put an additional 290,000 klicks between us and the heavy to prevent them obtaining a weapons lock. That's not far off three minutes' travel time, assuming we're at near maximum velocity when we fire our Ilstroms," said Burner.

Recker smiled. "I appreciate the effort you put into figuring that out, Lieutenant, but we're not going to be shooting from orbit. The cylinder is fixed in position and we can program the Ilstroms to fly straight for those coordinates."

"We'll break up if you're planning another high-speed pursuit through the atmosphere, sir."

"I'm just planning to get us out of here, Lieutenant. And if we can fire a few missiles into a Daklan super-weapon at the same time, all the better."

The words were easily said and Recker knew they'd be hard to live up to. He asked himself if it was even worth having another shot at the cylinder or if he should just take the chance to escape without risking a confrontation with the desolator. Duty was a bitch and sometimes Recker felt like its helpless servant.

"Lieutenant Eastwood," he asked. "How long will it take to ready the forward module for overstress?"

CHAPTER EIGHT

FIVE MINUTES WAS all it required to complete the preparations.

"On your command, sir," said Eastwood.

Recker's mind was already made up and he didn't hesitate. "Do it."

"Switching forward module to overstressed state."

The engine module suddenly howled, and Recker felt the hairs on his neck stand on end. He watched the output gauge climb to one hundred percent and keep going. The scale recalculated and the reading went past two hundred percent, while the howling transformed into something primal, different to anything Recker had heard before. When the gauge raced beyond three hundred percent, the sound was like the pinnacle of every known technology washing through his body. Still its increase didn't slow.

"You said three hundred percent, Lieutenant," he shouted over the noise.

"I did, sir."

"Then why's it at 350%?"

"I don't know. Should I attempt to cancel the over-stress state?"

That single word. *Attempt.*

"Let's see what it does."

To Recker's relief, the output stabilised and he exhaled.

"That's a 370% overstress, Lieutenant. Any idea why so high?"

"I wonder if it's because our ternium drive is an old one, sir," said Eastwood uncertainly. "The fabrication plant only ever tests the modules when they're new. Maybe the internal structure changes after an extended period. It sounds crazy, but it's all I can think of."

"You can put it in your report. Is everyone ready for this?" Recker asked without turning to check the crew's expressions.

"Hell, yeah," said Burner.

"Let's do it."

Recker's hands were already resting lightly on the controls and he wrapped his fingers tighter. This was going to be tough. Normal flight involved increasing power to the engines, depending on what you wanted the space-ship to do. With the module being overstressed, it was at constant maximum power which meant the *Finality* was fighting for full acceleration and the difficulty lay in restraining it. If Recker screwed up in the next few seconds, the ship was going to hit the side of the fissure at high speed.

With exceptional care, he eased the vessel sideways from the crack in which it was hidden. Usually, Recker listened to the variations in the engine note to help him fly. Now, that note was unchanging, making it tough for him to get a feel for the speed and movement. The sensor feeds helped and Recker checked them more than normal.

He made it into the main part of the fissure without hitting the side walls and held the spaceship in place to give Lieutenant Burner a moment to complete a scan.

"There's nothing overhead, sir. I only have a limited view of the sky."

"I'm taking us higher."

The extra resonance from the engine caused hundreds of smaller rocks to cascade down on the hull. It wasn't as if there was any new paintwork to worry about and the *Finality* could ride an impact from a hundred million tons of stone - or so Recker told himself.

At a depth of a thousand metres, he halted the spaceship again.

"Anything new?"

"No, sir. The visibility arc is still too narrow. Even if you came to the top of the opening, there're plenty of mountains that'll limit what we can see."

"In that case, I'll stop pissing about."

Recker brought the spaceship straight out of the fissure, marvelling at the responsiveness and the ease with which it gained speed. He planned to halt at an altitude of ten thousand metres but overshot by two hundred.

"There's nothing in visual, sir," said Burner. "If the desolator is at a high enough altitude, I'll need time to find it."

"That's fine, Lieutenant. If they're so far away, they won't easily see us either."

"Don't bank on it, sir."

Recker got the hint and he lifted the spaceship higher still, so that it was level with many of the surrounding mountains. He knew where he was going and accelerated along the route he had in his mind, which led directly away from the cylinder.

The *Finality* didn't so much gather speed as it threw itself at the horizon. Given the damage the hull had suffered, Recker didn't want it to heat beyond a couple of thousand degrees, so he held back. The distant groaning of distressed metal told him everything about the health of the spaceship and he willed it to hold together until the mission was over.

"Still clear," said Burner.

Every second increased the risk they would encounter the desolator, but Recker was determined that he'd get a good shot at the cylinder and that required plenty of distance. They made it halfway around Etrol and Recker decided that was enough. He brought the *Finality* to a halt, five klicks above an immense boulder-littered plain of light grey stone. The oblique angle of the sun made the shadows long and, for the shortest of times, the emptiness of it took Recker's breath away.

"Have you programmed the coordinates into the guidance systems, Commander?" he asked.

"Yes, sir. Front and rear clusters."

Recker was on the brink of giving the order to fire when he heard Lieutenant Burner swear with real feeling.

"Sir, we have to get out of here. Now!"

Eastwood had picked something up with his own monitoring tools as well and he also cursed loudly.

"Hold fire!" he yelled.

"Someone tell me what the hell is going on!" roared Recker.

"Something's about to show up on the blindside, sir," said Burner. "I'm reading the biggest damn ternium cloud I've ever seen."

Recker experienced a sinking feeling as he realized the opportunity was slipping away. A voice whispered that he should fire and have done, but this shot at the Daklan weapon was only a bonus and he wasn't prepared to throw everything away for it.

"What're we dealing with?" he asked, biting down on his anger.

"It's more than a single spaceship, sir," said Eastwood. "Ah, crap. The first one is a heavy lifter." He swore again. "It's taking effort to untangle the overlapped particle clouds."

A feeling of alarm sank deep into Recker's bones. The Daklan heavy lifters were enormous spaceships and, although they carried comparatively few armaments, they were an opponent far beyond the *Finality*. Even if they were defenceless, Recker wasn't sure a riot class had the capability to punch through a lifter's armour.

That aside, it wasn't the deep space lifter that had Recker worried. The *real* concern was its escort – wherever the Daklan lifters went, they usually had some firepower to back them up. *Serious* firepower.

"Preliminary data analysis suggests an annihilator battleship is about to take a shit in our coffee, sir," said Burner. "The ternium pattern doesn't exactly match that of previous sightings."

"Another new one off the production line." Recker wanted to curse like everyone else was doing. He bit his tongue. "Hold fire, Commander," he ordered.

"Ternium cloud decaying, sir," Burner reported. "Both vessels are now in local space and estimated to be no more than two hundred thousand kilometres from Etrol. The estimated positional data is on your tactical."

Recker hardly spared it a glance. The timing was a disaster for his hopes of delivering a surprise blow to the Daklan weapon. You didn't play games with an annihilator. Not in a riot class and probably not in any single HPA warship. From their assumed position, the enemy battleship crew would almost certainly detect the Ilstroms in flight. After that would come the pursuit and Recker didn't think the *Finality* had any chance of outrunning the annihilator, overstressed propulsion or not.

Backing down was harder than he'd imagined it would be. "There're calculated risks and there's suicide," he told the crew. "I'll order one, but never the other. Not here, not when we don't know the significance of the cylinder."

"We should attempt a return to base, sir," said Aston in agreement. "This is one for high command to deal with."

It was the right decision. Even so, Recker's heart was heavy as he increased altitude. The spaceship climbed eagerly, and he noticed the output gauge had crept up to 380%.

"Lieutenant Eastwood, check that out," he ordered, not wanting to spend time worrying about it at the moment. "And we can't forget there's a cruiser out there."

"I'm watching for it, sir," said Burner.

Although the spaceship wanted to accelerate without restraint, Recker didn't think the hull could handle another cycle of heating up and cooling down. The creaking and flexing noises were getting worse, like the spaceship would tear apart if it was treated carelessly.

"We're heading for Sarus-Q," said Recker. "The moment I'm convinced it's safe, we'll kickstart the aft module, ready the ternium drive and head for home."

"As easy as that," said Aston.

"Yes, Commander. As easy as that."

The *Finality* tore out of Etrol's rarefied upper atmosphere and Recker gradually increased the engines to maximum. Having become so in tune with a spaceship by listening to its propulsion sound, it was strangely eerie to feel the acceleration without any discernible change to the metallic howling coming from all around.

"No cruiser," said Burner. "Maybe they gave up."

"You think?"

"No, sir."

For ten minutes, Recker held the spaceship on course, heading directly away from Etrol. Lieutenant Burner didn't locate any sign of pursuit and with each passing second it would be harder for the Daklan to detect the *Finality*. The atmosphere on the bridge was tense and nobody spoke for a long time.

After thirty minutes, the output gauge topped 400% and Lieutenant Eastwood didn't have a precise answer as to why it had climbed so high. Even worse, he didn't have an imprecise answer either. The only positive was that as the output climbed, so did the *Finality*'s speed.

A full hour after departing Etrol, Recker was ready to

order the restart of the aft module. The output was 410% and hadn't changed in the last fifteen minutes. Lieutenant Eastwood ventured his opinion that it wasn't going any higher.

"We can do this kickstart in flight?" Recker asked, to confirm what they'd already discussed.

"Yes, sir. If it works, you'll want to slow us down for the lightspeed jump, otherwise we'll lose control over the destination."

"410% on the forward module has got to be enough juice," said Aston.

"You should see the modules they use at the fabrication plant, Commander. Those ones make ours look like a battery for your flashlight."

"I'll take your word for that."

Despite the importance of the coming minutes, Recker felt calm again and he twisted so that he could see how Eastwood was handling the pressure.

"You ready for this, Lieutenant?"

"Yes, sir. I made the final preparations on the way from Etrol. Say the word and I'll attempt the kickstart."

There was no benefit in waiting. "Do it."

For the first time since Lieutenant Burner put the forward module into a semi-stable condition, the howling sound reduced. The output gauge fell, climbed, and then the hull was shaken by a single expulsive thumping sound. After the thump, the howling returned - this time louder than before. Not only that, everything seemed to vibrate and Recker felt a sharp pain developing behind his eyes.

"Aft engine module active!" said Eastwood. "Output, 94%. Uh-oh."

Recker didn't need to ask the question – he could see the reason for the *uh-oh* right in front of his eyes.

"Output now at 110% and climbing. 130%. Tell me some good news, Lieutenant."

"I have none to give, sir. It seems like the overstressed forward module has kickstarted the aft module into an overstressed state as well."

"Did you know this would happen?"

"No, sir. I don't think anyone in the HPA would have known."

"Can you switch them back to a normal state?"

"I'm checking that out, sir."

There was more bad news.

"We're spilling particles again," said Eastwood. "Only this time it's not just for a few hundred klicks behind us. They're pouring out of that hull breach like a flood."

Eastwood wasn't exaggerating. The *Finality* was a long distance from Etrol, but the aft module was doing a damn good job of making the spaceship visible.

"We're too far away for the Daklan to see us," said Aston, like she was trying to convince herself. "Surely."

Suddenly, the numbers weren't adding up. The *Finality* required fifteen minutes to warm up for a light-speed jump and a Daklan annihilator could likely prepare in less than half of that time. If the enemy spotted the ternium leak, they could be here in plenty of time to spoil Recker's day.

"Lieutenant Eastwood, can you switch the modules back to a stable condition?" he repeated.

"Yes, sir. I think it'll take me a few minutes."

"We might not have a few minutes."

"The alternative is that we set a course and go," said Aston.

"It might come to that. Lieutenant Burner, will the Daklan spot us from here?"

"We're approximately five and a half million klicks from Etrol. If they're running wide area sweeps for incoming HPA spaceships, they'll spot us eventually."

"The Daklan don't usually make mistakes." Recker succumbed to temptation and crashed his fist onto the top panel of his console. "Set a course for planet Lustre," he said.

"The Topaz orbital is six hours closer, sir," said Aston.

"I know, but they don't have the facilities to deal with the *Finality*. Not like this."

"You think the Lustre shipyard will welcome us with open arms?"

"I'm not about to give them the choice. Lieutenant Eastwood, that's where we're going."

"It's five days travel, sir," said Aston. "Maybe we should aim for a shorter run that takes us to the middle of nowhere. That will give Lieutenant Eastwood time to stabilize the engines."

"What do you think of that, Lieutenant?" asked Recker.

"I'm worried we might not have a second chance, sir. The forward module shows no sign of additional instability. But still..."

"What does your gut tell you?"

"My gut tells me the forward module is going to hold as long as we need it." Eastwood reached out a hand and patted his console. "It also tells me the *Finality* isn't going to let us down, sir."

"What about the aft module?"

"We don't have time to wait and see how high that one goes. Not unless you want to shake hands with a Daklan annihilator."

Recker had no intention of making it easy for his enemy. "If I'm going to die, I'd prefer it to happen at light-speed instead of giving the satisfaction to the Daklan."

"Yeah, screw those bastards," said Burner.

Time was running out; Recker could feel it. He hauled the controls towards him and the spaceship's velocity readout fell with such rapidity that the life support was overwhelmed. The decelerative forces threatened to pull him from his seat and he quickly adjusted the position of the control bars.

"I guess they didn't expect the life support hardware would end up dealing with two overstressed engine modules," he muttered once the interior was stable again.

Soon the warship was reduced to a low enough speed that Eastwood was confident they'd exit lightspeed near to their target destination. Recker gave the instruction to set a course for Lustre.

"Not too close," he said. "I don't want us dousing every HPA citizen in ternium particles."

"There's no proven link with any known medical condition, sir," Burner reminded him.

"Maybe not, but there's a proven link with the amount of paperwork I'll have to complete and the amount of ear chewing I'll have to sit through if we turn up too close to Lustre with the *Finality* in its current state, Lieutenant."

"Point taken."

"Coordinates entered," said Eastwood. "Fifteen minutes for the lightspeed calcs."

"I'll let Sergeant Vance know what's happening," said Burner.

It was a nervous wait and Recker divided his attention between the sensor feeds and the aft module status readout. Within a short time, the rear engine output went beyond 300%, but the rate of increase declined, and he guessed it might stabilize at about 400%. The pain behind Recker's eyes didn't go away and it intensified with each increase in the propulsion output. His crew complained about it too, so he knew he wasn't suffering alone.

"Five minutes and we'll be out of here," said Eastwood.

"The size of our ternium leak is increasing as an exponent of the module output," said Burner. "This is crazy stuff."

"It'll give the research guys something to get excited about once we get back," said Recker, refusing to concede that their successful return was anything other than a certainty.

The five minutes felt as if they lasted an eternity. With a minute to go on the lightspeed calcs, Recker had his jaw clenched so tightly that the muscles ached. His mouth was dry again from the pulsing waves of adrenaline and he felt like he could sleep for a week.

"Twenty seconds."

"Particle cloud detected. Right on top of us," said Burner. His voice was rock steady, like he'd either completely given up hope or was absolutely convinced the *Finality* was going to make it out of here.

Recker could have said one of a hundred different things. Instead, he said nothing and only watched.

"Ten seconds."

"The ternium wave is at its peak. It's the annihilator," said Burner. "Cloud starting its decay."

"Five seconds."

"Deploying disruptors," said Aston. "Ready for their arrival."

A handful of drones wouldn't do much good. They wouldn't even put up a worthwhile show of defiance.

The annihilator appeared, so close that its dark grey sides filled the entirety of the starboard feed, blotting out the white speckling of faraway stars. Recker hadn't seen a Daklan battleship from such a short range and found himself hating this one with such an all-encompassing intensity that his body shook.

"Goodbye," said Eastwood.

Recker wasn't sure whose ears the farewell was meant for. The *Finality*'s propulsion thundered like the worst of storms and the spaceship entered lightspeed.

CHAPTER NINE

AS WELL AS his feeling of immense relief at escaping the Daklan battleship, Recker felt an almost equal happiness at the significant reduction in the howling of the two propulsion modules. Whilst the sound of it was intoxicating in small doses, it had rapidly become a pain in the ears and the ass, like a highly tuned sportscar that was great in short doses, but rapidly became draining on longer journeys.

For a couple of minutes, nobody spoke, though the crew didn't take a break. Like Recker, they ran through the extensive list of status checks required at the beginning of every transition into lightspeed. So far, there was nothing to report beyond the known issues from before the launch.

Eventually it was Lieutenant Burner who spoke. "That wasn't the most fun I've ever had."

"Nope," agreed Eastwood. "And now we've got to hope this old warhorse hangs together long enough for us to reach Lustre."

"It will," said Recker firmly. "The *Finality* hasn't let any of us down before and it won't happen this time."

"No sign of anomalies on either module," said Eastwood. "Everything looks fine."

"Five days to Lustre with all that extra power," said Burner. "How much longer would it have been without the overstress?"

"The improvement isn't as great as you might think," said Eastwood. "Time at lightspeed is governed by more than maximum propulsion output. A lot of it's down to how much processing grunt a warship is packing."

It sounded bizarre, but it was true. It didn't matter how many engine modules the HPA shipyards crammed into a hull, a spaceship was still limited by the number of lightspeed calculations its processing core could perform during the flight - and that had boundaries too.

Thinking about it made Recker's head spin. A warship at lightspeed created a tunnel towards its destination as it flew - a tunnel that required a combination of theoretical mathematics and the incredible output of a ternium drive to hold open.

Recker had once asked a member of the lightspeed research team to explain it to him in simple terms. The man had grinned, shrugged and that was all Recker had needed. In the case of lightspeed travel, it was best to accept that it worked and not think too hard about the specifics. So far for Recker, the method was working great.

"So how much time did we save?" pressed Burner.

"Three hours," said Eastwood. "If we had one of those new processing cores it would have been a whole lot more than three hours."

Burner let it drop, evidently satisfied with the response. "Five days to Lustre and then they might not let us dock for another five days on account of the hole in our armour and all the crap that's coming out of it."

"And when we finally set down, expect a fortnight in the debriefing room," said Aston with a theatrical sigh. "Followed by assignment to some old rust bucket that first came out of the yard sixty years ago."

"I was hoping they'd thank us for doing so well at Virar-12 and give us a few weeks off," said Burner. He raised his hands in mock apology. "Yeah, I know. I'm too optimistic."

There was plenty to discuss about the mission to the Virar-12 system, but nobody brought up the subject, as if they knew the hunt for answers would only result in frustration.

After six hours at lightspeed, the *Finality* hadn't broken up and the crew detected no new failures in the onboard systems. Everyone was exhausted and Recker realized he couldn't keep them on shift any longer. The spaceship's mainframe had the military's scheduling software installed and it produced a shift pattern based on details of the crew's circumstances.

"Commander Aston, Lieutenant Burner, you got your three hours."

"Three whole hours?" grumbled Burner. "I'm so wired it'll take me that long to fall asleep."

"Maybe you should trim your caffeine intake to a lean dozen coffees a day," said Aston sweetly.

"I'd rather lie awake."

The two of them left the bridge, leaving Recker stifling

a yawn. When he turned to check on Eastwood, the man raised a thumb, but the smile on his face wasn't enough to hide the tiredness etched in his features.

Recker paid a visit to the replicator for a water, a double-strength coffee and a nutrition block. His stomach craved something more fulfilling and he stared angrily at the malfunctioning device.

"Is there anything we can do to fix this?" he asked.

"You've only got to put up with it for five days, sir."

"I'll take that as a *no*, then."

"It's a self-contained unit. It gets plugged into the warship for power and that's it. I have no access except through the front panel interface."

Recker was briefly tempted to check out the machine's diagnostic reports, but common sense took over. A second machine was installed in the tiny mess area elsewhere in the ship – for use by the soldiers – and Recker promised himself he'd stop by when he got the chance.

He finished his water at the replicator and returned to his seat with the coffee and grunt fuel. Nothing had changed on the status panel – lots of ambers and reds, but the backups were running fine.

"Lieutenant Burner never finished analysing the sensor data we gathered from that cylinder," said Eastwood.

"Thinking of taking a look at it yourself?"

"Not me, sir. I'm not multi-skilled like most of the guys they're bringing in these days." He gave a short laugh. "Besides, I'm too tired right now."

"I know what you mean," said Recker. He wasn't exactly struggling to keep his eyes open, but his focus wasn't where it should be. Once more, he thought about taking one of the booster pills - Frenziol-13 was the name of the drug and Recker had no idea if that was an intentional joke or not. A single tablet would help him get through this shift at the expense of the three hours' sleep he planned to take when his turn came. He left the pills untouched.

"Anything to report on the propulsion modules, Lieutenant?" he asked. He was sure Eastwood would speak up if there was anything to report but talking helped Recker stay alert.

"The aft module is steady at 402% and the forward module hasn't moved since last time you asked."

"Think you'll be able to shut them down once we arrive at Lustre?"

"I know what steps I'll be taking, sir. Whether or not they'll work, I can't tell you. What'll happen if the modules won't come out of semi-stable?"

"They'll rescue us, tow the *Finality* someplace way out and send a maintenance team onboard. If the maintenance team can't shut the engines down, they'll take more direct action."

"By blowing the spaceship to pieces."

"I've seen it happen, though not for the same reason."

The conversation ended, yet Recker couldn't stop thinking about the likely destruction of the *Finality*. He knew it was stupid to become emotionally attached to a lump of alloy – *a tool* – but the spaceship had become an expression of his own determination to face the universe and come out of it unbowed by adversity.

Eastwood was a great engine man – the kind who

seemed to have an otherworldly sense for the hardware – and though he wasn't infallible, he wasn't far removed. If anyone could shut down the propulsion, it was him. Either way, the *Finality* was done. It would be quicker, cheaper and easier to simply scrap the hull and build a new riot to replace the loss.

Three hours after she departed the bridge, Aston returned. She looked surprisingly refreshed, with her dark hair pulled back and tied in a short ponytail. Five minutes later, Burner appeared, carrying a coffee and apologising - without much enthusiasm - for his lateness.

Recker completed the shift handover in a couple of minutes and headed for the bridge exit. He placed his hand on the adjacent security panel and the heavy door slid open to reveal a short passage leading to steps lit in the dull red of the internal alarm system.

He paused, noticing how hot it was, and humid like a tropical greenhouse. His spacesuit kept his body insulated, but he'd left his helmet on the bridge, leaving his head exposed to the heat. The scent of metal was stronger here and mingled with another sharp odour which was always present, with a source he'd never been able to identify.

The steps were narrow, and he could easily touch the side walls if he stretched out his arms. At the bottom, a corridor cut left and right. Here, the way was only just wide enough for two to pass and the lowness of the ceiling was made worse by the occasional pipe or grey-sheathed cable crossing overhead.

At the first intersection, Recker stopped. Straight ahead was the door to the officer's quarters. Left would take him to the mess area where the soldiers often gathered. It was a while since he'd shown his face and Recker knew from the internal monitoring that Sergeant Vance was currently eating. He ignored his fatigue and headed left.

The mess was a compact room about four metres by three, with a total of three exits. The replicator was on the short wall to the left, while to the right, a couple of steel tables were fixed to the right-hand wall. Uncomfortable benches provided limited seating.

Staff Sergeant James Vance was sitting with his back to the entrance and talking to the squad medic, Corporal Suzy Hendrix. She caught Recker's eye and nodded in recognition.

Recker didn't sit at once and he ordered a couple of burgers from the mess replicator. The machine was functioning properly, though that didn't mean too much. Two sorry-looking pale-grey lumps of reconstituted meat peeked out from between the halves of a seed-topped bun which looked like it had been dropped from altitude by a pack of quarrelling seagulls. Compared to the nutri-block, the burgers were gourmet dining at its finest and Recker bit into one as he made his way to the table.

"Mind if I sit?" he asked.

Pale blue eyes stared up. "All yours, sir," said Sergeant Vance.

Recker was a big man and while Vance was a little shorter, he was broader, with a fine-lined face and features which looked like they'd been hewn from a chunk of basalt. Somehow, he'd found the opportunity to shave recently and his blond hair was cropped to exactly the right length dictated in the grooming standards handbook.

If you could take every single stereotype of the battle-hardened sergeant and compress it into a single package, Vance was the result. On top of that, his combat record checked out, though it was unusual to have a rookie assigned to a spaceship.

There wasn't much room on Vance's bench, so Recker sat next to Corporal Hendrix. She was probably younger than thirty, but with hard features that made it difficult to determine her age just by looking, and her haircut was more severe than the military demanded. Hendrix gave him a tight, suspicious smile.

"We're on our way home, Sergeant. In less than five days you'll have that touchdown we talked about," said Recker. "How's the squad coping?"

"They're fine, sir. Sounds like we took a beating and came through it."

"That we did. The Daklan had plenty of firepower out there and my crew did a good job. On top of that, we got lucky."

Vance nodded at the word *lucky*. Recker had a reputation for many things, not all of them bad.

"What comes after this, sir?" asked Hendrix. She had a low voice, not quite husky, and an unusual accent.

"Due some shore leave, Corporal?"

"I'm due three months' worth, sir. Like most of us. I'm not holding my breath."

"If I had to guess, I'd say our feet will hardly touch the ground. Whatever we're assigned to, it won't be the *Finality*."

"What about my squad, sir?" asked Vance.

Recker understood the unspoken question. *Will we be*

coming with you?

"I don't know, Sergeant. If I had to guess, I'd say you're here to stay."

Vance nodded again, his expression unreadable.

Once his meal was finished, Recker didn't linger. It wasn't that he felt unwelcome – not that it would have made a difference to him anyway – more that he had nothing to say and nothing to learn. Recker was sure these soldiers had the skills, they just hadn't had a chance to demonstrate them yet. Maybe they'd get the opportunity before they were helplessly incinerated by Daklan missiles.

In his quarters, Recker barely glanced at the spartan furnishings. He was provided with a bed and a thin foam mattress, while a narrow doorway led into a cubicle with a toilet and a shower. An entertainment unit, bolted to the wall opposite the bed, could play any one of a million films or TV shows as well as providing a private comms link if Recker ever needed one. He couldn't recall the last time he'd switched it on.

Two minutes after rolling onto the mattress, Recker was asleep.

When his alarm went off, he woke with a grogginess that clung to him like a hangover. He hoped a quick shower would be enough to help him shrug off the lethargy and the hot water pelted him with the intensity of hailstones. Steam filled his lungs and the mixed sweat and grime washed into the drain, leaving him feeling considerably better than when he'd first woken up.

A few minutes later, he was dressed and back on the bridge.

CHAPTER TEN

FIVE DAYS WASN'T a long time to spend at lightspeed, but it was frustrating for Recker. The threat of hardware failure didn't go away, though he didn't worry about it. If it happened, it happened, and no amount of fretting would affect the outcome.

Instead, the frustration came from knowing that he was carrying potentially vital intel that he needed to put into the right hands. The Daklan were busy in the Virar-12 system and the HPA military should do something about it, Recker thought.

By day three of the journey, the crew had caught up on sleep and everything was running as smoothly as could be expected. Lieutenant Burner dedicated himself to analysing the data he'd gathered from the cylinder and the task kept him fully occupied. Recker was bored, agitated and irritable, and he checked through the status readouts for the hundredth time, waiting to see what his sensor officer would come up with.

"I think I'm done," said Burner at last.

"What kept you?" asked Eastwood.

"All the ones and zeroes in the raw data."

"Let's hear it, Lieutenant Burner," said Recker. "Anything significant?"

"Yes and no," Burner started. "Like I already told you, the cylinder is constructed from a material we've not seen the Daklan use in anything else. It's a metal alloy, along with some other bits and pieces that our sensors don't recognize."

"Still convinced it's a weapon?"

"From the information available, it's either a spaceship or a weapon," Burner said, in between sips of his coffee. "Or something so completely beyond our expectations that I have no point of reference to help me understand it."

"A weapon," said Aston. "I think we all got that feeling when we first saw the cylinder."

"Yeah," said Eastwood.

"Lieutenant Burner, you thought it was generating power," said Recker.

"It was, sir - a heavily suppressed output. Either the casing was blocking the sensor readings, or the energy source is so volatile that they need to keep a tight rein on it."

"Did you recognize the source?"

"No, sir. Again, it was nothing we've seen from the Daklan before." Burner took in a breath. "There again, they're advancing so fast and we know so little about them. This could be something new or it could be that we've simply not encountered it."

"All that time on the raw data and that's the best you

can come up with?" said Aston, her eyes twinkling. "Guesswork and maybes."

"Oh no, Commander. I saved the juicy bits for last."

"Don't keep us waiting."

"The cylinder emitted two wide area pulses in the short time we got to look at it. Until about an hour ago I couldn't find any reason for the pulse to happen."

"Comms?" said Aston.

"That's what I assumed. Anything military and the sensors on the *Finality* wouldn't be able to pick it up, so I guessed this pulse was something else. Maybe it came from a sensor scan or something, like the personnel on the cylinder were looking out for HPA warships."

"It was something else."

"Yes, sir." Burner finished his coffee and placed the cup reverently on the edge of his console, as if he was buying himself a moment to prepare. "It turned out there *was* something in the pulse. A data packet so small that I don't know how we managed to catch it."

"What was in the packet?"

"Nothing, sir. Or at least nothing readable. Just a blip."

"A *blip*?"

"That's the nontechnical term, sir. I mean the packet wasn't meant to carry anything."

"I'm lost," said Recker, mystified.

"The best explanation I have is that it was an acknowledgement of continued existence."

"A handshake?" asked Recker. A knot built in his stomach.

"Not that, either, sir. More like a *hello, I'm still here.*"

Recker felt suddenly cold. "Another cylinder?"

"Maybe. Or something else." Burner grinned, though it was an apologetic one. "There's more. I mentioned two pulses. The second contained an identical data packet, but this one was aimed elsewhere."

"You were right," said Aston. "You did save the juicy bits for last."

"Did we gather enough information on the travel direction to find where these transmissions were going?" asked Recker. "That's the important question."

"Short answer: I don't know. The pulses were travelling so quickly that we only caught a snapshot of each. In order to follow their paths, we'd need to know at least two points on their route and then we could draw an imaginary line between those points which would give us an indication of the destination."

"With some variance, given the likely distances," said Eastwood.

"Definitely. Anyway, right now, we only know a single point on the route."

"If you knew the transmission point from the cylinder, that would be a second point," said Aston.

"I was coming to that, Commander. I think I can narrow down the likely transmission source to one of three places on the upper four hundred metres of the cylinder. Unfortunately, each of these possible areas is a few dozen metres across and I have no way of pinpointing the precise location of the antennae."

"You're holding something back," said Aston. "I can see it in your face."

"I'm that transparent, am I?" Burner grinned again.

"The data packets were accelerating to lightspeed, which meant they left a trace blur across the raw data."

Recker hadn't heard the term before, but he could guess what Burner was getting at. "The packets left a tail?"

"Yes, sir," said Burner, puffing out his chest a tiny bit. "A really small tail."

"Which gives you a single definite point on the transmission path, alongside two other points which aren't so definite."

"And with a bit of manipulation and guesswork, we should be able to narrow down the destination of one of those packets."

"Only one?"

"I'm sure the antenna for the second was on the cylinder's blindside. We don't have enough information to trace it."

"One's better than none," said Recker. "That's good work, Lieutenant, even if it leads nowhere."

Burner's expression became rueful. "And it might well lead nowhere, sir. I ran a preliminary course projection and you can appreciate the divergence becomes greater as the distance increases. If Admiral Telar decides this is something to follow up, he's going to need a lot of spaceships."

Recker hid his disappointment. "We'll leave that for someone else to deal with when we get back. Maybe one of the deep space monitoring stations will be able to generate a list of candidates for further exploration." He grimaced. "Which in a way leads to a question of my own. What do you suppose that Daklan lifter was doing on Etrol?"

"Bringing something in or taking the cylinder away, you mean?" said Aston.

Recker gave her a nod. "It was an enormous ship."

"Maybe twelve klicks from end to end, sir," Burner reminded him.

"A real big bastard," Eastwood confirmed. "Something that size could fit an eight-klick cylinder in its bay and still have room for Lieutenant Burner's lunch."

"And it could also carry enough ground launchers and other armaments to keep Etrol safe from an HPA attack," said Aston. "It'd be good if we knew which it was."

Recker had already given the matter some thought. "Why would the Daklan want to remove the cylinder?"

"Because they suspected we found it," said Burner.

"In which case, they got a lifter out there pretty damn quickly."

"It could have been stationed close by. The Daklan have a knack of guessing what we're planning. I wouldn't be surprised if they were a stride ahead of us in this."

"Coincidences happen," Recker agreed.

"But you're a reluctant believer," said Aston.

"That I am, Commander." Recker leaned back in his seat and the artificial leather creaked like a cheap jacket. "I can't for the life of me imagine why the Daklan would install something as big as that cylinder and then want to take it away. Especially if it's a weapon."

"Didn't you say Admiral Telar is good at answering questions like this?" asked Burner.

"He's got a sharp mind and a dozen teams of analysts backing him up."

"In that case, he'll have something to say."

"I'm sure he will. That doesn't mean he'll say it to me," said Recker. "And I'm damned if I want to be left in the dark."

"The workings of the military, sir."

"I not a man who accepts the status quo."

"We noticed," said Aston.

Nobody had anything else to say about the data packets or the appearance of the Daklan heavy lifter, so Recker got to his feet and stretched his muscles. The *Finality* had a tiny gym that could accommodate two personnel and he considered paying it a visit.

Instead, he took himself for a walk about the *Finality's* interior, uncomfortably aware that this was the last time he might see these claustrophobic passages. Once the debriefing for this mission was over, he had no doubt that Admiral Telar would have a replacement riot class waiting for him. The same layout, the same weapons, the same everything. But different.

And to go alongside the new spaceship would be a mission that would take Recker and his crew somewhere out on the fringes – to a place that would certainly be both dangerous and out of sight. His face twisted angrily at the thought.

One of the soldiers approached from the other direction and Recker saw that it was a private called Eric Drawl, a man whose bulky combat spacesuit failed to disguise his wiry frame.

"Sir," said the man cordially as he squeezed by in the corridor.

"Soldier."

A few minutes later, Recker was in the mess, where he

picked up a tray of steak and potatoes for lunch. He returned to the bridge and ignored Lieutenant Burner's envious stare.

"Anything happen while I was gone?"

"Nope," said Aston.

The final two days passed in a similarly uneventful fashion, though Recker experienced renewed tension which he couldn't understand. Arrival at Lustre posed problems which might end up fatal, but he'd come to terms with the possibility long ago. Something else was bothering him and he didn't know what it was. The feeling gnawed at him.

Eventually, the journey's end neared.

"Ten minutes and we enter local space!" bellowed Eastwood.

"I'll make sure Sergeant Vance knows about it," said Burner.

With all the advance preparations done and with the monitoring tools checked and checked again, Recker could only wait for re-entry.

"Sixty seconds!"

"This is it, folks. You all know what you're doing."

"Ten seconds."

The *Finality* completed its last journey five seconds early. It rumbled and shuddered, the instrumentation jumped around and the sensors recalibrated.

"We completed the transition," said Eastwood. "We're back in local space."

At the same time, the engine note climbed once more to its deafening howl, reminding Recker how much he hadn't missed it.

"Switch the engines back to a stable condition," he shouted.

"On it, sir."

"I've sent a low speed comm to the Adamantine base requesting emergency assistance," yelled Burner. "We're eight million klicks out, so it'll be a few seconds until they receive it."

"There's a new red on the life support," said Aston. "Critical failure."

"Any way to get it operational?"

"Too early to tell."

Recker checked it out as well. As he was looking at his console, a red appeared on the navigational backup system and then another on the aft sensors.

"The *Finality*'s shutting down," he said.

"It got us home and now it's dying," said Aston, sadness in her expression.

"What about those engines, Lieutenant Eastwood?"

"I'm not having any luck, sir. They won't switch out of semi-stable. It might be because of a failure on the monitoring and control hardware."

"Keep trying."

"I've had a response from Adamantine, sir!" said Burner. "We're to stay put and they'll send someone out here to pick us up."

"Let them know we're in a bad way."

"Already done."

"And then send them every detail about the mission."

"That's just a bunch of unsorted data, sir."

"I don't care – get it on its way and I'll send a verbal report to accompany it." Recker glanced up at the sensor feeds. Lustre was a long way distant. "I'll have plenty of time to put something together."

The rescue craft were rapid in that they could match a riot class for speed. Eight million klicks was a long journey and they'd probably want to go to lightspeed for it. That plus the muster time and Recker guessed they'd be waiting a couple of hours. He wasn't planning on going anywhere.

"Best get your suit helmets on," he said. "We've got enough air to last, but we might as well be prepared."

The crew's helmets were stashed in a wall cubby along with a variety of small arms, a comms beacon and some medical supplies. Recker dropped his into place. A tiny motor whirred, and he felt the collar tightening around his neck to form a seal. It was disconcerting the first few times and thoughts of a motor sensor failure were hard to ignore.

With the rebreather humming softly, Recker instructed the helmet computer to link with the ship's comms, so he could monitor the progress of the rescue team. His breathing was loud and hollow, and for some reason he associated the sound with loneliness.

Two hours and five minutes after Lieutenant Burner made the emergency broadcast to the Adamantine military base, the rescue ship arrived to pick them up. In the circumstances, the team onboard were more cautious than usual and it was five hours later that the *Finality*'s occupants were back on the ground.

With no fatalities and plenty of useful intel, Recker knew he should have been elated at the outcome. All he felt was foreboding.

CHAPTER ELEVEN

TO RECKER'S SURPRISE, he was assigned an office in the central administration building and left to fill his time. The rest of his crew were ordered to report for temporary duty in other areas of the base, while the soldiers were sent to barracks.

That had been an hour ago. Recker cracked his fingers and breathed in the faintly musty air, detecting odours of polish and leather. The room he'd been given was suitable for a senior officer, with carpets, pale-blue painted walls and a few decorations, which had probably been brought in when the base was first constructed and which now looked like they should have been hanging in an elderly person's flowery-wallpapered living room.

A large wooden desk faced the door and a full-width, four-screen communicator terminal took up most of its surface. Every screen was switched on, allowing Recker access to any information available to his grade, as well as to his overflowing inbox. He scanned the latter once and then deleted everything. If any of it was important, Recker was sure someone would turn up at the office to fill him in.

Two windows looked out onto the wall of an adjacent building and the noise of spaceship and shuttle engines was distantly audible through the soundproof clear polymers which most people still referred to as *glass*. The sky above was tinged with late afternoon pink and – he longingly recalled - the air was refreshingly cool. Unfortunately, the windows weren't designed to open, leaving him to rely on the air conditioning. It didn't feel the same.

Recker wasn't the sitting down kind and he certainly wasn't a desk officer. The chair was both soft and supportive, but he couldn't get comfortable in it. However, he couldn't get up to pace the room, because something was going on and he was determined to find out what it was by means of the communicator.

Firstly, the crew on the rescue craft had been jumpy and uncommunicative. Recker was good at ignoring hints that he should stop asking questions and had talked to the personnel at great length. That was when he first became sure something had happened, and that it was a bad kind of happening.

The rescue crew didn't know any details, but they felt it. Usually the rumours would have coalesced by now – possible truth formed out of conjecture - but so far there was nothing other than that feeling.

Here on the ground, the unease was palpable, like the atmosphere in a hospital waiting room. Once again, Recker had tried to extract information from the personnel he met, only to come up blank.

He didn't like to be denied and combed through the

available information. In an organization as big as the HPA military it was hard to keep anything secret and Recker knew where to locate traces of facts that his superiors wanted kept hidden. He had a report to write, but as far as he was aware nobody ever read them, and he believed they were filed away on a data array and then immediately forgotten about. The verbal report he'd sent from the *Finality* would have to be enough for now.

In an hour, he'd uncovered enough. The HPA fleet had suffered a catastrophic defeat to the Daklan, fighting over an insignificant installation on an insignificant world. The more he unearthed, the greater Recker's anger became and he found himself shaking with the intensity of it. He closed his eyes. Maybe he was wrong. Maybe it wasn't so bad as he thought.

He tried to contact Admiral Telar, only to be advised by a computer PA that his commanding officer was busy. Since he was only speaking to a collection of ones and zeroes, Recker gave it an earful and then cut the channel. Ten minutes later, he tried again with the same outcome.

Having discovered the cause of the widespread trepidation, Recker was reluctant to dig further. This was something he'd prefer to speak directly with Admiral Telar about. Telar had faults, but he didn't sugar coat and that suited Recker fine.

Three hours later and he was still in his office, though now the light was artificial instead of entering through his windows. In truth, Recker didn't want to go to his quarters – in a building twenty minutes' walk across the base – and he didn't have anything to do here either. On Lustre, he had no friends and no family. Except his crew. He reached a hand towards the communicator, intending to contact them and find out if they wanted to talk crap in a mess room somewhere.

An inbound message halted his finger mid-air. He answered it and the comm system converted the text file to speech.

"Office 003. Briefing and debriefing with Admiral Telar. Immediately."

Recker stood from his chair and hesitated for a moment in order to study the direction map the computer helpfully provided. Office 003 was in the same admin building as his office, two floors down and in one of the far corners.

He left his room quickly. Telar didn't like to be kept waiting and Recker was keen to speak with him. Last he heard, the admiral was on Earth and FTL conversation would be slow and frustrating, but it was better to have the meeting done than to sit around on the Adamantine base for another few days. Briefing and debriefing, the message said. It sounded like he wouldn't be staying on Lustre very long at all.

Recker's stride lengthened. The admin building was well-constructed, with stone-effect cladding around a strengthened alloy frame. It was just the right side of opulent – enough to instil a sense of pride without prompting Representation members to ask too many questions about the use of taxpayer money.

The building was also filled with tech and that's where the architects had screwed up – the transition between classical materials and square-edged pieces of HPA hardware was jarring and Recker wondered if they should have done something different with the cladding. Like use it for target practice.

Even at this late hour, the corridors were busy with personnel. Fevered, almost. Officers of all grades hurried from place to place, most of them with one eye on a hand-held tablet or speaking loudly into comms headsets. Recker caught a few of the words – enough to realize that the cat was slowly clawing its way out of the bag. This meeting with Admiral Telar had come at just the right time and he was determined to get some answers, whatever it took.

The door to Office 003 was like every other – a veneered piece of alloy with a security panel to the side. Recker brushed his fingertips across the panel, the base mainframe verified that he was on the attendees list and opened the door for him.

He stepped inside.

"Hello, Carl."

Recker belatedly realised that an FTL meeting could have taken place in his existing office without dragging him all the way down here.

"Hello, sir."

Admiral Devon Telar wasn't on Earth. He was here on the Adamantine base, sitting behind a large, dark-wood desk, half-hidden by the desktop communicator.

Telar stood. He was about Recker's height, but slimmer of build, with short grey hair, piercing grey eyes, a straight nose and high cheekbones. In an unusual display of informality, he was dressed in dark blue travelling clothes, like he'd not long ago landed on the base. He gestured towards one of the two spare chairs opposite. "Take a seat."

"I thought you were on Earth, sir," said Recker, lowering himself into the green leather chair.

"I was. And now I'm here." Telar's voice was deep, while his accent was unusual and unidentifiable, like he'd grown up living in several different places. "Tell me what happened on Etrol, Carl. I've got teams checking out the data you sent, and I listened to your verbal report. It was light on detail."

That was an exaggeration, but Recker went with it anyway. "I was light on time, sir."

A hint of a smile played at the corner of Telar's mouth. "A weapon, you say?"

"That's what the evidence suggests, sir. My crew and I believe it's part of a network."

"I've already drawn a few conclusions of my own. Now, please give me the details again. Everything."

Ten minutes later and Recker was finished his explanation. Telar didn't give too much away about his feelings - if he ever decided to take up poker, he'd make a tough opponent, though Recker was beginning to recognize that the admiral's lack of reaction had its own meaning and in itself gave away clues as to what was going through the man's mind.

"You did well, Carl. Thank you."

"Everyone did well, sir."

"I know, but you're the one who's sitting in front of me."

"What are we going to do with the intel? Whatever's happening at Etrol, it's important."

"I need to think on it," said Telar noncommittally.

"But sir..."

Telar raised a hand for silence. "I'm not dismissing your assessment, Captain. Don't think that for a moment." He smiled, though it was a sad one. "Our situation recently became more difficult and until the dust settles, I can't just order a fleet to the Virar-12 system. Not with you confirming the Daklan have an annihilator and a desolator out there."

Recker didn't protest any further – Telar would do what he had to do. "You said our situation just became more difficult. We lost some ships, sir."

Telar didn't seem surprised that the secret was out, though his face twisted in a memory of pain.

"A lot of ships – eighty confirmed, a handful of others unaccounted. A bad result, Carl. A *real* bad result."

"What happened?"

"We had intel from DS-Quad2 – a Daklan installation on a dead world. We saw a chance and we went for it."

"What went wrong?" asked Recker quietly.

"They had a fleet stationed out there. We expected one and we compensated." Telar picked up a collection of papers from his desk and shook them angrily. "Probability reports, intel meetings, strategies, tactics, planning, you name it, we considered everything. Or we thought we did. What we didn't expect was three previously unrecorded annihilators to be out there, along with everything else we *had* assumed."

Three annihilators were enough to turn the tide of most engagements, but Recker got the feeling there was something else.

"Those battleships alone wouldn't be enough to wipe out our fleet, sir. Unless the rest of the Daklan presence already matched us for firepower."

Telar leaned across his desk. "Lightspeed missiles, Carl. High payload, lightspeed missiles."

Recker wanted to say that it wasn't possible - that the Daklan missile tech wasn't much better than what the HPA was producing. He kept his mouth shut, not wanting to waste his breath arguing against the truth.

"Range? Limitations?" he asked.

"We have no answers to either. The few details we have is that the missiles launch from specially-adapted tubes and then accelerate to lightspeed after a short duration."

Recker leaned back and ran the fingers of both hands through his hair. "It's a game changer we didn't need."

"If we'd found out about this new tech in a limited engagement, maybe we'd have enough time to adapt or come up with a counter. Losing eighty ships might be too much."

"Do you think the Daklan held back from showing their hand until they knew they could make the best use of these new missiles?"

"It doesn't matter too much, does it?" Telar smiled thinly. "For what it's worth, I think you're right, Carl. Those bastards are turning out to be cleverer than we are."

"That annihilator at Etrol looked new. It could have used a lightspeed missile against the *Finality*," said Recker in realization. He knew he'd escaped by the skin of his teeth and now he saw exactly how thin the margin had been.

"If it's any consolation, they aimed the missiles at our larger warships. We're working on the assumption the Daklan can only build them in limited numbers or that the cost of producing each is so outrageous they aren't prepared to waste them on the less capable members of our fleet."

Whatever the reality, it was sobering to learn that the enemy had developed a weapon with such terrifying capabilities and Recker fell silent as he considered the future. He remembered something else – a statistic which Aston had mentioned during the Etrol mission.

"I heard we're at a fifty percent chance they'll find one of our worlds within the next twelve months," said Recker.

Telar looked down at his desk, the contents of which were hidden from Recker's eyes by the communicator. Finding what he was after, he brandished some more pages. "This is the latest projection. I won't tell you the numbers, but it's not good."

Recker didn't press for specifics and wasn't sure if he wanted to know what was contained in the projection report. "We've talked problems, sir. What solutions are we working on?"

"Fleet Admiral Solan has obtained agreement from the Representation to transition our economy to total war."

Hearing the name *Solan* caused Recker's hackles to rise, but he kept his expression neutral. The shift to total war was significant and overdue - and probably too late, given the recent loss of eighty ships.

"When is that news going official? The whole military is expecting something."

"I know. Every base is seething like a pit of snakes and

that extends beyond Lustre. Before you leave this office, the word will go out and it'll be ten times worse than it is now. We're cancelling all leave and we're switching to twenty-four-hour operations in our shipyards, weapons factories and research labs."

"We don't have the personnel, sir."

"Not yet we don't. Total war is going to require sacrifices from our people and that extends to more than a few extra feds in taxes."

"Conscription?"

"Starting from tomorrow. Fleet Admiral Solan already has access to civilian records and databanks – he's got a team compiling lists of who we need."

"That won't go down well."

"I'm leaving that to the Representation. They can deal with the fallout, we'll handle the Daklan." Telar wasn't a stupid man and he met Recker's eyes. "And yes, I'm fully aware the military has been derelict in its duties so far, and I'm part of that."

"What are we planning to do about the Daklan? I take it nobody's talking peace?"

"We're talking peace, they're talking war." Telar's gaze was unwavering. "Do you understand the Daklan, Carl?"

Telar didn't like timidity in his officers, so Recker came right out and said what he thought. "They're warlike bastards, sir. They respect strength and bravery, though they give no quarter when confronted by either."

"I don't think they respect strength," said Telar with a slow shake of his head. "If anything, the strong don't have to be brave – they win battles without taking risks."

Recker thought he understood where Telar was leading. "They are the strong party in this war."

"Yes, they are now. A decade ago, they weren't. Back then, the HPA might have had the upper hand. At the very least we were evenly matched."

"The Daklan could make peace at any time and we'd accept."

"Think about the situation." Telar didn't drop his gaze and the intensity of it increased.

"They won't make peace because we keep asking for it."

"So I have come to believe. At one time, they might have respected us. Now, they may even hate us for our weakness."

"That's no reason for them to pursue the war so aggressively."

"I'm not so sure you're right. Maybe the Daklan want to destroy us completely."

"You don't think so."

"I think they'll come to a trigger point at which they feel honour – or whatever concept of it the Daklan hold – has been satisfied."

"When do you think that point will come, sir?"

"I don't know, Carl. I lie awake at night asking myself the question and I'm no closer to coming up with anything I can believe in. In truth, a part of me does think the Daklan will continue until we are extinct. We're dealing with aliens here and we have only a limited grasp of their motivations, despite the number of people we employ to try and understand them."

"What are our plans, sir?" asked Recker again.

"We should do our damnedest to regain the respect of

our opponents," said Telar, avoiding the question. "They hurt us, we hurt them."

"I don't see the difference. That's how we've always approached the war."

"We have been risk averse. We have allowed opportunities to pass us by in case the outcome resulted in too many casualties – casualties that the Representation might not accept. Losses that our funding might be inadequate to replace."

"We're going to take some extra risks?"

A fleeting something passed across Telar's features and Recker guessed that high command wasn't in complete agreement about what approach they should take.

"Some *limited* risks. When the moment is right. Our fleet has suffered and even though we have many part-built warships in our yards, our losses will take time to replace."

"Not all of those risks will be delayed for the *right moment*. That's why I'm here."

"You understand the realities, Carl." Telar sighed. "Several hours ago, I had few options. Now, I have many and little time to understand the potential outcomes of each possible success or failure." He leaned forward, offering a sheet of paper.

Recker took the printout, which was headed *Top Secret*. The text was small and there was plenty of it. He scanned the top few lines and found that he was holding a list of potential Daklan installations, gathered from the DS-Quad1 monitoring station's long-range scans. Against each line was a percentage, ranging from one to fourteen.

"A lot of sightings," Recker said.

"I have similar lists from our other three monitoring stations. A total of 615 leads to investigate, and not nearly enough warships to accomplish the task." Telar gave a half-smile. "Turn it over."

The printout was double-sided and continued all the way to the bottom of the second side. One line stood out – it was highlighted in orange and the percentage was higher than any of the others.

"Thirty-four percent," Recker grunted humorlessly. "I guess this one's mine."

"You're a damn good officer, Carl."

"Did you choose this? Or did instruction come from elsewhere?"

"The military picks the best personnel for every job."

Recker's anger climbed again. "Cut the crap, sir. I know how it works and you're going along with it."

"You don't know as much as you think, Captain!" said Telar, thumping his palm onto the desk. "There's a spaceship waiting on the landing strip to replace the broken one you came back in. You'll depart within two hours."

"What about a briefing, sir?" asked Recker coldly.

"Everything you need is waiting onboard. Now go!"

Recker stood and studied Telar's face for a moment, searching for hints as to what the admiral was thinking.

"Thank you, sir." Recker turned for the door.

"Carl?" The word was spoken softly.

"Sir?"

"I can't promise you a change. Not yet."

"I know, sir. This is my cross to bear."

With that, Recker left Telar's office.

CHAPTER TWELVE

GETTING hold of his crew wasn't an easy task given the late hour and Recker was required to send squads out to make sure they were roused. After that, he exited the admin building into the near darkness of late evening. The air was colder than before and filled with the sounds of countless vehicles passing along the roads nearby. From much further away came the dull bass rumble of something far bigger.

Without a backward glance, Recker made for the parking lot where vehicles were left for the use of senior officers. Personnel headed in every direction and the roads were in danger of becoming clogged. Troops of armed soldiers in full combat gear jogged from place to place. Directly ahead, the walls of another building loomed and everywhere he looked, Recker saw others like it, light spilling from their reinforced windows and figures visible inside.

The Adamantine base was predominantly right-angles, concrete and alloy. Aside from the central administration building, everything was designed with two things in mind: cost and resilience. Recker didn't hate it, but every time he came to one of the HPA's military bases, he was reminded why he preferred to be far away in space. There was beauty in emptiness. Here, there was little to be found.

Only a single vehicle remained in the lot and another officer brushed past Recker as he dashed towards it.

"That one's mine," said Recker calmly.

The man slowed and turned to look over his shoulder. He recognized Recker's insignia and gave a rueful smile. "Sorry, sir. All yours."

Recker was in too much of a hurry to offer the other man a ride and he strode past. The vehicle was square and basic like exterior of the buildings and he hauled open the door. He slid into the driver's seat and wrinkled his nose. A pile of crumpled fast food wrappers in the rear footwell told a tale of selfish laziness. Recker told himself it wasn't important and tapped his finger against the starter pad.

The vehicle's onboard computer completed a biometric scan and its gravity drive fired up with a gentle hum, lifting the car a couple of feet from the ground.

"Where to, sir?" asked the navigational computer with irritating obsequiousness.

"Take me to the *Punisher*. And don't piss about."

"Certainly, sir. By which I mean I will certainly take you to the *Punisher*, but I certainly won't delay."

"Shut up and go."

"Yes, sir!"

The car reversed out of the lot and headed into traffic.

This area of Adamantine was served by a road with five lanes in both directions. Even so, it was crowded – far more than Recker would have expected at any other time. Admiral Telar had promised that news of total war would go out and Recker guessed he'd made it onto the roads just in time. Another hour and he expected the base mainframe would have to take control of every ground-based navigational system just to keep things moving.

Recker's pocket buzzed and he tugged out his portable communicator. It had a flip screen and he opened it with one thumb to find confirmation that his crew were on their way. He closed the device with a clack and slid it back into his pocket.

For a couple of minutes, the car got stuck behind the broad hull of a tank, which occupied all five lanes and which didn't seem in a hurry. Recker gritted his teeth and considered opening a comms channel to the driver. A few seconds later, the tank turned left towards another area of the base, its twin-barrel guns almost scraping against the sides of the corner building.

After that, the traffic lessened, though the pavements were no less busy. The road widened to fifteen lanes in each direction as it carried on straight into the storage and warehouse area of Adamantine. In this area, the largest vehicles of all required access, though Recker couldn't see any of the huge crawlers which lugged supplies and ammunition from warehouse to warship.

The last of daytime's deep blue vanished from the sky, leaving thousands of artificial lights to produce an imperfect copy of midday here at ground level. Recker had always been impressed by the size of the military's storage facilities and he peered through the windshield at the sheer walls of concrete reaching high above.

At last, the car left the buildings behind and it raced onto the landing strip, which was illuminated by countless globes embedded in the ground. Ahead and in the distance, Recker saw the familiar outline of a riot class, while to his left was the much larger shape of a Teron class cruiser.

A surprise waited – the source of the rumbling engine he'd heard earlier turned out to be one of the fleet's battle-ships, which hovered so low to the ground that it might as well have been touching. The warship was showing its profile and Recker marvelled at the sleek, four-thousand-metre, dark shape that crossed his vision. From here, the front and rear charge cannons were the only visible protrusions in the purposeful lines of the hull. He guessed it was either the *Damocles* or the *Granite*, which were the oldest two battleships in the fleet.

"That's how Admiral Telar got here," he muttered. "No wonder it didn't take him long."

Telar didn't generally treat fleet warships as his own personal transport, so Recker assumed the battleship had another mission. Whatever that might be, he didn't know and didn't attempt to guess.

The landing strip occupied approximately one hundred square kilometres and was clad in a thick concrete which was reinforced with flexible alloy bars that could support the immense weight of a spaceship by bending rather than snapping. Vehicles of all descriptions – many of them automated – travelled in every direction. Recker spotted cranes and cargo trucks, along with the largest low-level crawler he'd ever seen. In the sky, shuttles flew, many of them with huge loads suspended underneath.

The landing strip was never quiet, but the activity was clearly increasing.

"Getting busy, sir," said the navigational computer.

"Yeah."

"We're going to kick some ass!"

"You think?" asked Recker without interest. He didn't normally waste time speaking to computers.

"Oh, absolutely, sir," the machine gushed. "I wouldn't like to be a Daklan when our fleet comes knocking."

"Thanks for the input. Now be quiet."

The car drove past a stack of Railer ammunition crates that were probably intended for the cruiser, veered sharply around the tail end of a crawler and then headed straight. The *Punisher* was still out of sight, parked up in the far corner of the landing field somewhere behind the battleship. Two more riots came into view amongst the organized chaos and then Recker caught sight of the ship-yard, several kilometres to his right.

The construction crews were working on something like always, and Recker remembered seeing the incomplete hull of a shard class destroyer in the visible trench when the rescue craft was bringing him in. The adjacent trench – currently out of sight – held a second destroyer and in the third was a cruiser, while the other two were empty. The HPA would need more firepower than two destroyers and a cruiser if it hoped to face down the Daklan fleet.

With each passing second, the battleship grew larger

in the windshield and Recker could feel the rumble of its propulsion whenever he touched an exposed metal surface inside the car. He now recognized it as the *Granite* from a slight variation in the angles of its rear section plating, resulting from repairs a few months ago.

The car didn't have permission to drive beneath the battleship and it diverted around. After what seemed like many minutes, the vehicle passed beyond the rear section of the warship and then Recker saw his new ride. The *Punisher* appeared tiny – insignificant – in comparison to the *Granite* and looked like any other riot class. From what he'd learned, this one only finished its trials eight days ago.

Recker thought back to Aston's words about them being assigned to a rust bucket and smiled. An old ship would go through the same extensive maintenance as every other warship, meaning they were as reliable as anything else in the fleet. Something new like the *Punisher*, on the other hand, might well have all kinds of underlying issues that would only make themselves known in the first few hundred hours of active duty.

Someone had a sense of humour, though Recker wasn't laughing.

The car slowed up and came to a halt at the *Punisher*'s forward boarding ramp. A squad of soldiers stood guard and a light tank patrolled nearby. The armoured vehicle seemed like an overkill deterrent for the HPA's army of civilian warship spotters – colloquially known in the military as *spaceholes* - but there were groups out there for whom it was a badge of honour to get onboard a military craft, even when the penalties for doing so were severe and occasionally fatal.

Recker had no sympathy. The military put on regular parades and displays, giving every citizen the opportunity to see the latest warships and armed vehicles from up close. There was no excuse for interfering with vessels on active duty.

"Good luck out there, sir," said the car. "And do your duty!"

Slamming the door with feeling, Recker headed the last fifty metres towards the guard squad. He counted fifteen men and women. They looked alert and were dressed in full combat gear, each carrying a standard-issue gauss rifle, a sidearm and two grenades. More than enough to deal with a bunch of overeager spaceholes.

The commanding officer advanced to meet Recker, offering him a salute of pinpoint accuracy. He'd read his briefing and knew who was coming.

"Captain Recker," said the man. "I'm Sergeant Tracker."

"Any problems, Sergeant?"

"No, sir. I checked out the test report. Everything's green to go."

Recker winced at the reference to a test report. The signoff guys were technical experts, but it was the everyday maintenance teams who knew the nuts-and-bolts ways of keeping a spaceship ticking, often locating faults even when the monitoring hardware reported everything was in tip-top shape.

"Thank you, Sergeant. I'm waiting for my crew and a squad of soldiers."

"Yes, sir. Commander Aston, alongside Lieutenants

Eastwood and Burner. I'll tell them to head straight onboard."

"What about the squad?"

"Staff Sergeant Vance, sir," said Tracker promptly. "I got word he's on his way."

"Send him to quarters once he arrives."

Tracker knew the drill and snapped out another salute, no less perfect than one which preceded it.

With the formalities over, Recker approached the *Punisher*. Its engines were running, though they struggled to make themselves heard over the all-encompassing droning of the *Granite*. The multitude of thick landing legs towered high, like a forest of alloy, and the spaceship's underside blotted out many of the stars. While the riot class were easily the smallest warships in the fleet, only an idiot would call one *small*.

At the end of the boarding ramp, Recker paused, trying to remember exactly how long it had been since he'd commanded anything other than the *Finality*. He took a breath and put his foot on the lowest step. The ramp weighed a few thousand tons and it didn't so much as echo beneath the weight of his tread.

Above, the light from the airlock was muted and Recker climbed into the enclosed space, which was reputedly designed to accommodate exactly fifteen soldiers with a full loadout. Whatever the truth, Recker knew the current record was twenty-eight soldiers, though he had no idea how the feat was accomplished.

A door at the far end of the airlock opened when he touched the access panel and Recker entered the ship.

The sight and the smell were identical to that of the *Finality* and he felt immediately at home.

Within five minutes, he was on the bridge and sitting in the command seat. A quick status check told him that all the onboard systems were online and showing green lights. He accessed the external sensors and focused one of the arrays on the landing strip. In the few minutes since he'd boarded, the quantity of visible traffic had increased noticeably.

Commander Aston was carrying a personal communicator and Recker connected to it.

"I'd guess we're ten minutes from the *Punisher*, sir. We got slowed by traffic. You said we had two hours before Admiral Telar expects us to lift off."

"And you can be sure he's standing with a stopwatch, Commander."

She laughed. "I'll bet. Anyway, we're coming as fast as we can."

The channel went dead and Recker accessed the mission briefing files, which he skimmed through once. With that done, he continued his pre-flight checks. His officers were a little more efficient at the task when it came to their own specialities, but it wouldn't hurt to give them a head start.

Sergeant Vance and his squad arrived in an ugly-looking armoured transport a few seconds before the crew, and Recker watched the soldiers file up the boarding ramp. He linked with Vance's comms unit and repeated the order to hunker down in quarters.

"Quarters it is, sir." Vance's tone didn't give away much of his feelings, though Recker was certain everyone in the squad would be pissed at the current turn of events. Or maybe they were experienced enough to have learned that you had to take the rough with the smooth.

Shortly after, Commander Aston entered the bridge, followed by Eastwood and Burner, the latter with his hair sticking up like he'd been fast asleep when his communicator started buzzing.

"Welcome onboard," said Recker. "Ladies and gentlemen, please take your seats. The clock is ticking and we have to be on our way."

"Where are we going, sir?" said Eastwood. "And couldn't it have waited until morning?"

"Nothing can wait until morning, Lieutenant - I thought you'd know that by now."

"You'd think," Eastwood grumbled.

"Let's not delay any longer, folks. I've done the basic checks and you've got five minutes to find anything I've missed. After that, we're taking off. The mission briefing gives me the usual limitations on disclosure."

"Nothing until we're at lightspeed, huh?" said Burner.

"Got it in one, Lieutenant."

The crew took their stations and got to work. Recker could see the tiredness in their features and Burner couldn't stop yawning. They had a long flight ahead, so there'd be time for sleep once the *Punisher* entered lightspeed.

"That's five minutes," said Recker loudly. "Anything to report?"

"All green, sir."

"Lieutenant Burner, we should have clearance to depart."

"That's confirmed, sir. Our window lasts another ten minutes."

Recker glanced at the clock and smiled. Assuming Telar had ordered the clearance window, he'd given the *Punisher* precisely zero additional time over the two hours.

"Tell the squad outside to get clear."

"Sergeant Tracker acknowledges the order."

The squad didn't hang about. Most of them piled into a nearby transport, while another climbed into the cabin of the truck Sergeant Vance had arrived in. Moments later, they were gone, leaving the area beneath the *Punisher* clear.

"We're ready," Recker said. He reached out and laid his hand on the two horizontal bars in front of him.

Almost every spaceship captain had preferences about the weighting on the controls and they could be adjusted through software. The resistance he felt when he pulled gently at the alloy bars told Recker immediately that the technicians had loaded his profile data.

He increased power to the engines. They hummed with increasing volume, accompanied by a droning and a faint vibration which was subtly different to that of the *Finality*.

"That doesn't sound right," he said. "Lieutenant Eastwood, check it out."

"Nothing to worry about, sir. The *Punisher* is carrying slightly larger propulsion modules than the *Finality* and our maximum output is approximately four percent higher."

"That'll make all the difference," said Burner.

"Eyes on your station, Lieutenant," Aston reminded him.

Recker didn't wait any longer and took the *Punisher* vertically into the darkness. Several proximity warnings bleeped to advise him of the traffic above the landing strip, but the base mainframe was programmed to halt anything that drifted too close to the warship's permitted flight path.

Higher into the sky the *Punisher* flew, gaining altitude steadily. There were no towns or cities nearby, but the military didn't permit its spaceships to create sonic booms in non-emergency situations.

"You never get sick of the views," said Aston, pointing at the starboard feed.

From this altitude, the sensors picked up the retreating planet's day, far in the distance. It was almost gone, leaving a thick curve of deep blue tracing across the edge of Lustre. Recker wanted to stare but had to focus on the warship's flight. It was sights like this which had first made him abandon his career as a ground soldier to become a flight officer.

On the underside feed, the sprawling Adamantine base dwindled, though the *Granite* was still visible. To one side, the construction trenches were thick grey lines, with specks moving around like a swarm of tiny insects. Recker noticed activity on the far trench and he wondered if they were expanding it in order to accommodate a larger hull for whatever was due to be built next.

"That's us at a thousand klicks," said Burner.

"Time to fly," said Aston.

"The first active duty stress test," Recker confirmed.

He rammed the controls forward and the *Punisher*'s

engines responded by throwing the warship towards the stars. The velocity gauge climbed rapidly, the rate of increase only slowing as it approached maximum speed.

"We've got clearance to hit lightspeed once we're at half a million klicks, sir," said Burner.

That was plenty of time for the *Punisher* to hit maximum speed and Recker held it there, enjoying the intoxicating propulsion note.

"No alerts," said Eastwood. "Looks like we got a good one."

The next big test was entry to lightspeed and Recker brought the spaceship to a halt at exactly half a million klicks from Lustre.

"You have access to the destination coordinates, Lieutenant Eastwood. Warm up the ternium drive," he said.

"Roger that, sir. On the star charts that shows up as a solar system called Exim-K. Four days travel time."

"That's right."

The warmup required fifteen minutes and although the crew talked lightly, it was a tense wait. A warship was tested extensively for lightspeed entry before it went into service, but for some reason, accidents still happened, predominantly on the very first active duty transit.

At exactly fifteen minutes, the warship's mainframe completed its calculations and the *Punisher* launched into lightspeed.

CHAPTER THIRTEEN

THE SPACESHIP'S instrumentation jumped around crazily, the sensors went blank and the comms links dropped, while the crew experienced nausea and a feeling of dislocation. So far, nothing unusual.

"We're not dead," said Lieutenant Burner.

"Doesn't seem like it," said Aston.

Recker concealed his relief. He hadn't expected the *Punisher* to break up, but he thought a few ambers might appear on the monitoring tools. As yet, the sea of green lights hadn't so much as flickered and he was beginning to wonder if his opinion about the reliability of new spaceships was no longer valid.

"As Lieutenant Eastwood said, the *Punisher* seems like a good one," he said. "But don't take your eyes off the equipment just yet."

"I can't keep mine open, sir."

"First duty break is in an hour and you're one of the

chosen two, Lieutenant Burner. The replicator's in the usual place if you need some temporary assistance."

"Thank you, sir," said Burner, rising at once to order a coffee.

Aston stretched luxuriously in her seat and rolled her head on her shoulders. "Are you going to tell us what's happening at Exim-K?" She stood and gave Recker a look. "And what are high command planning to do with the information we brought back from Etrol?"

"I hear we've gone to total war, sir," said Eastwood.

The crew had some pent-up questions and Recker did his best to answer them. They hadn't heard about the losses inflicted on the HPA fleet and they took it hard.

"That's a real kick in the balls," said Eastwood. "We're not coming back from that soon."

"It won't be easy, Lieutenant. The next few months are going to be the most important of our lives." He smiled grimly. "By which I mean the lives of every HPA citizen."

"We might lose this," said Burner, as if it was just sinking in. "All these years of fighting and now we're on the brink."

"We're not on the brink yet," said Recker, more angrily than he meant. "We've had setbacks before and this is another one to add to the list. You know what total war means – bottomless funding for new ships and new tech. The military is bringing in the finest minds from across the HPA. It'll take a few months for everyone to start pulling in the same direction, but that's just a challenge we'll have to overcome."

"I hope it works out, sir," said Burner quietly.

"It will. It has to."

"Lightspeed missiles," said Aston, shaking her head in dismay. "What can we do against technology like that?"

"We can learn fast, Commander. Same as we always do."

"And we're still non-the-wiser about what the Daklan were planning on Etrol," said Aston.

"It doesn't look like we'll find out any time soon, either," said Recker. He thumped his console, but the anger was already fading.

"Once we reach Exim-K, we're to investigate two of the twelve planets – Oldis and Resa," said Eastwood. "Neither of which have been scouted by the HPA. So what exactly is it we're looking for?"

"Nobody knows, Lieutenant. One of the deep space monitoring stations found something – a trace of whatever it is they hunt for – and the report ended up in Admiral Telar's hands. Now we're on our way to see whatever there is to be seen."

"What aren't you telling us, sir?" said Aston.

"I'm that obvious?"

"Sometimes."

"Admiral Telar had a big list of places to explore. The one we were given stood out as the most likely to be a site of enemy activity."

Aston looked shocked. "In that case, why aren't they sending a substantial force, sir?"

"Admiral Telar didn't say."

"But you found out."

"I checked the flight logs. There's a temporary hold on any mission that doesn't involve the defence of our estab-lished installations or resource-bearing planets. Presumably to give high command a chance to update their strategy."

"So the whole fleet's on lockdown apart from us?"

"As far as exploration and scouting goes, yes."

"Why is Admiral Solan still screwing with you after all these years, sir?" asked Eastwood. "And why does his father tolerate it?"

"Next time I see either of them, I'll be sure to ask," said Recker, clenching his fists.

The crew knew his background and they didn't scratch at the wound. For his part, Recker hated that they were involved and it was more than peripheral. Because Admiral Gabriel Solan held a pointless grudge, anyone assigned to one of Recker's missions could be sure they'd be exposed to the biggest risks, yet not so obviously that any evidence of it was left behind.

Recker hadn't even known it was happening for a long time and assumed he was getting all the bad missions because high command thought that a former ground pounder should be pushed harder than the other officers. Yet the bad missions kept on coming and eventually Recker found out by accident that his past *transgressions* weren't forgotten.

For a time, he revelled in his ability to take on those missions and turn a good result out of each one. Success was never enough and Recker suddenly knew he'd tolerated the situation for far too long. The manipulation was getting worse, not better, and soon he and his crew would be given a mission that no amount of skill or luck could pull them through.

Maybe this mission.

Although his expression didn't change, inside he raged and Recker told himself that enough was enough. When this trip to Exim-K was done, he'd put a stop to this. Even if he had to fly the *Punisher* straight through Admiral Solan's front window and set the warship down on the man's hand-knitted fireside rug.

Negative thoughts weren't going to help him through this mission and Recker pushed them aside. The shift break was due and he sent Aston and Burner to get their four hours sleep. Recker's muscles felt coiled and he longed to burn off some of his pent-up energy by walking around the spaceship, if just to familiarise himself with what was surely already familiar.

With Aston on shift break, Recker couldn't go anywhere except the replicator. This one was working fine, and they'd even upgraded the model over what was installed on the *Finality*. The steak and fries that appeared in the vend slot were almost indistinguishable from the real thing. Almost.

Lieutenant Eastwood didn't speak much and that suited Recker fine, since the day was beginning to catch up with him. Besides, he appreciated the quiet and used it to think about what might lie ahead at Exim-K. A thirty-four percent chance of finding something was too high to ignore, which meant the *Punisher* and its crew were likely heading into danger.

Luckily, much of what the deep space monitoring stations detected ended up as nothing out of the ordinary, so the mission could turn out to be an extended surface scan of two heavy ore bearing planets. A real optimist might hope to locate ternium deposits or some other rare metals. Recker smiled thinly at the thought.

At last, his time to sleep came and he accepted the opportunity gratefully, and by halfway into the four-day journey, the crew was fully adapted to the new routine. Recker spoke to Sergeant Vance and a few of the other soldiers and found they were more resigned than angry at being sent out again so soon after touchdown.

"I want to shoot some Daklan sir," boasted Private Wayland Steigers, one time Recker turned up in the mess room.

"No promises we'll find any, soldier."

"Don't listen to him, sir," advised Corporal Hendrix. "Last time Steigers fired that rifle he was holding it the wrong way and it took me three hours to patch him up."

"Hey, quit saying that, Corporal," Steigers protested. "I was there on Haldar. Fiver, too."

Hendrix laughed and Recker saw how different she might look when the fighting was over.

"Fiver," she said. "What a rot hole."

"What happened?" asked Recker. The war had so many flashpoints he couldn't keep up with the individual stories.

"What didn't happen more like," said Private Ken Raimi, leaning against the wall near the replicator and pretending to study his gauss rifle.

"Yeah," said Steigers. "Must have been ten thousand Daklan ground troops with tank and air support, trying to take one of our ore processing plants. Me and some of the guys..." he pointed at the other soldiers in the room, "...we were holed up for must've been days in one of those big storage areas. The Daklan kept on coming and we kept on shooting them."

"Good thing for us they wanted to keep the place operational," said Hendrix. "Else we'd have been toast."

"In the end, there was just too many of the bastards," Steigers resumed. "I was down to my last mag and all I could see was Daklan."

"And what happened?"

Steigers smiled, revealing pristine teeth. "A dozen of our warships came out of lightspeed and incinerated everything. Except the ore plant. That didn't have a mark on it." His smile faded. "But they took out Lieutenant Danny Steyne and most of his squad. Damn shame for those boys."

"Shit happens," said Hendrix, like she was trying to convince herself.

"And now it's going to get worse, Corporal," said Raimi. "Total war means the meat grinder's got a whole lot more bodies to chew through."

"I'm not going to be one of them," said Steigers. "I promised my wife and kid I'd get through this for them. And my daughter thinks her Daddy's a hero."

"You let her believe that?" asked Raimi in mock disbelief.

"Hey, shut up, man. It helps me get through, alright?"

"And taking the piss out of you helps me get through."

"How's about you kiss my hairy ass, Raimi?"

"I just ate, man. Don't make me bring it up again."

Recker listened, glad that the soldiers were opening up in his presence. A couple of months ago when they first came onboard, they were almost hostile - as if they resented him for leaving behind the ground corps and becoming something he didn't deserve to be. Maybe the attitudes were thawing and Recker hoped it was so.

He left the mess room and continued his circuit of the interior. A riot class wasn't a good place for the claustrophobic, though Recker found it strangely soothing to be here. Walking these corridors was the closest thing he could get to having some time alone with his thoughts.

At a nondescript door, Recker halted. He tapped his fingers against the control panel and the door rumbled open, revealing one of the two steep ramps leading to the underside bay. Recker headed down.

The bay was the largest interior space on the warship, though that didn't mean too much. It extended for thirty metres forward to aft and twenty from port to starboard, with a wide channel running down the middle where the incision class deployment vehicle was accessed.

It seemed as if the lighting was set at a lower level than everywhere else and it was freezing cold, like down here the vacuum was pressing at the fabric of the warship and trying to reach the warmth of life inside. With his head brushing the ceiling, Recker advanced across the floor towards the channel. At the edge, he stopped, not knowing why he'd come here.

The deployment vehicle was clamped to the underside of the thick, armoured slab which formed the bay floor. It was hard to make out the shape of the craft by what was revealed in the metre-deep channel, but Recker knew the vessel was sleek, cramped and lightly armoured. Two square hatches, five metres apart, allowed access and he checked the security panels on each to make sure there were no failures.

Everything was operational and ready to go, so Recker exited the bay and headed back to the bridge.

The remaining two days went by in a peculiar mix of double-time and half-time. When Recker thought about it, he reasoned that it all averaged out. At no point in the journey did the *Punisher*'s monitoring tools highlight any hardware faults, leaving Recker confident that the spaceship would hold together for the coming mission.

"We're going to drop out of lightspeed midway between Oldis and Resa. From the observations of DS-Quad2, they should be almost in alignment with Exim-K," said Eastwood. "The mission briefing doesn't make it clear which of the two we should be looking at first."

"You know why that is," said Aston.

"Because they didn't know."

"That's right, Lieutenant. We're here to find out."

"Still be nice to have some clues."

"I won't argue that one."

"Thirty minute and we enter local space," said Eastwood a few minutes later. "We'll get to do that *finding out* pretty damn soon."

Recker felt a chill of anticipation, like this mission to Exim-K was going to end up far more significant than anyone expected. He smiled inwardly. If his intuition was right, Admiral Solan might regret sending one of the fleet's least capable warships. However, Recker fully intended to show what could be accomplished with a riot class warship, a skilled crew and plenty of guts.

"Ten minutes! Get ready for re-entry folks!" yelled Eastwood.

The wall timer counted down and Recker could hardly take his eyes away from it. At two minutes, Eastwood called his final warning and the crew straightened in readiness.

At ten seconds, Recker took a deep breath and placed his hands on the controls. The propulsion system grumbled and the *Punisher* shuddered at the switchover to sublight engines. Without drama, the warship re-entered local space.

CHAPTER FOURTEEN

STATUS REPORTS!" shouted Recker, giving the engines maximum. A spaceship always emerged from lightspeed at a low velocity and made an easy target for anything hostile. The accepted tactic was to go to full thrust and execute evasive manoeuvres, launching disruptor drones at the same time if you were dropping into the middle of a battle zone.

"Weapons systems online and available," said Aston over the sound of the acceleration.

"No errors on the hardware," shouted Eastwood.

"Waiting for sensor calibration, sir."

"Commander Aston, I want you to help out on the local area scans," said Recker, banking the *Punisher* hard one way and then the other.

"On it, sir."

"Sensor recalibration complete," said Burner. "Positioning underway. We're in Exim-K. Commencing close range scans."

"Working on the fars," said Aston.

Recker could fly without conscious thought and he was able to study the bulkhead display to see what the sensors were picking up. Right now, there was plenty of darkness.

"Nothing on the close-range scan," said Burner. "I'm expanding the sweep radius."

If there was an enemy warship close by, Recker was sure it would have made itself known by now. Given that the *Punisher* wasn't going to be within easy sensor range of either Oldis or Resa, it was enormously unlikely the Daklan would spot their arrival. Even so, the tension in his shoulders and arms didn't lessen and he waited impatiently for his crew to paint him a picture.

"I've located Oldis, sir," said Aston. "Forty million klicks to port."

"Remember it's in near alignment with Resa," said Eastwood.

"Yes I got that, Lieutenant." Aston went quiet for a few seconds. "There's Resa – about forty million klicks starboard."

"An easy stroll in cosmic terms," said Eastwood dryly.

"What about the far scans, Lieutenant Burner?"

"Nearly complete, sir. Done. We're in the clear."

Recker backed off on the controls and reduced speed to half. "We made it here safely, so that's the first hurdle jumped. Commander Aston, Lieutenant Burner – check out those planets and see if you can determine which one we should check out first. Bonus points to the officer who pinpoints the location of a Daklan outpost."

"Let's get it done," said Aston. "I'll take Oldis." She

sounded eager and her hands flew confidently from place to place on her console.

"I guess that means I take Resa."

Recker would have liked to walk between their stations to see how they worked – it was always good to learn new tricks or see how other experienced officers did what they did – yet even the all-clear on the wide area sweep wasn't enough to make him abandon the controls. He didn't get a sense of impending danger but wasn't about to treat instinct as fact.

Lieutenant Burner was the first to report. "Resa - planet eight of twelve, with zero moons. We've got rocks, ice and a ten thousand klick diameter. From this range, there's not much else to be seen," he said. "I've attempted a penetrative surface scan to hunt for anything which might have triggered the lenses on the monitoring station." He exhaled in frustration. "We're too far out and I can't obtain an accurate geological profile."

"Commander Aston?"

"Just finishing the preliminaries, sir. Oldis – planet seven with an eighteen thousand klick diameter and again, zero visible moons. That's unusual for a planet this size. Surface imperfections indicate past upheaval. Given the relative proximity to Resa, maybe the two planets collided a few billion years ago."

"What do the surface scans show?"

"No conclusive evidence of anything Daklan."

"Well, shit," said Recker. He gave a short laugh. "I should stop expecting everything on a plate."

"We've got some work ahead of us, sir," said Burner.

"What're the options?" mused Recker. "Going to

either place will require a lightspeed jump or ten hours at sub-light. I'm not ready to commit until we've obtained every piece of information available to us from here."

"In that case, the options are to keep doing what we're doing," said Burner. "The sensors gather data more effectively from a fixed position. The two planets are diverging along their orbital tracks. If you held the *Punisher* in a fixed relative position to either Oldis or Resa, I could run a long-exposure scan of whichever planet. That would pull up a lot of raw data, but we might find something in amongst it."

"Leaving the second planet and two blindsides still to scan."

Burner shrugged. "Like you said, sir - it's not coming on a plate. The choice is between safety and speed."

"Right now, we'll stick with the safe option." Recker narrowed his eyes in Burner's direction. "Do you have a hunch about either?"

"I'm not sure, sir. Maybe Oldis first."

"Oldis it is. I'll hold at forty million klicks and you have an hour."

"That's not enough time, sir."

"I know. After an hour, we'll jump in to ten million klicks."

"If there are Daklan on the surface, ten million should be far enough to avoid easy detection," Burner confirmed. "I'll get started. Commander Aston's assistance will move things along."

"You've got it."

"I've sent my preferred coordinates to your console,

sir. Once the *Punisher* is stationary in that position, we'll gather a lot more raw data."

A green line appeared on Recker's navigation screen and he guided the *Punisher* along it. The planet was travelling at a little over eighteen klicks per second around its orbital track, which was an easy speed for the warship to maintain. A few minutes later, Recker finished the positioning and set the autopilot to hold at a precise distance from Oldis.

"Don't forget you'll have to compensate for the planet's rotation, sir. We need to be as relatively stable as possible."

"I didn't forget, Lieutenant. We're in place."

Aston didn't require micromanagement and she already had her face close to one of the screens on her console, her eyes darting across the data. Nearby, a paper notepad and a stubby pencil were her tools for jotting down ideas and discoveries. A few thousand years of technological advancement wasn't enough to make such basic instruments completely obsolete.

Ten minutes went by and then twenty. Since the *Punisher* was on autopilot and running smoothly, Recker didn't have much to do. He drummed his fingers, studied the sensor feeds, vended drinks for Aston and Burner, and tried not to waste time thinking what they might find here at Exim-K. Guessing was a fool's game, though one it was hard not to play.

"Some parts of Oldis are unusually patterned," said Burner eventually. "Others, not so much." It was the first time he'd spoken in about thirty minutes, which was probably a new personal best for the man.

"How so?" asked Recker.

"Hang on, I've got enough information to generate a rough topographic map. Here you go, sir – coming up on the centre screen."

It *was* a rough map and Recker narrowed his eyes, trying to spot the areas Burner thought were unusual. A grey representation of Oldis hovered on the screen, its computer-generated edges artificially distinct. At first and second glance, the topographical map could have come from any one of the thousands of other dead worlds that Recker had seen before.

"What am I looking for?" he asked.

"I'll add a highlight."

The outline of a red oval appeared on the far left of the disk, encompassing an area where the terrain vanished out of sensor sight towards the planet's blind side.

"See this - lots of different elevations," said Burner. "Do you notice the narrow gaps between these contour lines?"

"Steep slopes," Recker nodded. "Impact craters from a meteor storm?"

"Those would have a shallower incline."

"Then what?"

Burner pursed his lips, like he wasn't sure if it was the right time to disclose what he was thinking. "I'd expect to see craters covering more of the surface, while these ones are densely clustered. If you look a couple of thousand klicks east, there's a huge area that's almost flat. After that, there are signs of a bowl that might be five thousand klicks in diameter."

"The planetary impact Commander Aston mentioned?"

"It's possible. It's these craters I'm more interested in."

"Spell it out for me."

"The data isn't precise, but I believe this clustered area of craters is unnaturally circular." Burner left his seat and approached the bulkhead screen. He stretched out and traced his finger around the red oval. "You see how the oval distorts as it approaches the planet's cusp? That's to take into account the curvature as we see it from way out here. In reality, it's a perfect circle on top of this representation of Oldis."

Recker was interested. The area of craters was blotchy on the image, owing to the quality of the raw data. Even so, he could see how the indentations were all within the red oval.

"What's your feeling, Lieutenant Burner?"

"I'd prefer a closer look." He turned towards Commander Aston. "And a second opinion never hurt anyone."

"Well?" asked Recker.

Aston hadn't shifted her gaze from the image since Burner first put it up on the screen. She nodded slowly. "I hadn't made as much progress as Lieutenant Burner," she said. "Looking at this, I think we've got something to go on."

"But what is it?" asked Eastwood in puzzlement. "Are you saying the Daklan use this planet for target practice?"

"I'm not saying anything," said Burner. "Other than to point out that regular patterns don't often show up in an irregular universe."

That was enough for Recker to decide that Oldis required further investigation. "I promised you an hour to find something and you did it in half that. Will another thirty minutes allow you to refine your conclusion?"

"I don't think we should rush in, sir. On the other hand, we can see less than two-thirds of the target area from our current position. If we were positioned right overhead, that would make things easier for me and Commander Aston."

"What about the rest of the visible surface? Have you seen enough of that?"

"I've seen what I can given that we're sitting at forty million klicks. There could be a dozen Daklan installations down there that our sensors can't pick up from here. Of course we might jump to ten million klicks and find all we're looking at is a bunch of naturally formed craters from closer up," said Burner.

"But from that range you'll be able to rule out any possibility of an error in what you've concluded from forty million klicks?"

"Yes, sir. There is a chance those craters are entirely natural and the pattern might not even fit so neatly inside the circle as it appears from here. At ten million it'll take me about two minutes to tell you with certainty."

"The monitoring stations look for patterns, amongst other things," said Recker. "What we've found on Oldis must be what triggered that thirty-four-percent evaluation."

"Are we going in, sir?" asked Aston. "Speed or safety?"

"You've got another thirty minutes," said Recker. "It's not like we've got a mission timer running."

During those thirty additional minutes, Lieutenant Burner discovered the possibility of something else.

"The chance of a meteorite storm landing within a perfect circle is close to zero," he said, when half of the time was used up. "So I decided to focus on the exact centre of the area."

"You found something?" said Recker, feeling his stomach tightening.

"Maybe. The penetrative scans can't puncture the surface from here, but I think they've picked up something on the top of it, which the raw data suggests has a 28% chance of being metal."

"Could it be subsurface ores revealed by whatever made those craters?"

"Absolutely it could be, sir."

"We'll go check it out. Lieutenant Eastwood, warm up the ternium drive. We're aiming for ten million klicks directly above the centre of Lieutenant Burner's circle."

"Yes, sir. Coordinates entered. Fifteen minutes to warm up."

"A suggestion, sir," said Aston. "Lieutenant Burner and I could use that time to gather some data from Resa. If Oldis turns out to be a dead-end, then we'll have made a head start on the second planet."

"That's a good idea, please proceed."

Recker was happy with the progress of the mission so far and he was keen to see what Oldis had in store. If the Daklan had a presence there, ten million klicks would make it difficult for them to detect the arrival of the *Punisher*. However, something didn't quite add up and Recker asked himself why the aliens would have installed anything in the centre of their own target area. It was one of many unknowns.

"Have you found anything interesting on Resa?" he asked, five minutes into the warmup time for the light-speed jump.

"No patterns yet," said Burner. "It's a bit more mountainous than average, but other than that, nothing unusual. Of course, this isn't anything like a comprehensive scan and won't detect a Daklan ground base – even a large one."

"That's fine, Lieutenant. You've got ten minutes."

"Shit," said Burner suddenly, snapping his head up. "Particle cloud at three million klicks."

"Let me check that," said Eastwood. "Crap, something's inbound."

Recker closed his eyes and opened them, feeling like the relative calm of the mission so far was about to be shattered. "What is it?"

"You're not going to believe it, sir," said Burner. "The size and movement pattern of the ternium wave indicates it's a Daklan annihilator."

"Good spot, Lieutenant. Though it's the worst possible development."

"Their particle wave is a big one and I was looking that way already, sir. They're between us and Resa."

"Three million klicks," said Recker, his brain adding up the numbers. "Assuming the worst-case scenario and they detect us immediately, it'll take them twenty-four sub-light minutes to get into Odan launch range. Plus travel time for the missiles. We'll be gone in ten and they won't have a damn clue which way we're headed." The inconvenient truth was that an annihilator required much less than fifteen minutes to enter lightspeed and Recker felt obliged to remind everyone. "Unless they fire up their lightspeed drive and land on our doorstep."

"It is definitely an annihilator, sir," said Burner a second later. "They just entered local space and I've sent an FTL comm to base. There'll be no text response for hours."

Recker knew it. He also knew that if the military decided to send out a few warships to take on the battleship, that backup wouldn't be here for days. In truth, he feared that high command had been so badly stung by the recent loss of so many ships that they would be reluctant to take on the annihilator.

He remembered Admiral Telar conceding that the military had become too risk averse and Recker was sure that Telar didn't include himself in the cabal of senior officers who favoured a softly-softly approach.

"This is the time for risks, folks. If there's something on Oldis, we've got to find out what it is."

"In which case we'd better hope that enemy warship doesn't spot us quickly," said Eastwood.

"The arrival of a Daklan battleship vastly increases the likelihood of there already being an enemy presence in this solar system," said Aston.

"I know it, Commander."

"They might be heading to the same place as we are."

The annihilator was bigger, better and faster at everything. If the enemy crew were heading to the Oldis, they could exit lightspeed from their initial journey and still beat the *Punisher* into a second jump.

On the other hand, the battleship could easily have aimed for a destination point much closer to the Daklan base, assuming such a base existed in the first place.

A thought came to Recker. "What if that cylinder on Etrol wasn't made by the Daklan?" he said. "What if their own monitoring stations found it by accident and they sent warships to Virar-12 to investigate, thinking it was an HPA resource world?"

"And we arrived just in time to watch their escorted heavy lifter come to pick the cylinder up," said Aston.

"That's a lot of speculation," said Eastwood.

"Lieutenant Burner, what're the chances they'll spot us in the minutes between now and our departure?" asked Recker.

"I don't know, sir," said Burner, clearly reluctant to give an answer. "The Daklan tech seems to be improving all the time and they put the newest kit on the annihilators."

"Best guess?"

"There's a low, but not negligible, chance they'll detect us."

"Eight minutes and the calcs are done," said Eastwood.

"What's the annihilator doing?" asked Recker.

"Nothing," said Burner. "They came out of lightspeed and they haven't gone anywhere."

"Which suggests they aren't expecting trouble," said Recker, not sure if he believed it himself.

"Now they're accelerating, sir," said Burner.

"Coming our way?"

"Negative. Heading elsewhere. They're at twenty-two klicks per second and holding steady."

"Not in any hurry."

The seconds counted down and the crew watched the annihilator on the sensor feed. At this range and with the sensors on maximum zoom, the Daklan warship was little more than a grey patch on the backdrop of space.

"One minute until ternium drive activation."

"They're holding relative position with Resa," said Aston, clicking her fingers in realization.

Recker knew at once that she was right and suddenly a whole bunch of new questions jumped into his head. With the jump so close, he couldn't let his mind follow the threads and gave his full attention to the controls.

"Ten seconds."

"I think I detected..." said Burner, his voice laden with uncertainty.

A note in the man's voice was enough to fill Recker with alarm. He snapped around towards the calculation timer, in time to see it fall from one to zero.

The *Punisher* jumped into lightspeed, just as the Daklan missile exploded against its rear plating.

CHAPTER FIFTEEN

AT THE PRECISE moment the *Punisher* entered light-speed, Recker heard a thunderous detonation and every-thing shook, like the spaceship had been struck by a sledgehammer-wielding god. A split second later, the *Punisher* re-entered local space and the double impact of nausea from the in-out transition made Recker groan.

The noise didn't lessen and it was joined by the shrill note of the bridge alarm. The lighting went a deep red and Recker's warning panel seemed to turn a shade of crimson. He stared, his vision not yet recovered, and tried to grasp the extent of the multiple failures.

Recker's instinct was to pilot his warship away from the arrival point. A check of the life support told him the primary hardware had failed, while the backup was active and amber. He threw the control bars forward and snarled when the propulsion whined and the output gauge stayed on two percent.

"Lieutenant Eastwood! The propulsion won't come out of idle!" he shouted.

"I know, sir!"

"I need a status report!"

"Major damage to our external plating and our propulsion system," "Hull temps off the scale!"

"Sensors recalibrating," yelled Burner. "I don't know if they're going to come online. The comms hardware's stuck in a boot loop and the FTL transmitter's out of action."

"The interior's breached, sir!" said Eastwood.

"What about the internal lockdown systems?"

"I'm not sure...checking. They're active! Some of the aft doors are showing red – they must have lost power or been too badly damaged!"

"Lieutenant Burner, tell those soldiers to grab their suit helmets. This warship is no longer a safe place for them or any of us."

The shrieking alarm was already pissing Recker off. He thumped his hand angrily on the override button and the high-pitched wail stopped at once.

The ending of the alarm didn't bring silence. Although the shuddering vibration of the missile impact was fading, the creaking of distressed alloy came from every direction. Deep below the bridge floor, something boomed hollowly, while Recker's own console emitted a squealing that he'd never heard it make before.

"I need sensors!" he shouted.

"Working on it, sir!"

"The aft propulsion module is gone," said Eastwood.

"Get it back online!"

"No, sir. I mean it's gone. Whatever the Daklan hit us

with it had a massive payload. It took out the rear third of the *Punisher*. I think our entry into lightspeed is what stopped the entire hull melting – it must have quenched the plasma."

It was beginning to sink in. The unthinkable had happened and now it was all about dealing with the result. Recker swore and continued his rapid audit of the onboard systems. It seemed like everything was in a state of failure.

"Aft sensors offline and not responding. Topside and underside likewise," Burner intoned, like he was reading someone else's shopping list. "Yes!" he exclaimed with new excitement. "One of the forward lenses just came online!"

Recker felt a tap on his shoulder and he looked up to find Aston offering a helmet to go with his suit. She carried a second in her other hand.

"This is only going one way, sir."

The words forced Recker to confront the inevitable and his heart fell. He took the helmet and dropped it into place, hardly noticing the tightening of the seals. The sense of loneliness came at once, trying to fool him into believing he was remote from everything that was happening.

"I've got something on the forward engine module, sir," said Burner. "Thirty percent output. I'm not sure what'll happen if you tap into it."

Recker pushed buttons on the navigational system, trying to bring it to life. The single active sensor lens hadn't yet figured out where the spaceship was located.

"Lieutenant Eastwood, did the lightspeed jump execute correctly?"

"Yes, sir. I believe so."

"That means we're somewhere above Oldis."

"Ten million klicks."

"With that annihilator out there somewhere."

A wrenching groan came from deep inside the *Punisher* and it created a droning vibration that made Recker feel like his eyeballs were bouncing around in his skull. He knew what the sound presaged.

"We're breaking up," he said, rising from his seat. "Send the order. Everyone to the deployment vessel."

"Yes, sir," said Burner, his voice sounding distant through his helmet's chin speaker.

"Let's move!" said Recker. He felt cold from the many different emotions, the predominant one being fury.

Eastwood was closest to the bridge door panel and he pressed his hand firmly against it twice. The door moved reluctantly and Recker thought it might stop halfway, which would mean the power source for the internal security had failed.

To his relief, the door opened fully, and the crew hurried down the steps outside. The interior alarm was going and everything was bathed in red. A light appeared on Recker's helmet HUD, letting him know the air temperature – at a couple of hundred degrees Centigrade - was hot enough to cook an unprotected human in only a few seconds.

"This way," he said, heading left. Either direction would reach the deployment bay with the same efficiency, but he didn't want the crew to split up.

"There's a squad channel," said Burner, a few paces behind. "I'm putting us into it."

Additional lights – representing the soldiers already in the channel - appeared on the comms section of Recker's HUD and he felt a thundering wave of renewed anger when he counted only ten. He opened a channel.

"Sergeant Vance, please report."

"Five dead, sir. They were in the mess room when the heat wave came."

Recker's stomach clenched like it was being squeezed by a viciously strong hand. He couldn't allow himself to falter - the mourning would have to come later.

"What's your progress towards the deployment vehicle?" he asked.

"We've reached the bay, sir. Feels like the ship's going to break in half."

"That's exactly what it's doing, Sergeant."

"Damn. We'd better not stick around."

Recker turned right and then left, leading his crew past the mess room. He didn't want to see, but he couldn't stop himself – not out of a ghoulish interest in the dead, rather because he felt that those soldiers deserved more respect than him looking away.

The angle along the passage didn't grant a view of the entire room, but it was enough. One body was slumped across a table, facing the passage, skin blackened and smouldering.

Two others lay face-down on the floor where they'd fallen. Men or women, Recker couldn't tell. They'd brought their gauss rifles to the mess room but left their helmets elsewhere. The air temperature must have spiked at four or five hundred degrees to have killed the soldiers so quickly. Maybe they'd have died even if their helmets had been on the table in front of them. The thought was no consolation.

And then Recker was past, the brief sights converted to a vivid memory which he filed away with all the others, to be confronted when the time was right, if such a time ever came.

The door leading to the bay was already open and Recker dashed down the ramp. In the red light, he saw three figures standing near to where the deployment vehicle's primary access hatch was hidden by the floor channel.

One of the figures – Sergeant Vance by the size – straightened and motioned the crew to hurry. Recker stopped in front of the soldier and directed the others towards the open hatch.

"Is everyone inside, Sergeant?"

Vance's expression was impassive through his visor – the calm expression of a man who'd experienced everything and refused to let fear dictate his actions.

"Them that made it, sir."

Commander Aston paused at the top of the access ladder. "Sir, we don't have long."

Recker nodded. "Sergeant," he said, indicating Vance should go next.

Vance didn't hesitate and he climbed through the hatch towards the cold-lit interior of the deployment vessel. As soon as the top rungs were clear, Recker followed, grabbing the first rung and dropping nimbly into the shaft, where he descended until he was clear of the opening.

The security panel glowed dimly on the solid alloy

wall of the shaft to his left and Recker entered the command to seal the hatch. With hardly a sound, it slid across his vision, blocking out the crimson from the bay and with it, the harsh sounds of distress from the *Punisher*'s hull.

With practiced ease, Recker climbed, his feet making little noise despite his haste. At the bottom, he stepped off the lowest rung into the incision vehicle's interior. The bay was long and narrow, with curved walls, a flat ceiling and floor. It thrummed with the readiness of the underfloor propulsion and the chill, clean air seemed artificially pure. The eight rows of two seats were partially occupied and the narrow aisle between them led straight for the open cockpit door. Sergeant Vance was halfway along the aisle, squeezing his way through the clutter of guns and packs.

"Why are we still here?" shouted Recker into the comms.

"I'll give the order to break the clamps, sir," said Vance.

Recker had a thought. "Hold that order, Sergeant."

"Yes, sir."

"And grab yourself a seat - my crew will take the controls."

If the *Punisher*'s main crew hadn't been onboard, Vance would have normally been the one flying. When he heard Recker's command, the soldier stopped his advance on the cockpit and dropped into one of the seats near the doorway.

"Commander Aston, Lieutenant Eastwood, you're up here with me," said Recker.

He entered the cockpit. The space was not generous

and even more dimly lit than the passenger bay. Three bucket seats with harnesses were fixed in front of a basic, but robust control panel. The ceiling sloped towards the nose, while front and side view screens gave the impression of sitting in a gravity car.

One of the soldiers – Private Nelle Montero – was in the third seat and she'd brought everything online, including the screens. The view outside wasn't much to admire, being no more than the unmarked walls of the deployment spaceship's docking bay. Montero turned at Recker's arrival and her dark eyes met his.

"You're relieved, soldier. Find yourself a place out back."

She nodded and climbed from her seat. From her expression, Montero was finding it hard to stay on top of the fear.

"Worried, Private?"

"Hell no, sir."

"Good. This is going to be a piece of cake."

"Whatever you say, sir."

Recker dropped into the centre bucket seat, which was hard but comfortable. Time was running out and he ignored the harness for the moment. Aston and Eastwood took the other two seats and looked at him for guidance.

"Why the hold up, sir?" said Aston.

"We're ten million klicks from Oldis, Commander. That's twenty-seven hours travel time at this vessel's maximum velocity. There's a Daklan annihilator out there."

"So we're still going for the planet?" asked Eastwood in surprise.

"There's no change in the plan, Lieutenant. The *Punisher*'s forward engine module is at thirty percent – I'm going to use it to give us a speed boost."

He calculated the potential maximum speed of the *Punisher* with only one-sixth of its propulsion available. It worked out at 180 kilometres per second – much greater than that of the deployment ship, but not enough if the annihilator came looking.

Recker interfaced with the *Punisher* using his command codes and discovered that the lone sensor array had completed its positional calculations. Using that information, he commanded the *Punisher* to accelerate on a course directly for Oldis. He held one finger close to the launch button for the deployment vehicle and gritted his teeth at the distant sounds of distress he heard from the parent vessel.

"Still too slow. Lieutenant Eastwood, I want the *Punisher*'s forward module placed into an overstressed condition."

"I..." Eastwood thought better about protesting. "Yes, sir."

"I've entered my command codes – you should have authority to do it from here."

Eastwood entered a series of instructions into the right-hand panel of the console. He waited for an acknowledgement from the failing mainframe and then entered several more.

"Done?" asked Recker impatiently.

"No, sir. There isn't a menu option for this," Eastwood replied, tapping a long string of digits into one screen and comparing them to a readout on another.

A loud thud from outside made the deployment craft shudder and Recker accessed the *Punisher*'s top-level damage report. Everything was either at a red status or no longer receiving input from the monitoring hardware.

"We don't have long, Lieutenant."

"I know, sir. I can't work any faster than this."

"Try."

As the seconds went by, Recker expected to see the holding bay walls split apart, dropping the incision vehicle into space. He was taking a gamble – he knew it – but experience told him the *Punisher* was only going to break apart rather than explode. If its magazines hadn't gone up in the initial enemy missile impact, they weren't going to do it now. The panel before him showed the *Punisher*'s velocity climb past 150 klicks per second.

Eastwood rolled his shoulders, blew out noisily and clapped his hands together, the sound muffled by the padding of his spacesuit gauntlets. "Done. Engine output climbing."

"Nice work, Lieutenant."

The *Punisher*'s velocity gauge sped to 250 klicks per second and went on going. Even within the armoured shell of the deployment craft, the howling of the distressed forward module was clearly audible, and it got louder as the maximum output climbed.

"Three hundred percent," said Eastwood. "Let's see if it keeps going."

"The rate is slowing," said Recker. "320%"

After that, the module's output didn't go any higher, though the *Punisher* continued accelerating strongly.

Recker knew how high the velocity was likely to go and he watched the gauge closely.

"Four hundred klicks per second," he said. "Four-thirty."

A sudden shift in the view on the cockpit screens made Recker turn his head, where he saw that a ragged left-to-right tear had appeared in the wall of the holding bay. It widened slowly at first and then expanded so rapidly that the sides of the opening were lost from sight.

"It's happening," said Aston.

"Four-fifty klicks per second on the gauge."

The *Punisher* had given everything – far more than Recker could have expected from the warship. He knew it might have yet more to offer – it might hold together until it was travelling beyond five hundred klicks per second.

The time for gambling was over and Recker hit the release button. He heard the thumping of the holding clamps and the status screen indicated a successful release on eighteen out of twenty. The other two flashed red and Recker hit the emergency release which caused tiny explosive charges to blow out the failed clamps. Those two flashed alternating green and red, and the deployment vehicle was thrown automatically down its launch runners and out into space.

CHAPTER SIXTEEN

THE INITIAL BOOST which hurled the deployment vehicle away from the *Punisher* set it on a diverging course. Aston adjusted the sensors and the much bigger warship appeared as a dark shape overhead, which dwindled steadily.

Further adjustments enhanced the feed and Recker stared in shock at the extent of the damage. The stern was effectively gone, leaving plates of armour hanging loosely around the vast crater formed by the explosion of the light-speed missile. Elsewhere, much of the alloy hull was mottled and lumpy from the aftereffects of the plasma, leaving only the nose section undamaged.

"That missile really did a number on us," said Eastwood.

"I know, Lieutenant." Recker didn't want to dwell on it.

The *Punisher* was gone and there was nothing they could

do to change the fact. Despite that, Recker's eyes didn't want to look away and he studied the wreck for signs it was breaking apart. Larger pieces of debris fell away and then a vast tear appeared along the starboard flank. Recker stopped watching.

"We've inherited a velocity of 450 klicks per second," said Aston. She changed the sensor focus again and this time aimed the vessel's forward array at the planet Oldis. "If we coast, it'll take six hours to reach the place we're going."

"Wherever that is," said Eastwood.

The spaceship's sensors weren't designed to provide clarity at ten million klicks – more like a couple of hundred thousand at best. Consequently, the feed of Oldis resembled a grimy, grey disc. Luckily, Commander Aston was on the ball.

"I downloaded the latest feed data from the *Punisher*," she said. "The stuff that Lieutenant Burner caught before the missile hit us."

The sensor data the *Punisher* gathered at forty million kilometres was much clearer than that gathered by the incision vehicle at ten million. That didn't mean a lot and Recker still didn't have an idea what they were heading into.

"Lieutenant Burner, I need you in the cockpit," he called.

Burner showed up a few seconds later. "What can I do, sir?" he asked, leaning forward to check what the console was showing.

"The annihilator is out there still and we're six hours from Oldis."

"Are you expecting it to be safe once we reach the planet, sir?"

"I'm not expecting anything, Lieutenant. When the annihilator arrived, it was three million klicks away and then it headed along Resa's orbital track."

"Yes, sir." Burner's forehead wrinkled as he tried to guess where Recker was leading. "You want to know if they could have seen the cluster of indentations on the surface of Oldis from their arrival position."

"That's exactly what I would like to know. And also if they'd have spotted our exit from lightspeed."

Burner's forehead wrinkled some more, and he bared his teeth. "The second question's easiest. They probably didn't see our ternium wave when we re-entered local space."

"What about the surface craters? Would they have detected them?"

"If they were looking directly at the place, they would have had a worse view than we did, owing to the more oblique angle. However, their sensors are better than ours so that might not work too much in our favour. We can also assume they were mostly focused on Resa because that's where they were going." Burner lifted a hand to run it through his hair and remembered he was wearing a helmet. "On balance, I'd say we've got some time before the annihilator comes to Oldis, sir."

"Six hours?"

"Probably significantly more. It depends on how they approach the scan of Resa. A Daklan battleship is unlikely to tiptoe around like we did. Their crew might scan one side of the planet, lightspeed jump to the exact opposite side, scan and then decide they like the look of Oldis instead. I can't predict how they'll act."

"Thank you for your insight, Lieutenant, you've given me something to go on."

The cockpit didn't have much room, but Burner hung around anyway and crouched next to Commander Aston so that he could watch the sensors. It wasn't like he had somewhere else to go.

"From our approach angle we aren't going to get a sight of what caused the *Punisher*'s sensors to flag up the presence of metal," said Aston.

Recker checked their vector again – if the Daklan had an installation on Oldis, he didn't want to come down straight on top of it. The incision class were designed to drop through a planet's atmosphere out of the target's sight and then come in at a low altitude to minimize the chance of early detection.

"That's intentional, Commander. By the time we're close enough for surface scanners to detect us, the planet's rotation will have carried the target site around to the blindside. We'll go low to the surface and see what we can see."

"We don't have to do this, sir," said Aston. "The military will send someone out here to look for us eventually and this spaceship's replicator is carrying enough raw food paste to keep everyone onboard alive for a couple of years."

"There's nobody coming here any time soon, Commander. Not until high command gets its game together."

"What about the 34% chance, sir?" said Eastwood. "You said this was the most significant lead we had."

"It is. That doesn't mean a whole fleet is going to drop by for a look. We sent an FTL comm telling high command about the annihilator – they'll assume it took us out and that's why we've gone missing. We can't send them an update because this deployment vessel isn't equipped with an FTL transmitter." Recker took a deep breath. "After the HPA's recent losses, I don't know if there's anyone brave enough to chance another big defeat. For all Admiral Telar knows, the Daklan might have substantially reinforced since we sent the comm."

"Or we only detected one ship out of many," said Aston.

"That's right, Commander."

"I thought you said Admiral Telar was one of the brave ones, sir," said Eastwood.

"He is, or at least that's what I think. The trouble is, he's not the one making the final strategic decisions."

"The way you're talking, it's like you believe our guys will never show," said Burner.

"I'm trying hard to convince myself they'll come. Whatever happens, it won't be soon."

"And you've decided that whatever's on Oldis, it's not Daklan in origin," said Aston.

"That's what I said on the *Punisher* and that's what I believe now," Recker nodded.

"I count fourteen of us in total," said Eastwood. "And we're on a spaceship designed to knock out lightly-armoured surface vehicles and not much else. How are we going to beat that annihilator when it comes?"

"Nobody's talking about shooting it down, Lieutenant. We've got a head start on our enemy in finding out what's on Oldis and we're going to make use of it."

Aston narrowed her eyes in Recker's direction. "You're planning to do more than just look."

"Maybe. Don't think I'm intending to throw our lives away. I'm going to take this as it comes – at worst, we've got a chance to gather intel so that when we get back to base, we've got something useful to report."

"*When* we get back to base," said Eastwood, his face cracking a smile.

"You heard me right, Lieutenant."

"So. Another of those cylinders," said Aston.

"That's what it could be."

"The one on Etrol didn't shoot at us," said Burner. "It could be we're able to fly closer than we expect."

"Like I said – we'll take that as it comes."

The conversation died off and Recker concentrated once more on his console. The deployment vessel was running on autopilot, though he itched to grab hold of the twin control sticks which came up through the floor. It was a long way to Oldis and the trajectory didn't require any immediate manual input.

"Commander Aston, you're in charge," he said.

"Sightseeing tour?"

"Something like that."

Recker went to see how the soldiers were faring. They'd adapted quickly to the new circumstances and most of them were killing time by trading insults. Sergeant Vance wasn't taking part and Recker sat on the empty seat across the aisle to fill his officer in on the many details he was lacking.

When Recker was finished, Vance nodded slowly in thought. "Assuming you're right and there's an alien cylinder down there, you want to have a look inside."

"The time for hiding under the bed passed us by a long while ago, Sergeant."

"I'm glad someone's waking up to the fact," Vance growled angrily. "I could have told anyone the same thing five years ago. That's when I reckon the tipping point came."

"What makes you say that?"

Vance shifted uncomfortably. "Nothing scientific, sir. Five years ago, we'd throw a punch and they'd throw one back. We'd show up at a place and beat the shit out of the Daklan we'd find there. Meantime, someplace else, they'd show up and beat the shit out of us. Ever since the *tipping point*, me and my soldiers, we've seen what's coming. It feels like we survive every deployment by the skin of our teeth. Then, we arrive home and find out that some other guys we knew didn't make it. Hell, I can't remember the last time we got to celebrate a real big victory."

It was unusual to hear Vance speak so much and Recker paid close attention. Most people had an idea that the war was going the wrong way, but Vance had looked further ahead. He knew.

Recker knew it as well. When he commanded his first ship, the Daklan fleet wasn't anything to run from. Their warships were better at some things and worse at others. Now, just dreaming about an annihilator was enough to make half the military's commanding officers shit their white cotton sheets.

"I'd like to tell you something's going to change, Sergeant."

"It's times like this that it happens, sir. You could have pointed this spaceship the other way and told us that rescue was coming. Instead, we're flying into whatever lies ahead."

"I'm not going to let the Daklan win easily," said Recker. "Not while I've got the strength to stop them."

Vance didn't speak for a moment, like he was deciding whether to divulge something important. In the end, he kept his mouth shut and Recker rose from his seat. He looked towards the rear of the bay, which ten soldiers and their kit almost filled. The background drone of the engine combined with the subdued lighting and the confines of the space made Recker imagine he was in a spaceship from hundreds of years ago.

He smiled inwardly. Modern space flight was safe and reliable, except when you brought the Daklan into the equation. With those bastards flying around the universe, it was more hazardous than ever.

Recker returned to the cockpit and opened the tall weapons locker which was bolted onto the rear bulkhead. Inside, he found four gauss rifles, a comms beacon, spare ammo, a few explosive charges and a med-box.

"Got plans for those, sir?" asked Aston.

"Just checking to make sure we're properly equipped for any eventuality, Commander."

Recker took his seat once more and gave the instrumentation a once-over. Aston was thorough and none of the readouts offered a reason for concern. The sensor feed of Oldis hadn't visibly improved since the spaceship first exited the *Punisher's* bay and Recker wasn't expecting that to change for another three hours or more.

"Sometimes the shortest trips are the longest ones," said Aston, watching his face.

"I know what you mean."

The flight continued and the annihilator didn't show up. After a while, Burner took over Eastwood's seat in order to find out if he could extract anything from the sensors that Aston had missed.

For a long time, he came up with nothing and the centre of the cratered area was taken blindside by the planet's rotation. Then, with the deployment vessel about a million kilometres from Oldis, Burner began to discover some things that the *Punisher* had missed in its earlier forty-million-klick scan.

"Have a look at this, sir," he said.

An image appeared on one of Recker's screens, showing a circular indentation in rocky ground. The image was rough, over-enhanced and indistinct, but not so much that he didn't recognize it.

"This is what we thought was a crater," he said.

"Yes, sir. Except it's not – it's a massive, cylindrical hole in the planet's surface."

Recker squinted, trying to judge the size of it. "Don't tell me it's an exact size copy of the cylinder we saw on Etrol."

"No, sir, this is much bigger. The diameter is approximately ten klicks and while I can't get an accurate depth, I guess that hole goes down thirty klicks or more."

The image on Recker's screen changed and this time it showed another cylindrical hole. "Identical to the first?" he asked.

"Smaller. This one's less than a thousand metres across and maybe three thousand deep."

A third image appeared.

"This one's much larger than the other two," said Burner. "Fifty klicks diameter and it probably goes way down into the mantle. I estimate that an area of Oldis with a diameter of four thousand klicks is covered in these things, big and small."

"Ideas?" asked Recker.

"None."

"Anyone else?"

Aston shrugged and Eastwood didn't say anything.

"If there's one of those metal cylinders in the middle of this area, I'd say that's the likely cause," said Burner.

"Except we didn't find anything like this on Etrol," Eastwood pointed out.

"Keep searching, Lieutenant Burner," said Recker. "Once we get closer, everything might become clearer."

At an altitude of half a million kilometres, Burner unearthed something else.

"The sensors on this spaceship weren't designed for rock analysis, but they do collect basic information," he said. "I believe there are some pretty big deposits of tenixite beneath the surface where those holes are."

"Ternium ore?" said Recker sharply. "Could these be extraction points?"

"Not likely. And they certainly don't resemble any methods of extraction we've seen the Daklan use. There's probably enough tenixite on Oldis to build three more fleets the same size as the HPA's existing one."

All of which made Oldis a place of immense strategic importance to both the HPA and the Daklan. However, Recker wasn't convinced that ore extraction was the reason for these holes in the planet's surface, though he couldn't think of an alternative explanation.

The spaceship flew ever closer to the planet and his hands reached of their own accord for the control sticks. The deployment ship wasn't built to travel so fast, and deceleration from this velocity would put the vessel under greater strain than normal. Recker prepared for the approach.

CHAPTER SEVENTEEN

FOR SEVERAL MINUTES, the incision vessel's engines howled, while an intense, grating vibration coming from under the floor made Recker's seat shake like he was on a roller coaster car heading up the first big incline. The planet filled the forward feed and more details become apparent as the spaceship's sensors came within their intended operational range.

"Ice-rimed stone, near-zero atmosphere," said Burner. "There'll be some atmospheric friction once we reach a low altitude, but nothing our hull can't handle."

Recker glanced at the tumbling velocity gauge. "Still travelling at 175 klicks per second," he said.

"When I said nothing our hull can't handle..."

"You meant sensible speeds. I understand, Lieutenant."

The area of Oldis they were approaching appeared almost featureless, barring some irregular lines which may have been ridges. From the current altitude, the place looked flat, though Recker wasn't fooled - he was sure the planet would be rough going for anyone on foot.

"Two hundred thousand klicks to impact," joked Aston.

Recker ignored the vibration which now seemed to come from everywhere and maintained the deceleration, putting his faith in the reliability of the HPA engineering. It hadn't let him down yet.

"The area we're approaching will be day side, six thousand klicks from the edge of the circular area," said Burner. "A fast skim over the surface and we'll be there."

"Let's hope it's so easy," said Recker. His eyes kept going to the console, expecting to find a bunch of warning lights. Everything was clear.

"Altitude: one hundred thousand klicks," said Aston.

The velocity readout was at ninety-seven klicks per second and Recker slowed the rate of deceleration. Immediately, the vibration lessened and the respite was welcome.

"Don't get used to it, folks," he warned, watching the instrumentation closely.

Recker couldn't stop thinking about the annihilator and how it might turn up at any moment, so he left the final period of deceleration as late as possible. The sensors were still on maximum zoom, making it seem like the deployment vessel was on the verge of crashing into the plain of stone below, and he was glad the padding in his suit gloves deadened the renewed vibration coming through the controls.

"Fifty klicks per second," said Aston. "Forty."

At an altitude of fifty klicks, Recker levelled the spaceship out with the vessel travelling at twenty klicks per second. The planet's atmosphere was thin like Burner had said, though it was enough to cause the hull temperature to increase slowly. It wasn't a concern and Recker wouldn't need to pay it any attention unless he was required to fly lower.

"From this altitude we should see the first of the craters in not much more than four minutes, sir," said Burner. "Then an additional two minutes to find out if there's anything in the centre of that circle."

"Anyone excited?" said Aston.

"I don't know what I feel, Commander," said Recker. "Excitement probably isn't high up the list."

In truth, he felt a growing sense of anticipation. Recker believed they were on the brink of a discovery, though he didn't know how significant it might be. He was also acutely aware that he wasn't exactly holding a hand full of aces – fourteen men and women in a sixty-metre deployment craft with a nose gun wasn't much challenge to a Daklan battleship.

With an inward smile, Recker told himself that sometimes the mouse got the cheese and escaped the cat. The cynical part of his brain reminded him that nature ensured cats and mice had a certain equilibrium. There was nothing natural about an annihilator.

The incision craft sped across the planet's rolling plains. Here and there, the sporadic covering of ice glistened on the feed from the distant light of Exim-K, making it seem like the spaceship flew over a patchwork of sharply contrasting greys.

"The edge of the target area should be in sight any

time now, sir," said Burner, making some changes to the sensor panel. "I'll try and get us a sharp image."

"Look at that," said Aston, peering intently at the screen.

A dark line appeared on the horizon, becoming thicker with each passing moment. Gradually, the details resolved and Recker could see that he was looking at thousands of individual holes in the planet's surface. It was a sight he was expecting, yet it appeared much more dramatic – more destructive – from such a close range.

"Why?" Aston asked simply.

"Don't ask me, Commander. Maybe we'll find out soon."

"Sixty seconds and we'll have a view of what lies at the centre," said Burner.

"And no way to pass the intel back to base," said Eastwood.

"If it's important enough, we'll head into space and lay low for however long it takes for the HPA to send another warship," said Recker. "I'm bringing us lower."

It was still possible the Daklan had an outpost here on Oldis and he didn't want them getting an early sight of the incision craft. He reduced altitude, watching the ground come up to meet the spaceship.

"Ten klicks," he said. "Five."

"We're getting warm," said Aston.

Recker didn't reduce velocity – the incision craft were designed for rapid deployment and that meant their hulls could withstand the heat for long enough to deliver their cargo of troops. At such a low altitude, the spaceship shook with the turbulence and he made constant small adjustments to keep it steady. If he made an error at this speed, it would be catastrophic.

Soon, the spaceship was directly over the area which was covered in holes and the sight was a mixture of bizarre and impressive. The placement and size seemed completely random – sometimes there were large gaps between the openings, while at others they were nearly touching.

"I'm getting a reading from the bottom of those holes," said Burner, sounding puzzled.

"What is it?" asked Recker. "Do I need to worry about it?"

"Checking. It's a material I haven't come across before. There's nothing in the databanks of this vessel either, sir."

"Let's not worry about it, Lieutenant. I want to find out what's ahead of us, not what's underneath."

"Yes, sir."

Recker held on tightly. It was a long time since he'd flown a craft like this in anger and it was testing his skills in a different way to flying something bigger like the *Punisher*. A fleet warship was far too dense and heavy to be affected by mere turbulence, while this incision class felt like it was right on the edge of flipping over in mid-air and crashing to the ground.

"Got it!" said Burner excitedly. "A metal object... another cylinder, sir! This one is on its side."

"Any sign of Daklan?"

"I can't find anything on the ground and there's nothing visible in the sky."

Recker knew the limitations of the incision craft's sensor hardware. There could be Daklan a few thousand kilometres overhead and Burner wouldn't find them easily. Hell, the enemy could hide an entire fleet in some of the larger holes and the first anyone on the deployment ship would know about it would be when the missile detonated against the nose section. This mission had always been about risk and nothing had changed.

"Tell me what you can, Lieutenant," said Recker. "I need to know if we're sticking around or running for the stars."

"It's taking a moment to enhance the feed."

Burner got a high-quality stream up on the forward screen, which gave Recker an excellent view of what lay ahead. The cylinder was lying crossways to the spaceship's approach, in the middle of a thousand-klick-diameter area completely clear of holes.

"It's damaged," said Recker.

"More than damaged," said Aston.

The alien object was the same size as the one on Etrol and would likely have been identical in appearance were it not for the dozens of holes in its casing. When he saw them, Recker understood at once that they were created by high-yield missiles, which had ruptured the cylinder's thick outer plating and left wicked-edged blades of torn alloy jutting in many directions.

"What knocked it over?" asked Eastwood, leaning against the back of Aston's seat so that he could get a closer look at the sensor feeds.

Recker wasn't sure and the approach angle made it hard to see how much damage the cylinder had sustained at its base. He banked slightly, hoping they might get a better view.

"Still no sign of hostiles," said Burner. "There again, the Daklan could have a battleship parked on the opposite side and we wouldn't see it from here."

He was right – the cylinder's two-thousand-metre diameter meant it blocked the sight of anything which might be on the far side. Recker knew he could increase altitude in order to improve the viewing angle, but he didn't make any changes to the vector in case the deployment craft became easier to detect.

"If the Daklan have something parked up out of sight, they don't know we're coming either."

"And the moment we show our faces, they'll have a shot at us."

"Assuming they're in a better state of readiness than the desolator on Etrol," said Eastwood with a humourless laugh.

"You're forgetting about those incendiaries, Lieutenant," said Aston. "They got those into the air quickly enough."

Recker wasn't paying much attention to the conversation and he slowed the deployment vehicle. He didn't think it likely the Daklan had a spaceship on the far side of the cylinder, though he wasn't ready to dismiss the possibility entirely.

"There's nobody firing at us yet," he said. "Let's take a close look at the cylinder and see what information we can gather."

The deployment vehicle sped across the undamaged area of the planet on which the cylinder lay and Recker saw nothing to distinguish this ground from the vast plain where they'd first entered the atmosphere.

At thirty klicks from the cylinder, he slowed the spaceship to little more than a crawl and reduced altitude to a thousand metres.

Ten klicks from the cylinder, he slowed again. From such a close range, the sensors left no detail unrevealed. Recker knew the object was a massive construction from his encounter on Etrol but seeing it here from the vulnerable position of the deployment craft drove home what an awe-inspiring demonstration of technology it was.

"Nobody does alien quite like aliens," said Aston.

Recker didn't say anything. Now that he didn't have to think about turbulence or hull temperatures, he could give the whole of his attention to this discovery on Oldis. The cylinder was incredible, yet the damage it had suffered made it seem even more so and added a feeling of threat that went beyond the possible appearance of a Daklan battleship.

Recker's eyes jumped from place to place, counting the visible impacts the object had suffered. Some of the detonations must have hit weak points and they'd torn open irregular holes, one of which was in excess of four hundred metres across. In other places, the breaches were smaller and not all the missiles had penetrated the armour.

"The outer plating on this thing is more than two hundred metres thick," said Burner. "And whatever type of missiles it got hit with, they ripped it wide open."

The lowest fifteen hundred metres were still anchored into the ground, though they were no longer perfectly vertical and Recker could see that the lowest section of the cylinder was completely solid and made from a material so dark it was nearly black. Above that, the place where it was sheared had been subjected to a combination of intense missile fire as well as a huge lateral impact.

"There," he said, pointing at a place midway along the fallen section. "Looks like an indentation and we can only see part of it from this side."

"An indentation," Aston repeated. "Something crashed into this cylinder. A spaceship."

The crew studied the fallen object for what felt like a long time. Lieutenant Burner did what he could to gather information but declared the sensors on the deployment craft were too primitive to analyse the composition of the cylinder.

"I can't even tell you if it's generating power, sir," he said. "And there's no chance of finding out if it's still broadcasting to anywhere else on the assumed network of other cylinders."

Having flown the deployment craft two full lengths of the cylinder, Recker brought it to within a hundred metres and drew it to a halt outside one of the openings about halfway along.

"What can we see inside?" he asked.

"I didn't have a good angle from ten thousand meters, sir. The parts I could see just looked part-hollow – thick armour, some supports, and an open space."

"Show me."

Burner aimed the sensor array into the nearby opening and enhanced the feed. Like he said, it was mostly hollow, though Recker could see what he thought were thick support beams, along with an even thicker central column. Other than a few additional, indistinct shapes, much of the cylinder on the other side of this breach was empty.

"Let's check out a few of these other openings," said Recker.

"Shouldn't we have a look on the opposite side as well?" asked Burner.

"I thought you were convinced the Daklan landed a battleship over there, Lieutenant."

"On balance, they probably didn't, sir."

Recker flew the vessel sideways, so that the nose remained pointing at the cylinder. "Let's see what's through this next opening first. It's a big one."

"You are not going to believe this," said Burner. In a startlingly unusual display of anger, he punched his console and then did it again.

"Lieutenant!" shouted Recker angrily. "What is it?"

Burner was already talking – babbling, almost. "Ternium wave, sir. Five hundred klicks up. Annihilator."

Recker didn't believe in fate – or told himself he didn't. At that exact moment, he felt as if the universe was conspiring against him, either to make his life as hard as possible, or maybe just to piss him off.

With the lives of everyone on the deployment ship measured in seconds, Recker knew what he had to do. He threw the controls to the side. The opening approached and it required perfect timing for Recker to halt the ship directly opposite. Hardly had it come to a stop than he slammed the controls forward.

The opening was large, and the deployment ship's hull was slim and tapered. It vanished into the cylinder.

CHAPTER EIGHTEEN

THE SPACE within was unlit and Burner worked the sensors to try and give Recker an idea where he was going. The deployment ship had lights, but it wasn't a good time to be using them. Rather than risking an impact, Recker halted the spaceship the moment he was sure its stern was out of sight.

"Here you go, sir," said Burner, his anger having quickly dissipated. "We're on the far side of the plating, but only just."

Shapes and lines defied Recker's eyes and then his mind pieced much of it together. The deployment ship was about twenty meters beyond the inner wall of the cylinder's armour and the view from the rear sensors was strange. He couldn't remember seeing a detonation crater from this side before and it took a split second for his brain to accept the sight.

As soon as he was content the annihilator wouldn't be able to detect the deployment ship from above, Recker studied everything else the sensors were showing him. The entry point was about midway along the 6500-metre broken-off top section of the cylinder and it wasn't quite so empty as he'd first thought from outside.

The most notable feature was the dark central post, which had a diameter of five hundred metres and appeared to go all the way from the top, to the sheared end of the cylinder. Recker was certain this was more than a structural support, though he wasn't sure why – the post was smooth and with nothing to indicate it had a different purpose.

A huge inner structure of 100-metre-diameter, circular beams supported the post, keeping it in place when the outer shell toppled over. These beams were amply spaced for the sixty-metre deployment vessel to fit between, but at the same time they impeded the view.

"We should go deeper inside," said Aston. "If that annihilator comes in low, they might see us."

Recker nodded and piloted the spaceship vertically, halting when it was a hundred metres above the opening.

"They'll have a job spotting us now," he said. "Unless they press their eye right up against the hole."

"Do you have a plan, sir?" asked Eastwood.

The expectation that he'd have an instant answer to everything came with the promotion to captain and Recker had long ago come to accept the fact.

"Working on it, Lieutenant." He thumbed over his shoulder. "In the meantime, put your head through that door and let Sergeant Vance know what's happening."

"The door's been open all along, sir, and most of the

squad's bunched up in the seats outside. I don't think they need any extra explanation."

"I should've guessed," said Recker, who hadn't been granted even a moment to look behind since the deployment vessel first came to Oldis. "If anyone would like to offer some input on our situation, I'd appreciate the ideas."

"What about keeping our heads down until the annihilator crew gets bored and go somewhere else?" said Burner. "Or is that too easy?"

"I wasn't expecting you to come up with a way that would involve taking down a Daklan battleship," Recker assured him.

"But he wants more," said Aston. "I can read it in his face."

"I do want more, Commander. And there's nothing stopping us from doing some exploration while we're in here."

"Some of the missile holes are in the exposed upper surface," Burner pointed out. "And plenty of others on the opposite side to where we came in. If the annihilator does a thorough close-range scan of this cylinder, we're going to have a real tough job avoiding detection."

"They don't know we're here, Lieutenant." Recker paused for a moment while he thought of something. "As I've already told you, I'm becoming increasingly certain these cylinders weren't constructed by the Daklan," he said. "Yet they're hunting for them and I don't know why."

"It's not likely to be for the good of our health," said Eastwood.

"Aren't you missing the real big thing?" asked Burner. "If the HPA didn't make the cylinders and the Daklan didn't, that means there's a third species of intelligent life. And, since we don't know what attacked this place, maybe even a fourth species. Unless the third bunch was at war with itself."

"It's a big universe," said Aston. "Finding other life was only going to be a matter of time."

"And that's as much surprise as you're going to show?" asked Burner in disbelief.

Recker shrugged. "I understand the significance, Lieutenant, and if we get out of this situation, I'm sure I'll feel some major shock. For the moment, the Daklan are interested in this tech and that's bad news for the HPA."

It seemed like Burner was having a hard time grasping it all and for a moment, Recker felt real fear that his sensor officer was on the verge of a breakdown. The imminence of death combined with this potential complete shift in humanity's place in the universe was difficult for anyone to handle.

"Screw it," said Burner. "What doesn't kill you makes you stronger."

"That's the spirit," said Eastwood. "When the captain gets us out of here, we'll sink a few cold ones back on Earth and talk some shit."

Recker was pleased that his crew were pulling themselves together, but less happy at the direction of the conversation.

"We've got the here and now, gentlemen. Let's not forget how deep we are in the crap."

The words seemed to spur on Burner, and he came up with an idea. "The cylinder on Etrol was broadcasting, which means this one likely does the same. That means there's a comms station somewhere here. If we gain access, we may be able to locate the other nodes on the network."

"Good idea, Lieutenant. I remember you detected the likely transmission point on the Etrol cylinder."

"Yes, sir. One of three places on the upper four hundred metres."

"Think it's a manned station?" asked Eastwood.

"Worried about running into aliens?" asked Recker. "Anything living on this cylinder must have been killed in the attack."

"Only curious, sir. We're here for answers and if we turned up a few dead bodies, that would be something."

"I've had another thought," said Burner. "If the Daklan control the Etrol cylinder, they'll have an opportunity to locate the transmission station on that one. And if they carried the whole damn thing to one of their home worlds on that heavy lifter, they'll have the facilities to copy the technology."

"They're ahead of us, Lieutenant. Nothing we can do to fix that, so let's do our best to draw level in the race. After that we can think about getting our necks in front."

"It doesn't seem like the Daklan are happy to stop at one cylinder, or however many they've got," said Aston. "They're still looking because there's something they want."

"I don't entirely agree with that, Commander. If the cylinder on Etrol was their first discovery – and we're only guessing that's true – they won't have completed a fraction of their investigation into the tech. For all the Daklan know, they'll benefit from capturing as many of these things as possible. At the very least they'll want to stop the HPA gaining access."

"I won't argue that, sir. Maybe this isn't the time to talk about it."

"I agree. We should head for the upper section," said Recker.

He switched his attention to the sensors again and tried to figure out a path between the spokes linked to the main inner pillar. Burner was a fast worker and he enhanced the visible missile holes on the feed, adding transparent green cones to represent the predicted visibility arc of the annihilator sensors.

"These predictions aren't exact, sir. If the battleship comes near enough and the crew are persistent, it'll be a struggle to keep out of sight."

"You'll also have to take it slow and steady," said Eastwood. "Our propulsion will create a detectible resonance."

"Anything else to worry about?" asked Recker dryly. He knew the dangers, but this was still a unique situation and he was happy to listen to whatever input came his way.

The crew didn't say anything else and Recker flexed his fingers in preparation. Every time he looked at the sensor feed, with the overlaid visibility cones, the route seemed more convoluted, and the spokes prevented him planning too far ahead.

"Too many overlaps on those cones for my liking," he said.

With the utmost care, he increased power to the engines. "Exactly how evident will the resonance be to the Daklan, Lieutenant Eastwood?"

"There are too many influencing factors for me to give you a definitive answer, sir."

"Figures."

Eastwood had another shot at giving a worthwhile response. "The enemy will be looking through the missile craters, so I'd suggest you take it extra easy when we're near one."

"I agree," said Burner.

Slowly, Recker turned the deployment craft so that its nose was pointing towards the pinnacle of the cylinder and added some figures in his head. The entry point was halfway along this 6500-metre length, meaning the target area was about three thousand metres further. At any other time and in any other place, the distance would be insignificant. Right now, it felt to Recker like he was setting off on a walk from Earth to the sun.

The propulsion note rose and the spaceship accelerated slowly. Recker's eyes darted over the sensor feeds.

The entry point is below and there's an opening to the left, with a second ahead and above. Too many spokes to avoid the visibility arcs unless I head towards the base and find another route through.

Recker didn't change course and the spaceship flew towards the left-hand opening, which was a couple of hundred metres in diameter. Shards of alloy created by the initial blast intruded and he piloted the craft beneath them, doing his best to avoid the visibility arc from the larger opening ahead.

"Past one," he said.

A spoke cut diagonally across his path, forcing Recker to fly deeper into the cylinder.

"Coming into that upper arc, sir," said Burner anxiously. "If the Daklan are watching, it's most likely to be from directly overhead."

"I hear you."

A slight movement on the joysticks took the spaceship higher towards the curved inner wall, around the visibility arc.

"Shit, got another opening above and to the right, sir," said Burner, frantically adjusting the sensors. "Adding an overlay."

Recker swore under his breath. The missile breach Burner had detected was more like a ragged tear, as if two warheads had detonated in the same place, and the central pillar had kept it hidden until the deployment vessel came to this part of the interior. The visibility arc was enormous and Recker tried to figure out the best way to stay out of it. Only the spokes and the pillar interrupted the view from the outside.

"Oh crap, it's here," said Burner suddenly.

An immense, dark grey shape slid across the missile breach, completely covering the opening. The annihilator wasn't yet stationary and Recker caught a brief glimpse of a square Graler turret before it disappeared from sight.

"They're trying to get a sensor lens aimed into the gap!" said Burner in alarm.

Acting on instinct, Recker rotated the spaceship and flew it sideways as close to one of the spokes as he dared. A moment later, the interior of the cylinder was flooded with a stark white light, which illuminated a huge area and created lines of deep shadows which criss-crossed the outer walls.

"Lights?" said Eastwood in disbelief. "What the hell do they need light for?"

"Improved sensor efficiency," said Burner without looking up from his console. "Cutting it fine, sir," he continued.

On the feed, Recker saw the tightness of the margins.

"Two metres from hitting that spoke," said Aston.

"Our hull's tough enough if I get it wrong, Commander."

"It's the noise I was worried about."

"Hold it steady, sir," said Burner.

For long moments, Recker did just that, wishing inside that the engines weren't so damned loud. His grip on the controls was too tight but he didn't dare loosen up, as if any disturbance in the situation's balance would result in destruction.

"How long?" he asked through gritted teeth. The light hadn't gone anywhere.

"If they weren't suspicious, they'd have moved away already, sir," said Burner.

"What reason have they got to be suspicious?" Recker demanded. He took a calming breath. "I don't expect you to answer that, Lieutenant."

Abruptly, the light cut out, leaving the surrounding area in darkness once more. The change wasn't reassuring and Recker was rapidly coming to terms to how tough this short trip was going to be.

CHAPTER NINETEEN

"HAVE THEY MOVED ON?" asked Recker. It was an effort not to talk quietly. The Daklan annihilators had an aura, like they were technologically infallible and capable of picking up a human voice through the hull of the deployment ship.

"I don't know, sir," said Burner. "Their propulsion output is about a million times ours, so even the crappy sensors on this deployment vessel know the annihilator is out there. The hard part is reading the direction of the resonance with it bouncing around the interior."

"This is what they pay you for, Lieutenant."

"They don't pay me enough for this, sir. Checking... they've moved away!"

"Heading for a look through a different hole," said Eastwood.

"More than likely," said Recker, piloting the spaceship away from the spoke and towards the large central pillar.

"I've detected two additional openings," said Burner. "One dead ahead and the other right."

Recker guided the ship along the pillar, though he recognized that the cover it offered was illusory.

"Listen out for that battleship, Lieutenant."

"I am sir. The sensors on this deployment craft aren't meant for this kind of work."

"Do what you can."

No sooner had the words left Recker's mouth than Burner shouted a warning, and the annihilator's stark light came through an opening a thousand metres closer to the cylinder's pinnacle. The only way for Recker to get the incision craft into cover quickly enough was to give the engines plenty of juice and hurl it towards a spoke three hundred metres away. For a split second, he felt trapped between two bad options – make noise or stay out in the open.

He held the spaceship in place.

"We're not in their visibility arc," said Burner a second later.

Recker checked to make sure they weren't in any other visibility arcs and made a small adjustment to the space-ship's position. He was given cause to wonder about the nature of luck when a second light came on, shining through another hole about four hundred metres from the spaceship's position. The illumination was harsh on the central pillar, right on the place Recker had just moved away from.

"We're in shadow," he said.

"Everything going to plan," said Burner, his voice arti-ficially light.

"Absolutely, Lieutenant."

This time, the lights stayed on for almost an entire minute, like the Daklan knew the deployment ship was inside and they were hoping their quarry would make a run for it. Recker wasn't stupid enough to try.

Eventually, the lights went out, though the lesson from the incident was already learned; at four thousand metres in length, the Daklan ship was large enough that it could look through more than one opening at the same time.

"They're changing position," said Burner.

"Let's do the same," Recker answered.

Under his control, the spaceship accelerated along the central pillar. Each slow metre travelled was a victory bought through the endurance of great frustration and Recker found this small journey harder than any he could recall.

"Tell me what's waiting for us, Lieutenant Burner," he said. "We're about fifteen hundred metres from the pinnacle and I'd like to know what we're about to run into."

"There are too many of these spokes, sir. It's like they added extra ones at the end."

The light returned, though to Recker's great relief it was far behind his spaceship. It seemed like the entire lower end of the cylinder was turned to shadow-strewn daylight and his hopes faded that the Daklan would make only a cursory inspection and then wait for a heavy lifter to enact a recovery.

"They're too interested," he said.

"That's the same feeling I have," said Aston.

Recker trusted her instinct – even more so when it coincided with his own. "We're like rats in a trap," he said.

"I don't remember having much choice about where to hide," she said. "We took a risk, and this is where we ended up."

Recker had no regrets. Like he told his crew, any kind of victory against the Daklan would require sacrifice, risk, and, he admitted, plenty of luck.

"The enemy are still checking out the opposite end of the cylinder," said Burner. "I think I can see through these spokes in front of us."

"Let's find out what we've got," said Recker, lifting the deployment spaceship over a place where two of the support beams joined with the central pillar.

He banked left, around one of the final visibility arcs and suddenly the view became much clearer. At first, Recker felt disappointment – the top section of the cylinder was capped by a solid circle of alloy, making it separate from this central space. Then, his eyes made out a platform which continued around at least part of the perimeter. Lieutenant Burner performed some magic with the sensors and the clarity improved tenfold.

"Looks like a ladder," he said. "And a ladder has got to lead somewhere."

Recker stared closely at the feed and thought he could make out the faintest outline of a hatch at the top of the ladder.

"Those rungs are halfway up the inner curve," he said. "If there's no life support operating in here, it's going to be difficult to get that hatch open."

"The sensors on this craft aren't capable of detecting the presence of a life support field, sir," said Burner. "However, there may be more suitable openings - just not visible from here."

"We'll soon find out," said Recker. It was beginning to dawn on him how difficult it would be to explore the upper section of the cylinder if there was no life support stabilisation for the topmost levels. Not just difficult, he corrected himself. *Impossible.*

"Got something!" said Burner.

Recker saw it too. As the deployment craft emerged through a gap between two spokes, a large shuttle-type vessel came into sight, clamped to what would have originally been the ceiling of the cylinder's inner space and not far from the central pillar.

"Daklan?" asked Eastwood, stepping closer to see.

Recker's first question had been the same – that the enemy had somehow got here first. Now he was sure it was otherwise. "It doesn't look like a Daklan vessel, Lieutenant."

"There's no vessel with that hull shape in our databanks, sir," Aston confirmed. "Either it's a Daklan design we've not encountered, or it was inside this cylinder during the attack that knocked it over."

"150 metres long and fifty across the beam," said Recker, staring at the boxy shape and the rounded edges of the clamped spaceship. The craft was pale blue, though he didn't know if the colour was a property of the construction material or just a smart paint job. One thing was sure – the Daklan only went for grey in their fleet.

206

"I'd guess it's designed for heavy lifting," said Aston.

"That would make sense," said Eastwood. "It could be a maintenance craft they used to finish off the interior of the cylinder once the outer plating was sealed."

The sighting of this shuttle hadn't made Recker forget about the annihilator and he checked to make sure it was still searching the far end of the cylinder. Abruptly, the searchlight went out and he cursed under his breath as he piloted the incision craft beneath a cluster of three spokes.

"There are some unoccupied clamps to the left of that shuttle," said Burner, pointing at twin rows of dark grey cubes fixed to the ceiling, which looked identical to the HPA's gravity clamps. "That means..." He took a breath. "Yes - there's a second shuttle on the floor beneath us."

Recker glanced at the updated feed. The area below was filled with spokes and two smaller missile breaches were visible on the curve to the left. Poking into sight and mostly obscured by the central pillar, he saw the nose section of a second shuttle.

"Must have broken free when the attack happened," said Aston. "Or it was already flying around on maintenance duties and the crew got taken by surprise."

"We'll never know," said Recker.

Aston turned so she could get a better view through his visor. "We're going in?"

He nodded. "There's a hatch opening in the centre of those clamps. I'm going to find out if they'll take hold of us when we come close."

"We might not get free, sir."

"Do you have another suggestion, Commander? We're

at the mercy of the Daklan and the way I see it, we might as well do what we can while we have an opportunity."

Aston gave him a smile. "I know, sir. It's my duty to speak the alternatives."

"Thank you, Commander. I'm going to dock with the cylinder."

With the same care as before, Recker took the incision craft towards the ceiling. The uppermost two hundred metres contained no spokes, though the main pillar continued, and he suspected it went to the very top of the cylinder. Even with the view partially obscured, the size of the alien device was more apparent than ever and Recker found himself increasingly worried about the purpose of these cylinders.

Manoeuvring into position wasn't difficult, since the spaceship wasn't travelling fast and Recker aimed the tail towards the ground in order that he could line up with the rows of gravity clamps. He drew close to the docked lifter shuttle and even this made the deployment craft appear tiny and frail in comparison.

"I don't think the annihilator has given up, sir," said Burner with a new note of worry in his voice.

"Where is it?"

"Nearby, sir. Either above or to our right, on the side where we first approached."

The light came back again – this time shining through one of the upper missile breaches about five hundred metres from the deployment vessel. Recker got a sense that the beam was shifting, like the battleship was moving slowly back and forward in order to get a better view inside.

"Why don't they piss off?" said Eastwood with feeling.

"Because they know how to fight and they know that winning takes effort, Lieutenant."

"I know that, sir. Sometimes it would be nice to run into a lazy crew." He grunted in anger. "I'm just letting off steam."

It was understandable in the circumstances and Recker didn't say anything more about it. Besides, his hands were full with the effort of fine-tuning the deployment craft.

"We're in position," he said, looking at the gravity clamps on both sides of the spaceship. Like the shuttle, they seemed huge from close range.

"The clamps haven't activated," said Burner. "Maybe there's a docking computer waiting for a handshake."

"That's something we can't offer, Lieutenant. If this isn't automatic, we've got trouble."

In truth, Recker had a backup plan involving the portable laser cutter the deployment craft was carrying in its tiny aft storage bay. The cutter could slice open most things in time, but he expected the hatch into the cylinder's upper levels to be a metre or more thick and that would take some work to get through.

Not only that, Recker wasn't sure they had a lot of time left to them. The persistence of the battleship had him thinking that the Daklan weren't going to scan the interior and then hover patiently overhead waiting for a heavy lifter. Deep down, Recker believed the Daklan would launch a shuttle full of soldiers and that shuttle would head straight for the hatch leading to the upper levels. At that point, they'd learn the HPA had got here first and then the shit would really start flying.

The outcome would be death for everyone on the deployment vessel.

He couldn't tolerate the dark thoughts and he pushed them from his mind. At that point, he felt something tugging the spaceship and he took his hands from the controls. The gravity clamps made no sound, but Recker had docked often enough that he knew they'd taken hold.

"We're docked," he said. A green light came up on the forward hatch monitor. "Seems like their hatch just formed a seal with ours."

Recker turned to see the expressions of the others. They didn't know what to make of the situation and Lieutenant Eastwood looked more bewildered than anything.

"I guess that means we're going to send Sergeant Vance and his squad to check out what's inside the control area of this cylinder," he said.

"Almost right, Lieutenant," said Recker. He stood, feeling the tenseness in every muscle.

"You're going with them?" said Aston.

"Damn right I am. If the hatch opens."

"It did just open, sir," said Burner. "The security sensor on our hatch has a view into the exit shaft."

A tiny secondary screen showed the feed. A ladder led up a lit shaft, which became an open space about ten metres up. Any other details were difficult to make out.

Aston knew when a battle was lost before it started and she didn't argue Recker's decision. "I'll watch this ship, sir, and give warning if the Daklan send a shuttle this way. Problem is, we're clamped, so it won't exactly be a fair fight if you're expecting me to shoot them down."

"I know, Commander. Find out if you can interface with this cylinder's docking computer, which might offer you control over the clamps. Failing that, the moment you see the enemy, escape through the hatch."

"Roger that, sir."

"What about me and Lieutenant Burner?" asked Eastwood.

"I'm not expecting to encounter hostiles inside," Recker said. "The most likely requirement will be for trained technical personnel, so you're coming with me. Choose yourselves a rifle each from that cabinet."

The preparations didn't take longer than a few seconds. Sergeant Vance and his squad were born ready and they were keen to get off the deployment vessel. Recker could understand their motivation.

"Sergeant Vance, I'm in command of this one," he said.

"Yes, sir," said Vance, his voice giving no indication what he thought of the order. "There's a new squad channel. I sent you an invite."

Recker accepted the invitation and then brought Eastwood and Burner into the channel. He took a rifle for himself and put a couple of spare magazines into the leg pockets of his spacesuit. It felt like it had been too long since he'd handled a gauss rifle and memories came flooding back – blood, death, and thudding recoil.

Despite the danger, Recker felt a surge of excitement and his breathing deepened. He stepped out of the cockpit into the crowded troop bay. One of the soldiers – Private

Hunter Gantry according to the ping from his comms unit
– was already clambering up the exit shaft.

"Any time you're ready, sir," the man said. "Just give
the order."

"No point in hanging around, soldier. Open that hatch
and let's go see what's inside this cylinder."

CHAPTER TWENTY

SPACE within the deployment vessel was tight and Recker had to wait for the soldiers in front. Luckily, Sergeant Vance and his squad were accustomed to rapid departures and they vanished into the exit hatch with a speed which indicated how aware they were that their lives depended on it.

"We've got active life support up here," said Gantry on the comms.

The discovery was great news and when his turn came, Recker climbed eagerly, his muscles appreciating the honest exercise. With each step upwards, he felt them loosening and his heart rate increased with the burden of his loadout. Above him, the boots of Private Steigers clunked against metal and Recker matched him rung for rung.

The airtight seal showed as a thick line and there was a step formed by the extra width of the cylinder side of the exit shaft. A brief giddiness informed Recker that he was passing from one life support field to another, but he felt no other ill effects. The continuation of the ladder was on the opposite side and he was forced to turn and lean outwards so that he could grab one of the rungs. After that, he half stepped and half pulled himself across, before resuming the climb.

He glanced below to see that Lieutenant Eastwood was struggling to keep up. The military required a certain level of fitness in its warship crews, but it demanded a higher level from its foot soldiers. Recker came from the ground and he refused to let his body decline.

The space he'd seen from the hatch security monitor went all the way around the shaft and had plenty of room to accommodate the entire squad, who were spread around the opening. The ceiling was low and Recker bent his neck so that his suit helmet wouldn't knock against the solid alloy above him.

"We've got two doors, sir," said Sergeant Vance. "One here and another on the opposite side."

The doors were grey alloy, a little wider than most doors in the HPA, and bore no markings.

"Any way to get them open or are we going to be hauling up that laser cutter?" asked Recker.

Private Drawl was standing adjacent to the nearest door and he moved aside to reveal a green light on the wall.

"Access panel?" said Recker.

"A button, sir." Drawl spoke the words slowly, like his speech reflected his name. "Want me to push it?"

Recker turned to see how last man Lieutenant Burner

was progressing and found that he was just emerging from the shaft, his cheeks flushed from the exertion.

"Go ahead, Private."

The squad shifted in readiness. Private Gantry was enormously thickset, and he carried the squad's MG-12 high-calibre repeater, which he pointed straight at the door. The MG-12s were heavy, but they could sure as hell hold a choke point. Or chew through a watermelon harvest in double-quick time.

With his finger extended in an exaggerated fashion, Drawl poked the button. It must have offered greater resistance than he expected and he had to give it a second try, while a couple of the squad laughed nervously at his failed effort.

Drawl's second effort was successful, and the door moved slowly into a side recess to reveal steep steps leading upwards. The environmental sensor in Recker's helmet detected no significant change in atmospheric pressure and reported that the air was breathable for humans, though the temperature was below freezing. The significance of the atmosphere wasn't lost on Recker – it suggested this part of the cylinder once had a crew - a crew he had to keep reminding himself was certainly dead.

"Clear," said Drawl, having checked up the stairwell.

Recker sensed the hesitation in the squad and he swore at himself – he'd taken command and here he was standing dumbly and waiting for Sergeant Vance to get things moving.

"Private Drawl, up you go," said Recker, striding closer to the doorway. The moment Drawl was gone, he stepped into the vacated space and looked up the steps. They had high risers and were steep, though they didn't climb too far. Recker estimated they ended after twenty metres, which probably indicated the thickness of the armour separating the main bay below and the command levels above.

"It's big up here. No sign of hostiles," said Drawl on the comms. "And it's filled with some kind of alien tech shit."

Recker was seized by the urge to find out what secrets the cylinder held, and he ascended the steps rapidly, beckoning Sergeant Vance to come with him. He emerged into another space, much larger than the one below and with a three-metre ceiling. The curved inner and outer walls indicated that it wrapped around the central pillar and two straight walls suggested this room formed one quarter of a complete circuit. A diffuse light came from half-metre circular disks, flush with the metal overhead. These disks illuminated the area evenly and dispersed most of the shadows.

The *alien tech shit*, as Private Drawl had so eloquently described it, didn't look like anything too unusual. Ceiling-mounted racks carried bundles of thick pipes or cables, which emerged from the central pillar and then disappeared into the ceiling or the walls. Blocky, chest-high, single-screen monitoring stations were fixed to the floor in numerous places directly beneath these racks. Slender posts rose from the top of each station and connected to the racks, which Recker guessed was how the flow along the pipes and cables was monitored.

A few bulkier pieces of kit were bolted to the outer wall, twenty meters from the top of the steps. These consoles didn't have screens, but levers protruded next to panels of oversized mechanical switches.

"Manual overrides," said Vance, pointing briefly. "Everything looks ancient."

He was right – the tech *did* look old, though the overall sense Recker got from the cylinder was that it was far in advance of anything made by the HPA.

There were no threats to the squad in this room bar ones they'd make for themselves, so Recker ordered the squad to move up.

"If I see anyone pissing about with the hardware, I'll shoot them myself," he said, so there was no misunderstanding.

The soldiers hurried up the steps and he ordered them to secure the area. They split and most took cover behind the maintenance stations, whilst others hunted for exits.

"Maintenance area," said Eastwood, with evident interest. "Want me to check out any of these panels, sir?"

"Maybe later, Lieutenant. We've got to find the comms station."

"None of this is comms," said Burner, telling Recker what he already knew.

Although this room was huge, Recker estimated that it occupied only a small fraction of the cylinder's diameter. The interior was 1100 meters across once you deducted the outer armour and the space occupied by the central pillar from the total. This room was approximately 120 metres deep and 400 metres along its curved length, which meant that the outer walls here were either extremely thick or there was plenty of exploration to be done. Not only that, there was potentially space for another eight or ten levels above this one if the builders had decided to cram them in.

"Find the exits," Recker ordered. He looked about but couldn't see any obvious doors. "Lieutenant Burner, you're with me," he continued, setting off towards the longest wall.

To Recker's surprise, Burner held his rifle confidently and he followed at once.

"If this cylinder's like the one on Etrol, I'd guess the comms station is on the level above this one, sir. Depending on how they spaced out the floors."

As a pair, they jogged along the wall, which seemed to have been formed from a single piece of alloy. The override panels didn't look any more sophisticated from up close and Recker wondered what sort of tech required manual intervention if things went wrong. No sooner had he asked himself the question than a dozen answers jumped into his head. The HPA had plenty of kit that could be manually overridden in the event of power failure, such as the internal doors on a spaceship.

Recker and Burner didn't locate a door, but one of the soldiers did.

"Here, sir," said Private Montero, over by one of the straight walls. "I've found a door." She made a clicking sound with her tongue. "This one has a red light on it."

"Got another door this side, sir," called Private Raimi. "Red light as well."

"Leave it and get over here."

Private Montero lounged against the wall adjacent to the door, like this was the easiest mission she'd ever had the good fortune to be sent on. Recker wasn't fooled by the act – Montero's eyes didn't stop moving and her rifle barrel was only a few inches low.

"Want me to try this switch, sir?" she asked.

Recker waited until the others were settled nearby, either in cover behind the monitoring hardware or crouched with guns aimed at the door.

"Go for it."

Montero didn't make the same mistake as Drawl and she pushed firmly with her thumb. The light didn't change and the door didn't open.

"Try again," said Recker.

A second push of the switch produced the same outcome as the first.

"The lock on this door might indicate a vacuum on the far side, sir," said Lieutenant Eastwood.

"Good point."

Private Titus Enfield was carrying a pack full of explosives and he rose from cover when Recker beckoned him over.

"Private Enfield, this door thinks you can't handle what's in that pack," he said.

"Let's see about that, sir."

Vacuum depressurization would be strongest near the door, so Recker made sure everyone was far enough clear.

Like Recker expected, the members of this squad were skilled and efficient. They talked too much crap on the open channel, but that didn't slow them down and Private Enfield had eight shaped charges fitted to the door frame in less than a minute. Once he had the last one in place, he raced away with his pack in one hand and rifle in the other.

ANTHONY JAMES

"Remote detonation," he said gleefully. "Avert your eyes, people."

A second later, the charges ignited, producing a fizzing sound from the plasma burn, followed by a shaped blast to rip the door clear.

"Depressurization commencing," said Vance.

The air in the room was sucked through the doorway, producing a muffled drone. Recker leaned from the cover of his maintenance console to check Enfield's work.

"Clean," he said approvingly.

Enfield had taken the door out neatly and the slab of metal lay flat on the far side of the door, its edges red-rimmed from the plasma heat. The air shimmered slightly as it vanished through the opening and Recker tried to make sense of what was on the far side.

"Something wrong through there," said Vance.

"Looks like."

Recker went ahead and peered around the doorframe, taking care that his suit didn't touch the hot alloy.

It was difficult to be certain if this new room had ever been a copy of the old, because it was all burned. A layer of char clung to every surface and Recker saw misshapen lumps and bulges on the floors and walls. What he assumed were pipe racks and cable trays drooped from the ceiling.

The source of the damage wasn't hard to find. A couple of hundred meters from the doorway, a near-circular hole had taken out most of the wall and part of the ceiling. The angle wasn't good enough for Recker to see far into the opening, but he had no doubt this was also the cause of the vacuum.

"What the hell made that?" said Vance.

"It was no missile," said Recker. "A beam weapon of some kind."

"Must have been a hell of powerful one to penetrate so far into the cylinder," said Eastwood. "Far more intense than anything we've got in the HPA and probably more than anything the Daklan fleet is equipped with."

"Two warring races," said Corporal Hendrix. "Neither of which we've met."

Recker had already surmised most of this and here was yet more evidence in support. When news of this came back to high command, he expected soiled pants, resignations and plenty of finger pointing. Maybe some of the crap would land squarely on top of Fleet Admiral Thaddeus Solan and his son Gabriel, though Recker expected it would slide right off leaving only the stench behind.

"We need to find a way up, Sergeant," he said, clearing his mind. He turned to look at the squad and found they were waiting for him to act.

Getting rusty.

Recker strode into the new room, watching carefully for anything hostile or dangerous. It didn't seem likely he'd find enemy forces – Daklan or otherwise - but caution cost nothing.

"Find me a way up," he repeated. "Stairs, lifts, or a rope ladder. I don't care what it is."

He advanced deeper into the room, finding himself drawn to the place where the beam weapon had breached the cylinder. The char was dry underfoot and it crumbled where he trod, leaving imprints in his wake. He paused for a moment next to a waist-high lump on the floor and rubbed at the black coating. The top layer flaked off, revealing heat-darkened alloy beneath.

The beam from the unknown weapon must have been an easy fifty metres in diameter and the damage it created was almost precision. The light from the lower room didn't extend too far into the opening and Recker didn't want to switch on his helmet torch in case it somehow alerted the annihilator. What he could see was melted walls and not much else.

Standing so close to the effects of the alien weapon made Recker feel insignificant and powerless. He backed away, suppressing a shiver.

"Over here, sir!" called Corporal Givens.

The soldier was nearby and was using one hand to rub at a section of the longest wall. A green light shone through the coating of char.

"Another door," said Recker, hurrying closer.

Within a minute, the squad was gathered, and the door was open. A set of steps – even steeper than the last ones – climbed into darkness.

"Whatever's up there, it's got to be better than walking through this shit," said Private Steigers. The greys of the man's spacesuit were smeared in black and Recker noticed that his own wasn't much cleaner.

"You'll be happy to learn that's exactly where we're going, Private."

Recker was taken by the sudden feeling that he was approaching a crossroads. He'd never gone slow on life's road and he felt more excitement than fear. With his rifle ready, he ascended.

CHAPTER TWENTY-ONE

THE STEPS WERE BARELY WIDE ENOUGH for two people to pass. With no railing to hold, Recker leaned into the climb to keep himself balanced, which made it harder to keep his rifle pointing in the right direction. From what he'd seen of the operational area of the cylinder, Recker didn't think it likely that many personnel ever worked here – nothing indicated it was geared up for the presence of a large crew.

He arrived at a landing and the steps switched back, continuing to another landing visible in the low light of the stairwell. Recker went up and the squad followed, keeping a five-step distance between each member. After four switchbacks, the final landing was larger than those preceding it.

"A door," said Recker. "Got another red light on it."

"Time for Titus to save the day," said Hendrix, slurring her voice stupidly to piss off the other soldier.

"Aw shit, does that mean we've got to get clear of these steps?" asked Gantry.

"MG-12 too much weight for you, Private?" asked Vance. "Want me to give it to Private Drawl instead?"

"Hell yeah, hand it over," said Drawl, who probably couldn't lift the MG-12, let alone wield it effectively in combat.

Recker demanded quiet. "I've got a better idea. Who's last man?"

"That'll be me, sir," said Private Joiner.

"It's your lucky day, soldier. Go back and close the bottom door. There's a chance this upper door won't open while the life support detects a vacuum."

Joiner didn't grumble and he returned to the stairwell entrance.

"I'm ready to press this lower door switch," he said on the comms.

"Don't let us keep you, Private," said Recker.

"Done."

The light on the upper switch immediately turned green.

"Private Joiner, get yourself back up here," said Recker.

He turned to make sure the rest of the squad wasn't bunched up and then activated the door switch. It was stiff and he felt the mechanism click. The door slid open and Recker stared with momentary disappointment into a long passage with no side turnings.

"Another door at the end," he said.

"With a green light," said Vance, coming up to stand next to him on the landing.

Recker's impatience was getting the better of him and he marched along the passage. "Sergeant Vance, with me. The rest of you stay back."

The step counter in his helmet informed Recker that the passage was eighty meters long. When he reached the end, he nodded once at Vance and then pressed the switch. The door opened and what lay on the other side was enough to convince Recker that he was in the command area of the cylinder.

He didn't wait in the confines of the passage and sprinted for a semi-circular console to the right of the doorway, which he crouched behind for cover. Sergeant Vance went left and dropped behind an identical console.

The two men cautiously scanned the room, which seemed to form an uninterrupted circle around the central pillar, though it was impossible to be sure because of the curve. At forty metres front to back, the space was comparatively narrow, with a sub-zero, but breathable atmosphere.

"Full of tech," said Vance.

The words were an adequate description. Three rows of the semi-circular consoles appeared to go all the way around the central pillar and every one faced the centre. Recker swept his gaze over the console in front of him – it was a mixture of primitive and advanced in a way he couldn't immediately grasp. A few of the switches were lit and he could hear a quiet humming from within the housing.

The three wide screens were either switched off or connected to an offline system. Belatedly, he noticed the lack of a seat, which struck him as unusual. From his experience, most operators liked to park their backsides during long shifts.

"Move up," Recker ordered.

Within seconds, the first members of the squad entered the room.

"Sergeant Vance, take over. Secure the area."

The soldiers got on with business and Recker waited for Lieutenants Burner and Eastwood to join him at the console. At the same time, he checked in with Commander Aston.

"Looks as if we've reached the control centre," he said. "I think the power is on."

"There's no sign of the Daklan sending a shuttle, sir. However, they haven't stopped shining those lights into the holes."

The words made Recker uneasy. The Daklan interest hadn't waned and eventually they'd get bored with looking through those missile breaches. An annihilator carried a lot of troops and the shuttles to deploy them.

He cursed sourly. "Any intel we gain from this cylinder is only useful if we bring it back to base."

"Nothing about that has changed, sir. Don't forget to look for the docking clamp controller. I've tried interfacing from this deployment craft, but the cylinder hardware isn't answering."

"I didn't forget, Commander."

If he couldn't locate the docking controller, the next option would be to blow the clamps and that would be dangerous work, no matter how talented Private Enfield might be. Recker felt his earlier excitement eroding beneath the weight of reality.

Burner and Eastwood watched him carefully.

"You know what we have to do, gentlemen. Get this hardware online and find out what we can from it. Lieutenant Eastwood, your priority is the docking clamps."

They all knew that the shuttle wasn't going to carry them home since it wasn't fitted with a lightspeed drive - that meant they were waiting for the HPA to send help. None of it mattered unless the annihilator's commanding officer decided to take his warship elsewhere and that wasn't an outcome worth laying bets on.

The road ahead ends at a cliff edge and I'm probably the only one denying it.

Burner and Eastwood took the consoles at either side and Recker turned his attention to this one. He knew it had power and he pushed a few buttons to see if he could get the screens to turn on. Recker had a knack with hardware – always had – and he quickly got all three screens lit up. Each one showed the same alien characters, while a cursor blinked slowly, awaiting input.

The computer in Recker's helmet had some advanced software installed that was originally used to interpret the Daklan spoken and written word. Now the Daklan language was well-known, but the translation software was still installed as standard. Recker stared at the alien characters and the software kicked in automatically. A message appeared on his HUD from the translation module.

ALTM> Insufficient data for translation.

Recker's eyes landed on a ten-by-ten cluster of square-shaped, ivory-coloured keys, positioned exactly where an operator's right hand might comfortably rest. He pushed several of the buttons and each time he did so, a character illuminated on the surface of the key. Then, one of the keys he randomly pressed caused the illumination to stay on permanently.

By the time Recker had experimented for a full minute, the top two lines of the screen were filled with spidery alien letters and he had no idea how to delete them. It probably didn't matter, since the translation software could only learn from full words and sentences, rather than the crap he was typing out.

"If we can't access the software, the translation module isn't going to learn," said Eastwood, struggling with the same problem.

"Even if we get a greater exposure to the language of the species that built this hardware, the module will only have a rudimentary understanding anyway," said Burner.

The enormity of the task made Recker swear again. "I'd hoped we might find something different to this," he said. "Maybe a star chart on a big screen, or something more pictorial that we could take a recording of and bring home with us. The military has teams who can look at stuff like that and extract all kinds of useful data from it."

"This is what we've got, sir."

"Don't I know it, Lieutenant."

Recker spent another couple of minutes randomly poking at keys, to see if he could stumble on the right combination to access the control menus. The method was a failure and neither Eastwood nor Burner were faring any better.

Taking a step away, Recker studied the console, hoping for inspiration. A flat, grey rectangular area at the far left of the console's upper panel reminded him of the wireless antenna on the HPA equivalent hardware. Those antennae doubled up as interface ports and the memory of it gave Recker a sudden idea.

He stepped over to what he now hoped was the console's interface port and instructed his helmet computer to begin hunting for an option to link. A green light appeared and Recker requested a connection. He smiled when the link formed.

With no option other than to make some assumptions on how this alien hardware operated, Recker drummed his fingers as he considered his approach. He'd long believed that some methods of doing things were simply better than others, which was why human and Daklan tech operated so similarly – the two species had naturally and independently figured out the best way to achieve the same outcomes.

With that in mind, Recker attempted to upload the HPA language module. The file was accepted, and he waited to find out if the contents would simply be dumped in a databank, or if they'd be scanned and acted upon.

He got his answer soon enough, though in a way which surprised him. A return file was offered, and he loaded it into his suit databanks. It was a language file, but his suit computer wouldn't activate it before completing a security scan on the contents. The scan didn't take longer than five seconds and then the file was moved alongside the other language modules, where it become active. At once, the characters on the screen and the alien keyboard became understandable.

"Interface with the port on the left and upload your language files," Recker instructed Burner and Eastwood.

They didn't require any more instruction.

"Done," said Burner.

"Me too. That's going to help."

Seconds later, Recker discovered how to bring up the main control menu.

"Defence Platform: Tenixite Converter - Primary Node," he said, reading the words at the top of the menu.

"Primary node?" said Burner. "No wonder the Daklan are interested in this one."

"They can't know," said Eastwood. "Hell, it might mean nothing. Given the size of these damn cylinders every one might be its own primary node."

"I'm more concerned with what a tenixite converter does," said Recker, thinking about the cylindrical holes on the planet's surface outside.

"It must generate juice," said Eastwood.

Recker was determined to find out as much as possible and he went rapidly through the menus. The hierarchical arrangement, which was remarkably similar to that of the HPA's main control suite, reinforced his view that intelligent species, wherever they were found, would do the same tasks in strikingly similar ways.

He came across the monitoring tools and brought up a series of gauges on the left-hand screen.

"The central pillar is the power generating source for this whole place," he said. "If I'm reading this the right way, the sustained output from that single source could supply everything on Earth without breaking into a sweat."

Saying the words made Recker feel giddy and he double-checked, only to discover that the potential output was far greater than the sustained.

"The historical readings show a bunch of short-duration output spikes," he said.

Recker stared at the chart, which displayed time stamps for the activity. Unfortunately, even with the exchange of language modules there was no point of reference to tie in the alien method of recording time with that of the HPA. One thing was certain – the spikes came in rapid succession and they happened a long time ago. After that, the output levels remained constant.

"War happened and this node got taken out," said Recker. "Or so its enemies thought."

Sergeant Vance came on the comms. "Sir, we've found bodies. Lots of bodies."

Recker looked up from his console and spotted Vance further around the circle, waving to get his attention.

"I'm coming over, Sergeant."

Reluctantly, he backed away from the console and ran towards Vance. For a few seconds, Recker couldn't see the bodies at all. Then, a darkly twisted heap of discoloured forms came into view – they were piled up next to the central pillar, out of sight from the console he'd been working at. With each stride around the curve, Recker gained an increased view of the dead and he prepared himself mentally for the close-up.

He slowed at the last minute and shook his head at the sight. The corpses were blackened and shrivelled, wearing charred clothing of indeterminate original colour. Their limbs were intertwined like they'd known the end was upon them and they'd gathered to say their goodbyes. Recker tried to understand how they'd appeared in life and the best he could judge was that the aliens were taller and slimmer than humans, with the same two arms, two legs and a head.

Corporal Hendrix and Private Raimi were close by, the former crouched next to her med-box and holding a probe against one of the bodies.

"How many?" It was the first question that came to Recker's head.

"Two hundred. Maybe more," said Hendrix. "Must have been the entire crew of this control level."

"Heat death," said Recker.

"Yes, sir. Best guess is this cylinder got attacked and the crew weren't expecting it, else they'd have been wearing protective suits." She reached out her free hand and pinched a section of the burnt clothing which was wrapped around the corpse in front of her. "They had clothes on, but they didn't provide much protection."

Recker added everything up. "The heat from that beam weapon on the lower level was enough to kill everyone up here," he said.

"That's what it looks like," said Hendrix.

"And the crew huddled, in the hope that the personnel in the centre would be protected until the life support cooled the air again."

Hendrix straightened and Recker could see that she was affected. "They say that life is what you make it, sir. That doesn't mean much when someone comes and takes it away."

"It's a shitty war we're fighting, Corporal."

"And from this..." Hendrix indicated the mound of bodies. "...it looks like we're about to crash someone else's party as well."

"That's not in the plans. My gut tells me this happened a long time ago and we've found the leftovers."

"Maybe not such a long time ago, sir." Hendrix's face looked pained. "It's cold enough in here to keep them preserved but tissue decay indicates these poor bastards died eighty years ago."

Recker had been hoping this unknown war was centuries past and the truth of it must have reflected in his expression. He met the eyes of Hendrix and then turned to look at Vance. They understood what this meant, and they desperately wanted it to be otherwise.

"Eighty years is a long time," said Recker at last. "The species fighting this could be dust in the wind."

"In my experience, when two sides fight, there's always a victor, sir," said Vance.

"Let's hope that whoever won this one, they're a long way from here, Sergeant."

The words sounded hollow to Recker, even as he spoke them. He'd always accepted that the universe held plenty of secrets and had, in his younger days, imagined what it would be like to unearth some of them himself.

Now the moment had come, and the emotions weren't anything like he'd expected. Recker wasn't given time to worry about the ramifications. A channel opened in his comms unit and Aston spoke. Her voice was even, though the effort required to keep it so dripped from every syllable.

"Sir, a Daklan shuttle entered the cylinder."

It was the news which Recker hadn't wanted to hear. The Daklan were on their way and they usually came in big numbers. He swore and kicked out at the nearest console.

CHAPTER TWENTY-TWO

ASTON WAS IN DANGER, but she was also in the best position to gather intel.

"Have they found the deployment vessel?" asked Recker, forcing himself calm.

"Not yet, sir. They must have entered through one of the further openings. I caught sight of them flying between two of the spokes."

"Heading your way?"

"That's unclear, sir."

"What about the troop capacity of the enemy vessel?"

"Again, that's unclear, sir. The shuttle was larger than the deployment vessel, but I didn't recognize the type."

"Was it alone?"

"I only saw one. I'll keep watching."

"No. Leave the sensors running and if needs be, we can view the stream through our suit comms. Now get out of there," said Recker.

Aston didn't argue. "Yes, sir, I'm on my way."

Recker stayed in the channel and he could hear her breathing as she ran from the deployment vessel.

"I guess you didn't find a way to turn off the clamps," she said.

"Lieutenant Eastwood's checking it out, Commander. Seems like he's going to be too late."

Aston had been following the squad's progress on the open channel and she didn't require directions, allowing Recker to exit the channel and turn his attention elsewhere.

"Sergeant Vance, the Daklan sent a shuttle into the cylinder."

"An armed shuttle?"

"We'll assume so. Troop capacity unknown. It's certain they'll locate our deployment vessel."

"Will the annihilator destroy the cylinder when that happens, sir?"

"Negative," said Recker with conviction. "That shuttle came inside for a reason and I have a feeling the Daklan will be keen to find out what's on these upper levels. I'd like you to take charge of the squad and stop them."

Vance smiled dangerously. "They won't find it easy getting their shuttle docked and climbing up the shaft will be a hundred times harder."

"That depends how much destruction they're willing to commit in order to reach their objectives, Sergeant. Some of their shuttles carry missile launchers and I would hate for you and your squad to be caught unawares."

"We'll handle it," said Vance with such utter certainty that Recker didn't doubt the words. "Permission to take whatever action is necessary, sir?"

Recker understood the meaning. "If you have to plant explosives on the deployment vessel, do so."

"Yes, sir. What about the shuttle that's clamped next to ours?"

"Do what you have to, Sergeant, but I'd rather we didn't burn every bridge."

Vance laughed. "I don't think Enfield's carrying enough explosives to take out both anyway, sir." The laughter faded. "Do you need me to leave anyone here with you?"

"No – the Daklan can't reach this level without coming through you and the squad. I'll stay up here with my crew and Commander Aston's on her way. I've got a feeling we're on the brink of discovering something here."

"If this cylinder is a weapon and its power source is online, maybe there's a way to use it, sir."

Vance's words cut through the fog and focused Recker's mind. He nodded in acknowledgement. "I've been thinking too much about intel and escape, Sergeant."

"Nothing wrong with either of those things, sir." Vance turned to his soldiers. "Raimi, Hendrix, if you don't want to join those dead bodies, pick up your shit and follow me."

The words galvanised everyone. Vance sprinted away with the two soldiers, shouting orders on the squad channel. Meanwhile, Recker cut across the room towards his console. As he ran, he created a separate comms channel for his crew and invited them to join. It was important that Recker could hear the squad and he remained in their channel to receive updates and to provide updated orders if necessary.

"Were you two listening to what I said to Sergeant Vance?" he asked Burner and Eastwood.

"Yes, sir. The Daklan are coming," said Eastwood.

"And we've got our hands full with the alien hardware," added Burner.

Recker approached his console between the two men and found it exactly as he'd left it. "Discovered anything new?"

"Mostly technical stuff, sir – output charts, monitoring readouts, schematics - without an explanation as to how everything is tied together," said Eastwood.

"Makes sense," said Recker. "Why would the original personnel need documentation telling them what their own kit does?"

"That's what I said to myself. I'm still hunting – I reckon there's plenty to be found, it's just going to require me to dig a lot deeper."

"What about you, Lieutenant Burner?"

The other man looked up. "I'm pulling out some good data, sir. This tenixite converter is one node out of twenty-four."

"Can you locate the others?"

"Yes and no. As far as I can gather, each node only communicates with two others and this cylinder has received a fail response from one of those two."

"What about the second?"

"Coming through loud and clear."

"Why the limitation? Why don't all nodes speak to the others?"

"Security, sir. Whoever created the defence platform

didn't want the entire network being compromised if one node was taken over."

"Can you pinpoint the location of the active node this one is speaking to?"

"Again, that's a yes and no answer, sir. This node holds only a limited star chart and I assume that's also for security. The connected node is visible, but I have no way of tying the position of the stars with the HPA chart." He tapped the side of his head. "The suit computers only carry a fraction of what a warship navigational computer holds."

"You're about to tell me another problem."

"Yes, sir. Whoever built this cylinder plotted their sky map from totally different positions and I don't even know if they record the same celestial data as we do."

"Is there a way around that?"

"Extensive study and a bunch of high-end processing cores, sir."

Recker grimaced. "Can we get any of this back to base?"

"I've recorded the transmission direction to the linked nodes. That should be enough for us to locate the two other cylinders, even if it sounds like one of them is offline or destroyed."

"The top-level menu on this console names this cylinder as a primary node."

"I think they're all primary, sir, which means there's some secondary kit elsewhere. I don't think we should waste our time guessing what that does or where it's located."

"I agree. Now, gentlemen, we're in the crap and I want

us to concentrate on finding out exactly how this defence platform works. I didn't yet come across a method of defence that didn't involve blowing an attacker into small pieces."

"I don't think the high-level command options are available on these consoles here, sir," said Eastwood. He pointed at the nearby hardware. "Notice how every station is identical?"

"What's your point?"

"The senior personnel had different consoles and they sat elsewhere."

Recker swore. "There's no time to explore this whole damn cylinder."

"Maybe we don't have to, sir," said Burner. "Could be that one of the squad came across a command station and didn't mention it."

It was worth a go and Recker got onto the open channel to ask.

"Me and Steigers saw something counter-clockwise of your position," said Drawl. "Three other consoles facing outwards not inwards."

It was tempting to ask the soldier why he hadn't reported it at the time, but Recker held his tongue. "How far?" he growled.

"A hundred or a hundred and fifty metres. We were searching for exits, sir, and not looking out too closely for anything else."

Recker let it slide and switched to his crew channel. "You heard the man. 150 meters that way."

The three of them ran along the aisles in the direction indicated.

"Where are you, Commander Aston?"

"I'm nearly with you, sir."

They arrived at the place Drawl had described. Three larger consoles faced the others and had some extra space around them. A chest-high rectangular device stood nearby, looking suspiciously like a food replicator, though Recker wasn't of a mind to investigate the produce.

He chose the centre of the three command stations and studied it for differences. This one had five screens instead of three, as well as an extra keypad and some other touchpads that weren't on the smaller consoles.

"Let's fire this one up," he said, waving over Commander Aston, who'd just emerged through the far door.

Within a short time, Recker had the command console online. It presented the same menu as the others, though with a bunch of additional options.

"Paydirt," said Eastwood.

Recker was distracted by words from Sergeant Vance.

"I think we just lost the deployment vehicle, sir."

"Is that a visual confirmation?"

"No, sir. The sensor feed dropped. I was just about to send Enfield to fix some charges in the shaft."

"Lucky man. Any idea if they took out the second docked shuttle?"

"I've got a couple of soldiers looking for a way to get onboard that one. I'll let you know when we find out."

"The Daklan won't hold back, Sergeant."

"I know that as well as anyone, sir."

Aston arrived, hardly out of breath from her sprint across the operation room. Without asking questions, she stopped at one of the smaller consoles, her eyes searching for the interface panel.

"I'll upload the language module and then do what I can to help out."

Recker nodded, his mind elsewhere as he explored the additional options available on the command console. It seemed like the senior officers on the cylinder used the same software as everyone else, with the benefit of a few hundred additional options.

"The sensors are offline," he said.

"I just found that out, sir," said Burner. "There's no indication of hardware failure – they may have gone into sleep mode because of extended inactivity."

"I've got plenty of new stuff to look through," said Eastwood.

"More than I was expecting," Recker admitted. "Let's get on."

It was slower going than he anticipated. He guessed something was chewing through the converter's processing core cycles because navigating through the command menus was taking an age, like the backend software was housed on a dedicated unit situated elsewhere and the data connection between this console and the remote hardware was running at a crawl.

"Sir, the Daklan used a missile to destroy the deployment vessel," said Vance, after a couple of minutes. "The wreckage is still held by the clamps, but the enemy is using their own shuttle to knock it free. They'll be able to dock in the next few minutes."

"What about the second shuttle?"

"I've got someone watching the hatch above it, sir. If

any of those alien bastards poke their heads through, they're going to be eating gauss rounds."

It sounded like the squad was on top of things, though it was possible the Daklan could be carrying a few surprises on their shuttle. Recker's impression of Vance was that he was a shrewd operator and wouldn't let his soldiers be sucker-punched by anything so crude as a shoulder launcher missile coming up the shuttle exit shaft.

He continued his search, with Aston looking on. She asked few questions and Recker was sure she'd have the alien tech figured out soon enough.

Recker's earpiece came to life again and he could hear the background fizz of gauss rifle discharge.

"Sir, we have engaged the enemy," said Vance. "They have superior numbers and a shoulder launcher."

"What's your assessment of the situation, Sergeant?"

"My assessment is that we have a fight on our hands, sir."

"Nothing you aren't accustomed to."

Even under fire, Vance could find the humour. "A walk in the park."

The comms went quiet and Recker found the urgency helped clear his mind. A moment after that, he found a new option in the control software.

Targeting. Sounds promising.

He accessed the menu, which gave him access to a list of targets the cylinder had acquired while operational. The majority were clustered a long time ago – he assumed eighty years past, when the attack came. Worryingly, some others happened more recently, though Recker couldn't be sure how far back. One target, however, he was sure about.

"The cylinder is aware of the annihilator," he said. "The targeting software assumes the battleship is hostile."

"Aim and fire," said Burner at once. "Shoot those bastards out of the sky."

"There's no obvious way to give the command," said Recker.

He dug around further, without finding what he was looking for.

"Sensors coming online," said Burner proudly. "Let's find out what they show."

The four other screens on Recker's console – which had so far been awaiting input - lit up. The annihilator was on one, its menacing features revealed in sharp detail, like the sensor tech on the cylinder was twenty or thirty years in advance of the HPA equivalent.

From the angle, Recker guessed that the enemy ship was above and a couple of thousand metres to the side of the sensor lens, so that its underside and flank were visible. His eyes roved across the multitude of turrets and launchers, along with a single dome the purpose of which he didn't know. The warship's hull was unblemished except for the faintest signs of particle erosion along its nose section.

"I think this is the same battleship we encountered at Etrol," Recker said. "Either that or the Daklan put more than one into service recently."

He stared at his enemy for long moments, trying to feel something that wasn't hatred. His fists clenched and it seemed to him like this battleship had become his unwanted nemesis.

Aston appeared at his side. "There's got to be a way,

sir." She pointed at the other screens. "Tactical." She leaned closer to another screen. "Another feed here - seems to be aimed directly at the surface of Oldis."

The final screen was also running a sensor feed and inexplicably it was targeted at a distant planet. A text overlay indicated it was 120 million kilometres away, which he assumed meant it was planet nine in the Exim-K system. He struggled to recall the name.

Tanril.

Recker had plenty to be getting on with, but he felt an enormous curiosity.

"Lieutenant Burner, when you get a chance, find out why this feed is looking at Tanril."

"Yes, sir."

"Oh crap, see this on the tactical?" said Aston.

Recker gave it his attention. The annihilator was represented by a solid red circle and the cylinder was green. A second red circle – much smaller than the battle-ship – had appeared.

"They launched another shuttle," he said.

The course overlay indicated the vessel was heading for the upper part of the cylinder.

"What are they doing?" said Eastwood.

The answer came to Recker. "That particle beam opening is fifty meters across and goes all the way through the armour," he said. "Shit – the Daklan could fly a shuttle straight through it and deploy their troops on the level below."

"I'm trying to get a sensor lock, sir," said Burner. "This alien hardware is slowing me down."

Recker didn't need the sensors to confirm it - the

tactical screen gave him all the information he required. The Daklan didn't like the resistance they'd found below, so they were taking a different approach.

He accessed the squad channel.

"Sergeant Vance, I've got some bad news for you."

CHAPTER TWENTY-THREE

VANCE TOOK the change of circumstance in his stride. "We'll fall back to the next level up, sir, and try to hurt those alien assholes when they deploy. If that fails, we'll withdraw to your level." He took an audible breath. "Are we fighting for something other than pride, sir? It'll give the squad motivation if they know you've got a trick up your sleeve."

"We're bringing things together here, Sergeant. If this cylinder is a weapon, we'll figure out the way to use it."

It wasn't much of a reassurance, but Vance didn't complain. "I'll let the squad know, sir."

Recker checked to make sure his crew knew what was happening. To his memory, only Aston had any significant experience of ground combat, while Burner and Eastwood simply accepted the reality and continued what they were doing.

"I've found out why there's an array locked on Tanril,"

said Burner. "This cylinder performed something called a core override on one of the warships attacking it."

"Core override?" said Recker. "Is that the name for cylinder's main weapon?"

"I don't know, sir."

A sudden thought prompted Recker to check the audit logs for the tactical. He located what he thought was the right entry.

Core override success. Target destruction unconfirmed.

He ground his teeth in frustration. The tenixite converter held countless secrets and he wished for the time to unearth them all. Unfortunately, the Daklan were after those same secrets and Recker had no intention of making it easy for them. He was sure this cylinder had destructive capabilities and he didn't want the enemy figuring out how to turn this as-yet unrevealed firepower on the HPA.

"We've fallen back to the level below," said Vance.

"What about the Daklan on the first shuttle?"

"Private Enfield left them a gift, sir. I don't imagine it'll hold them up for long."

A glance at the tactical told Recker that the second shuttle was stationary, not far from the cylinder. He didn't know what was keeping them – maybe the entrance hole was obstructed.

"The enemy are stalled outside, Sergeant. I don't know if that's a permanent situation for them."

A rumbling boom came though the comms link and Vance unleashed a stream of obscenities.

"Sergeant, please report!" shouted Recker.

When Vance answered, he was clearly running full

pelt. "We found out the reason they stopped, sir. It was to send a missile into the opening."

"Casualties?"

"Private Joiner was lookout, sir. He was standing right where the missile landed."

It was another death on Recker's watch. "Withdraw from that level, Sergeant. If the shuttle fired a missile, there's nothing stopping the annihilator doing the same and the payload from one of those will be enough to incinerate everyone in the room."

In truth, Recker didn't think the battleship would send a plasma missile into the cylinder, but then again, he hadn't anticipated the shuttle firing one of its standard explosives inside either. The Daklan must know a lot more about these tenixite converters than he did and they might be happy to destroy some of the less important hardware in order to flush out the HPA troops.

Or maybe they're so scared we'll find something that they'll take drastic action to prevent it.

"What's this, sir?" said Aston, indicating a readout on one of the screens.

"Core override: charging," said Recker. "What the hell?"

A moment later, the text changed.

"Core override: discharge successful."

Recker didn't understand what had happened but realised he should do his best to find out damn soon. The tactical screen provided him with a partial answer.

"That shuttle's gone into freefall," he said.

Sure enough, the smallest dot on the tactical was plummeting towards the ground.

ANTHONY JAMES

"Got a sensor lock," said Burner.

The feed was near perfect and on it, Recker watched the boxy Daklan shuttle fall. It plummeted out of the viewing arc of the locked sensor, only for a different array to take over in time for him to see the enemy ship crunch into the ground. The Daklan built everything to last and the shuttle's armour plating buckled only slightly.

Recker waited to see what would happen, both with the transport and – more importantly – the battleship.

"The shuttle isn't moving," said Burner. "And these sensors can read propulsion output. That ship is stone, cold dead."

"The cylinder's got automated defences," said Aston. "I wonder if the crew on the annihilator know about them."

"If they didn't before, they do now," said Recker. He watched and waited – the danger hadn't passed yet. After another few seconds, he let out his pent-up breath. "They're holding fire," he said. "This cylinder is too valuable to them and now they've got that core override to worry about."

"Why the hell didn't the converter on Etrol do the same to the *Finality*?" asked Eastwood. "We hit it with plenty of missiles."

"I don't know, Lieutenant. It's looking increasingly likely there was a malfunction on that one."

"Good thing for us."

"I've discovered how to link these alien comms with the units in our suits," said Burner a moment later. "I'll take over communications with Sergeant Vance."

"Thank you, Lieutenant. I'd appreciate that." Recker

250

looked towards the doorway – the squad should be arriving soon, though he couldn't blame them for being cautious after the Daklan missile.

Burner soon confirmed the same. "Sergeant Vance held the withdrawal until he was sure the explosives had stopped. He's bringing the squad up here now and reports that the Daklan aren't pissing about - those from the first shuttle are pushing to the level below us."

"Any idea of the numbers?"

"Shitloads."

It was a nontechnical term that conveyed the situation almost as well as a precise figure. The Daklan were coming and the scent of blood would only make them press harder. Recker lowered his gaze to the console once more.

The tenixite converter promised many things, yet so far, the only demonstration had been in the form of the core override discharge. It left Recker feeling like he was holding a treasure map that might well lead to unimagined wealth or may be nothing other than a lie to tempt the desperate.

Recker wasn't sure what made him look up from his screen. On the curved outer wall, a door opened, fifty metres offset left to where he was standing. The conscious, thinking part of his brain was partway through forming the conclusion that Sergeant Vance or one of the soldiers had discovered a new way to this level.

The unconscious part of his brain – the part that operated on an instinct fine-tuned by his years in the military – already had him reaching for the gauss rifle propped upright against the front face of the console.

Recker pulled the gun's stock into his shoulder, just as the figure of a Daklan soldier appeared in the doorway. The aliens were hulking bastards and the wide shoulders of this one's grey combat suit, combined with the angular chest plate, exaggerated the effect, making it seem like a giant carrying a five-foot thick-barrelled gauss cannon.

It didn't matter that the Daklan were big, strong and mean - bullets killed them fine. Recker pulled the trigger on his rifle once, twice, three times. Daklan combat armour wasn't proof against the HPA's gauss rifles and each shot produced an expanding patch of vivid red. The alien fell back through the doorway, where movement indicated the presence of others.

"Get down!" Recker snapped at his crew. He got onto the squad channel. "Sergeant Vance, we've been flanked – numbers unknown. I need immediate backup."

As he spoke, Recker watched and waited to see if the Daklan would reveal enough for him to shoot. None appeared and he fired twice more into the doorway - the enemy were staying out of sight, but he might catch one out with a lucky ricochet.

"Our withdrawal is under pressure here, sir," said Vance. He swore. "We're on our way."

Recker didn't mention that it was impossible to continue working on the consoles while under fire and he was sure that Vance understood the urgency. The situation on the converter was becoming impossible - the Daklan must know they were only facing a small opposing force and that would make them bold.

The aliens were tough opponents and Recker didn't want to present them with an easy target. He crouched far enough that he could see over the top of his console. Unfortunately, this cut down his visual arc, making it possible for the enemy to crawl into the room and take cover behind the secondary consoles. Recker wasn't carrying grenades, but he was sure the Daklan troops would have explosives.

"This isn't a good situation," Aston observed. She was also in a half-crouch and every few seconds she rose in order to watch out for the Daklan coming in low.

"If they get into cover, we're screwed," said Recker.

He straightened in time to see movement. A second Daklan surged through the doorway. The aliens weren't any faster than a human, though their size made them appear superficially clumsy. This Daklan was ready and it snapped off a shot with its hand cannon, the slug cracking against alloy somewhere close by. Recker was just as fast and his aim was better. He tracked the sprinting enemy soldier, pulling the trigger three times. The Daklan crashed out of sight behind a console and Recker heard its rifle skittering across the floor.

"Incoming," said Aston, her own rifle whining as it discharged on automatic.

Another two Daklan sprinted from the doorway immediately after the first, firing as they ran. The enemy met a hail of slugs from the other members of Recker's crew and they were thrown to the ground, blood spraying from their wounds.

A glint in the darkness of the doorway made Recker crouch, just as a fifth Daklan soldier fired. The shots cracked against hard surfaces nearby and others struck the inner wall a short distance behind Recker and his crew.

These slugs were intended to keep the defenders low so that other Daklan could advance to cover, and he knew it was vital to keep the enemy at bay for as long as possible.

Taking a chance that the enemy were firing blind, Recker looked over the top of his console. He heard a scraping he recognized as coming from a gun being pushed across the floor and spotted a shape passing across the gap between two of the outer consoles. Recker shot quickly, before ducking once more, guessing he'd scored a nonfatal hit.

The gunfire from the doorway didn't let up and Recker knew that the enemy were getting a foothold in the room. He stood higher again and was immediately driven into a crouch by the bullets clattering off the far edge of his console. Recker answered by firing his own rifle blind at the doorway.

Nearby, Aston crouched, her expression determined and without fear. Eastwood and Burner were left and right respectively, each staying low and partially hidden from Recker's sight by the curve of their consoles.

"How far can a Daklan throw a grenade?" Aston asked with a grim smile.

It was a question Recker had already asked himself. "They could side-arm one from that doorway easily enough."

He looked over the top of his console again. The enemy weren't visible, but he fired a volley of shots into the opening.

"Will they risk explosives, sir? Or will they be worried about destroying the hardware?"

"They'll use stun grenades if they've been ordered to keep this place intact."

Recker stood higher, just as a Daklan rose from behind a console near the doorway. The alien soldier had its arm drawn back like it was about to throw and he shot it three times in the chest, killing it and making it fall out of sight.

A moment later, the stun grenade it had been holding detonated with a flash and a thunderous crack of expanding air. Recker was ready for it and he averted his eyes, while the coating on his visor darkened automatically. The sound was loud, but he was far enough away that it didn't even set his ears ringing.

The moment the light faded, he was up again, firing into the doorway, hoping the flash of their own stun grenade had caught the enemy soldiers unawares. He dropped low again and checked the readout on his gun.

"Reloading," he said.

A magnetic field held the rifle's square magazine in place. When Recker flicked a tiny switch - which was an easy thumb reach from the trigger point - the magnetic field was cancelled, allowing him to slide out the almost empty magazine. He let it drop to the floor and slotted in a full one he took from his leg pocket.

The magazine change only took five seconds, but during that time, the incoming enemy fire became far more intense and Recker guessed the Daklan had run out of patience. A second grenade went off on the far side of the console and this time the burst of light left afterimages on his retinas, while the sound produced a pain in his ears. Luckily, his suit helmet was designed to limit the debilitating effects of flash grenades and Recker experienced no deafness and his balance felt fine.

"Sergeant Vance, what's your progress?" he asked. "We're pinned down with no easy way to get out of the firing line."

"Nearly with you, sir."

Recker crawled sideways to the edge of his console and looked along the aisle. The arrangement of the consoles interfered with his line of sight, preventing him from seeing all the way to the door. A grey shape darted between two consoles and Recker's shot came too late. He spotted a second Daklan and this time he got a bullet into its leg.

Anticipating another grenade, Recker half-stood. He and his crew were within throwing range, but the Daklan would have to be standing to make the distance. Recker's timing was good and he shot an enemy soldier as it was rising from a crouch. The alien was much closer than he was expecting – within twenty metres – and Recker knew that time was running out.

As he lowered himself into a crouch again, he spotted other grey shapes moving swiftly from the doorway and coming in his direction. Once again, Recker lifted his rifle and sprayed bullets in the enemy's general direction. Two more stun grenades went off, one of them right on top of the adjacent console.

"Argh, shit," said Burner, dropping his weapon and pressing his hands to the sides of his helmet.

"Get up, Lieutenant!" yelled Recker, trying to ignore the pain in his own ears. He fired another dozen slugs into the room, knowing it was no use. The Daklan were ruth-less and they didn't like a stalemate.

Sergeant Vance and the rest of the squad arrived through the far doorway and Recker heard the clink-clink-clink discharge of Private Gantry's MG-12 repeater, the sound muffled by the temporary damage to his eardrums.

Recker wasn't a man to keep his head down while others did the dirty work. When he judged the moment was right, he put his head over the top edge of his console. Vance and his soldiers were to the right, advancing along the aisles.

"Grenade out!" yelled Drawl.

The man was scrawny as hell, but he had a tremendous throw and he arced a grenade about sixty metres across the room. Drawl wasn't throwing the nonlethal stuff and his plasma grenade detonated in the aisle between two consoles, producing a white-hot blast and a thumping expansion of air. Drawl sent over a second grenade and then a third.

Two more stun grenades went off, closer this time to Vance and his squad so that Recker avoided the worst of the effects. Several Daklan charged through the doorway to his left, trying to tip the balance back their way. The position of Recker and his crew meant that the aliens were under fire from two directions and they went down before they'd made it more than half a dozen paces.

The gunfire continued for another minute or two and then it died off. Sergeant Vance ordered the squad to guard their initial entry point and he ordered Private Enfield to do what he could to seal off the other doors into this level. The soldier had charges in his pack that could weld metal shut as well as blow it open and he got on with the job.

"We're holding back the tide, sir," said Vance.

"I know it, Sergeant. Give us the cover we need, and we'll activate whatever weapon this damn cylinder contains."

While Vance strode across the room, waving his arms and shouting at his squad, Recker hurried to where Commander Aston was checking on Lieutenant Burner.

"Do you need Corporal Hendrix to check you out?" asked Recker loudly.

Burner groaned and uttered a few oaths. "I can't hear out of my left ear," he said, tapping that side of his helmet. "But nothing that's going to going to stop me, sir."

"On your feet and let's get something out of this situation," Recker said, hauling the other man upright.

Burner's balance was off, and he stumbled before grabbing the edge of his console. "I'm good," he promised, once he'd got himself steady.

Watching carefully, Recker released his hold and the other man stayed on his feet. Without delaying further, he returned to his own console and got on with the job.

CHAPTER TWENTY-FOUR

THE NEXT FEW minutes were frustrating. Recker felt like he was becoming familiar with the alien hardware, yet the most important command functions eluded him.

"What am I missing?" he snarled angrily. "I've accessed the weapons panel, but most of the options are greyed out, like it's waiting for data."

"We're attempting to learn a comprehensive command and control suite in fifteen minutes while under pressure, sir," said Eastwood.

Recker leaned on his knuckles, hoping for some inspiration. Over by the second entrance, Private Enfield activated one of his charges to seal the door and slow any further Daklan attempts to attack from that direction. The charge burned with a harsh light which made Recker think of a bulb illuminating in his head.

"Something I saw earlier..." he started, checking through a couple of the menus which had initially seemed unimportant. Recker found what he was looking for. "Surface scan: idle," he read from his screen.

"We're standing in a tenixite converter," said Aston. "Maybe it scans for ternium ore."

"Tenixite is a damned big source of potential energy," said Recker. He could have kicked himself, having earlier thought about how the converter might have created those cylindrical holes on the surrounding surface.

"I know how to start the scan, sir," said Burner. "I'll do that now."

A moment later, a green progress bar labelled *Scan Progress* appeared on one of Recker's screens and began its advance towards 100%. Meanwhile to the right, the sound of MG-12 discharge drew Recker's attention to where the fighting had resumed.

"Sergeant Vance what's happening over there?"

"Daklan, sir. Coming up the stairwell."

A grenade exploded in the doorway and Recker wasn't sure which side had thrown it. Private Enfield sprinted that direction, fishing in his pack for one of his charges.

"Still scanning," said Burner.

The progress bar raced along until it was almost at the end, where it stopped for long seconds, flashing slowly and infuriatingly.

"Dammit," Recker swore. "Does every single damn computer operation in the entire damn universe stall at 99%, just to piss me off?"

The temptation to punch the hardware increased. At last, the bar moved an extra fraction and new text appeared beneath.

Scan complete.

Hoping he was on the right track, Recker navigated through the menu system. One of the greyed-out options was now available and he accessed it.

Conversion ready. Target?

"Hell, yes," he said.

The software linked in with the tactical screen and there he found, exactly where it had always been, the red circle of the annihilator. With a fingertip, he selected it as a target. Immediately, a red semicircle appeared above the green dot representing the tenixite converter, with the battleship right within the bounds. Text appeared on the screen.

Selected target range within permitted minimum.

"Minimum range for what?" said Eastwood.

"The big one," said Burner. "Whatever that is."

"If the battleship's too close for discharge, how do we fix that?" said Aston, leaning in closer to have a look.

"I'm not sure," Recker growled in frustration. With his teeth gritted, he chose a different option. "There's got to be a way to limit the effects of the weapon so that it will target the enemy ship."

"Any sign of an override option?" asked Eastwood.

"Do we even want to override?" asked Burner. "Failsafes are there for a reason."

Recker came across another sub-menu where he found the tenixite conversion was already set to minimum. The sliding scale made him wonder exactly what this cylinder was capable of if he turned the dial all the way up to ten.

"We're on the lowest level discharge already," he said. "I'll look for that override."

"The radius of this dead zone is two hundred klicks," said Aston. "And we're on the *lowest* level discharge?"

"We're going to fire this damn weapon, whatever the consequences," said Recker.

"I guess we don't have much choice anymore."

The gunfire from the doorway intensified and when Recker listened in to the open channel, he could tell that squad's control over the stairwell was fraying. Suddenly, the soldiers fell back, sprinting from the outer row of consoles and throwing themselves into the cover offered by the inner row. A huge explosion went off, far bigger than any grenade and Recker thought he could feel the blast through the soles of his boots.

In the aftermath, a temporary lull came and Recker stopped looking at the doorway. He was sure the tenixite converter was designed to tap into the ore on the planet's surface and make it do something unpleasant. Unfortunately, the annihilator was within the cylinder's dead zone and the Daklan had no reason to take their spaceship elsewhere. Recker's hands were tied and the enemy had far more soldiers at their command than he did.

"We've got another shuttle coming from the battleship," said Burner. "They must be running out of bodies down here and need to send some fresh ones for us to shoot."

"We can't handle another transport full of their soldiers," said Recker. In truth, he didn't know if they could deal with the number already inside the cylinder, though he suspected that Vance and the squad had made significant inroads into the ranks of the alien scumbags.

"The sensors are detecting another incoming spaceship," said Burner suddenly. "It's pushing a big ternium wave ahead of it."

It seemed to Recker that every time his plate was halfway clean, the cosmos served up another ladleful of ordure for him to spoon his way through. "What've we got this time?"

"The sensor databanks don't have a record of this vessel type, sir."

"Get a visual on it as soon as you can."

"A Daklan heavy lifter!" Burner exclaimed. "Altitude: two hundred thousand klicks."

The huge vessel appeared, with its boxy midsection and flat nose that had always reminded Recker of a sperm whale. It was unmistakably Daklan and could only be here for a single purpose.

"I guess they don't need to kill us before they begin the recovery operation," said Eastwood sourly.

"It's descending," said Burner. "Heading our way."

The moment he saw the enemy lifter accelerate towards the cylinder, Recker knew what he was going to do. He deselected the annihilator as the target and touched his finger on the new arrival. A red ring appeared around the lifter, moving with the spaceship. At the same time, the tactical screen updated and Recker's heart jumped.

Depletion burst available. Discharge?

"Depletion burst," said Aston, rolling the words across her tongue like she didn't quite care for them. "I wonder what it does."

"We're going to find out, Commander. The question is, can we catch two fish in the net?"

The lifter didn't seem like it was in a rush. Presumably, the crew onboard had been advised by the annihilator that everything was in hand. On it came, inevitable yet unhurried, while Recker scraped his teeth together in frustration.

At the doorway, Sergeant Vance and the squad were finding it progressively tougher to hold the Daklan. A shriek of propellant caused Recker to glance over in time to see the rocket from a shoulder launcher detonate in a massive burst against the ceiling about thirty metres from the door. Figures on the periphery of the blast scrambled away, patches of corrosive plasma chewing at the protective polymers of their combat suits.

The blast rumbled across the floorspace and Recker spotted a pale blue shape arcing in the other direction – towards the doorway. Enfield set off his pack charge remotely and a second thunderous explosion lit up that area of the room. The MG-12 fell quiet, since Gantry was too experienced a soldier to fire into the fading blast, and Recker noticed the absence of the weapon's comforting sound more than anything else.

"Hold steady, Sergeant Vance," said Recker. "If I'm right, we're about to unleash hell."

"We won't bend before we break, sir."

The light from the blast faded again and the MG-12 started up once more, joining in with the other weaponry. Another grenade went off and then two more.

"Lifter at fifty thousand klicks," said Burner.

"It's not the lifter I'm interested in," said Recker. "It's the lower limit of the depletion burst sphere."

With the annihilator only two thousand metres above

the cylinder, the margins were tight and Recker had no idea what would happen to anything on the periphery of the unknown weapon's effect. The battleship was a tough vessel and it seemed likely it would survive on the fringes. Recker knew that if the enemy warship remained operational, the game was up for him and everyone on the cylinder.

"Come on," muttered Aston.

"Lifter at twenty thousand klicks," said Burner.

"It's got a long way to go before the annihilator falls within the depletion burst," said Recker.

A shot cracked against a solid surface nearby and he looked around instinctively, expecting to discover that the Daklan had found a way through one of the other entrances. There was no sign of the enemy nearby, but Recker crouched lower into cover.

"Lifter at ten thousand klicks," said Burner. "What's the range on its gravity chains?"

"A hundred klicks for an object this size," said Recker.

The lifter didn't slow its descent and soon it was within a thousand kilometres. The lower edge of the depletion burst sphere seemed like it was within touching distance of the battleship and Recker prepared to activate the discharge.

Then, at five hundred klicks, the lifter slowed and, at 220, it came to a standstill.

"That's more than a hundred klicks," said Burner. "The sphere is eighteen klicks short."

Recker didn't need it spelling out and he clenched his jaw.

"I thought a hundred klicks as well, sir," said Aston. "What are they waiting for?"

"I don't know, Commander. Maybe they learned something from the cylinder on Etrol and aren't ready to come any closer."

It didn't quite add up and Recker knew he was clutching at straws.

"They're opening their bay doors, sir," said Burner. "They're getting ready for a lift!"

On the sensor feed, Recker saw the lifter's underside doors retract into its double-skinned hull. Elsewhere, the second Daklan transport arrived at the particle beam opening and he watched it manoeuvring into position.

"Running out of time," said Aston. "Even if this depletion burst takes out those spaceships, we're going to be overrun."

"I don't want to die, Commander, but if it's going to happen, I'll happy knowing the Daklan lost a battleship and a primary lifter at the same time."

"The lifter's moving again, sir!" said Burner. "And the annihilator's turning. Must be so close it'll interfere with the gravity chains."

Watching the tactical display with its moving dots and text overlays gave Recker all the information he required. The battleship rotated and rose at a diagonal, on a course that would take it straight across the top of the cylinder. Directly overhead, the heavy lifter dropped lower, and the annihilator was enveloped in the sphere.

Without giving the matter anymore thought, Recker activated the weapon.

CHAPTER TWENTY-FIVE

DEPLETION BURST: activation successful.

The words glowed on the screen, loaded with promise. For a moment, Recker thought that nothing had happened. Then, he noticed a perfectly circular section of the planet's surface – viewed on one of the sensor feeds – crumble into a dust which sank into the newly-created hole.

At the same moment, a blast of pure darkness, lasting for less than a second, blotted out the stars overhead. This sphere of destructive energy didn't expand from a point of origin like a conventional explosive, rather it appeared fully formed and then disappeared like it had never existed.

When the blast cleared, the heavy lifter was gone, both from the sensors and the tactical. The annihilator, however, wasn't gone and Recker stared in horror at what had become of it.

The depletion burst had stripped the warship of every

single protective armour plate, as well as several billion tons of what lay underneath. What remained was a ragged, uneven shape which bore no resemblance to the proud construction of savage beauty which had once risen from a Daklan shipyard.

Large pieces broke off from the ruined hull and tumbled towards the ground, while a huge cloud of smaller flakes made the battleship seem like it was surrounded by a miasma of disease.

"It's coming down," said Burner.

Recker's eyes darted towards the tactical. The predicted trajectory overlay told him the unwanted story.

"Right on top of us." He smashed his fist on the console. "Why is it never easy?"

"It's going to miss the top section," said Burner. "Not by much."

Recker wasn't so sure. Though the annihilator was no longer accelerating for orbit, some of its propulsion modules were still firing underneath the corrosion and the warship began rotating at the same time as it fell. All Recker could do was grit his teeth. Even in its death throes, it seemed like this battleship wasn't finished with him.

"Is there anything we can do?" said Aston.

Slowly, Recker shook his head. "For once, we'll have to let this one play out."

The tactical updated constantly as the converter's sensors tracked the battleship's change in orientation. Debris continued to scatter everywhere, as though the disintegration was ongoing and Recker noted how the warship's entire nose section was attached precariously to the rest of the spaceship.

"It's breaking up," he said. Recker accessed the squad channel. "Sergeant Vance, good news is, the enemy battleship is destroyed."

Vance was quick on the uptake. "And the bad?"

"What's left is coming down straight on top of us."

"I'll tell the squad to keep their helmets on."

"Impact in approximately thirty seconds. Hold the enemy at bay and good luck to us all, Sergeant."

"Amen to that, sir."

The annihilator's nose section – about five or six billion tons' worth - broke away, while the rest of the warship's structure remained intact. To Recker's eye, the disintegration had slowed and the trailing cloud of alloy particles was no longer so dense as it was.

"That's going to make a hell of a splash," said Burner.

With ten seconds until impact, it became clear that the annihilator was going to miss the uppermost section of the tenixite converter. If the life support units didn't fail, there was a chance Recker and everyone inside the cylinder might survive.

"Now," said Eastwood.

The nose section crunched into the centre of the cylinder, while the rear section of the annihilator clipped the lowest part where the converter had sheared from its base. One of the external sensors had a partial view of the impact and Recker watched as the cylinder simply crumpled beneath the impact.

"Best hold on," he said.

The shockwave flowed through the walls, the floor and

everything else, producing a bone-deep rumbling that made Recker think of a thousand lifter shuttles taking off at once. The shaking was so violent it seemed like the floor had become a liquid with a surface of fast-rolling waves. Recker found himself on the floor, though he wasn't sure how he got there, with his head ringing like a hammer-struck bell.

For long moments, the rumbling and the shaking continued and Recker became faintly aware of voices on the comms, though he couldn't make out if they spoke words or simply made sounds. With an effort, he rolled over and saw Aston nearby with her face twisted in a grimace of pain.

He kicked his legs, instinctively trying to get to his feet again, though he was sure he would fall again at once if he were to succeed. Somehow, he got a foot beneath him and pushed, using his hands to keep himself steady.

And then, the shockwave faded rapidly until Recker could feel it no longer. He looked about the room, expecting everything to be broken and smashed. Instead, it was as if nothing had happened – the consoles and screens were exactly where they'd been before the battleship crashed down.

"Sergeant Vance?" he said. Recker's first attempt was croaky and he wasn't sure if it was loud enough to be heard. He tried again and his voice came out stronger. "Sergeant Vance, I need a status update."

The walls of the cylinder groaned in distress and a booming noise drowned out Vance's response. He repeated it, louder this time.

"We got knocked about, sir. I don't think the Daklan came out of it any better."

The gunfire started again, though it lacked the ferocity of earlier, like this small-scale battle was no longer so important. Even as Recker was checking over the other members of his crew, the rifle discharge reduced from constant to sporadic.

With relief, Recker found that his crew had suffered only minor injuries. Their combat suits were built to take a beating and nobody would suffer more than bruises, though Burner's hearing still hadn't recovered from the earlier stun grenade burst and Eastwood had somehow managed to catch his balls on the edge of a console when he was thrown from his feet.

"What's the plan, sir?" asked Eastwood, leaning against one of the consoles and taking deep breaths to try and counter the pain.

Recker didn't answer the question at once. Instead, he got on the comms to Vance again. "Did you kill the enemy, Sergeant?"

"They're mostly dead, sir," Vance confirmed. "The Daklan don't give up easily, so there may be others nearby, thinking up ways to catch us by surprise."

"Casualties?"

"A few damaged suits and not much else. I call this a lucky result."

"I don't think luck played a part. We're getting out of here, Sergeant."

"I'm sure the squad will be glad to hear it, sir. Exactly how are we planning to do that?"

"The Daklan destroyed our incision craft and stole our dock. It seems only right that we steal their shuttle."

"If they left it unguarded."

"Failing that, there's another shuttle docked next to it. If it's capable of flight, I'll get it up into the air. Watch the doorway and wait for my word."

"Yes, sir."

Recker gave his attention to the members of his crew. "Before we depart, I want every single piece of useful data we can extract from this cylinder."

"I think we've got most of it already, sir," said Burner. "I've got the transmission vector for the two linked tenixite converters – assuming the failed link was to Etrol, that gives us a shot at locating the second."

"You want to shut this cylinder down," said Aston.

"If I can. Seems to me like the Daklan were too interested in this one for me to think they got everything they needed from the converter on Etrol."

"They haven't had time to study that one, sir."

"I know, Commander. My reasoning may be flawed. Still, the Daklan have a far greater chance of recovering this cylinder than we do. I'd like to deny them any advantage."

In the end, the task wasn't so easy and the tenixite converter's software and databanks couldn't be deleted or disabled from this control level. Recker knew enough about how these things worked that he was sure the command could be given from elsewhere on the cylinder – maybe on the levels above this one.

During the few minutes he allowed himself for the task, the shuttle outside the particle beam opening accelerated hard away across the planet's surface. Recker assumed the Daklan onboard had seen enough and didn't want to suffer the same fate as the annihilator and the heavy lifter.

With reluctance, he admitted defeat in his efforts to delete the contents of the cylinder's databanks. Having pulled through so many near-misses, his crew and the squad deserved this chance at life, where previously there had been none. Risks could often win wars, but Recker admitted that as far as this mission went, he'd taken enough, and it was time to move on.

"Sergeant Vance, we're ready to leave. Any sign of Daklan on those stairs?"

"No, sir. I sent Gantry down for a look and all he found was bodies."

"We're on our way."

Recker led the way towards the far doorway and had to stop when Burner stumbled to the ground.

"Looks like something screwed with my balance, sir."

Leaning forward, Recker offered a hand and hauled Burner to his feet. "Lieutenant Eastwood, help me out," he said.

Between the two of them, Recker and Eastwood kept Burner upright and they made it to where Sergeant Vance was waiting. The squad members were still hunkered down behind the nearby consoles and most of their combat suits were turned brown as a result of the polymers being exposed to the heat of nearby explosions.

With a wave of his hand and a single barked order, Vance brought the soldiers out of cover and they gathered at the top of the stairs. They were still wary, reminding

Recker that the Daklan might still have a presence on the cylinder.

"Corporal Hendrix, this man keeps falling over," said Recker. "Have you got anything for him?"

Hendrix fished in her side pack and came out with a familiar booster injector.

"Sorry, Lieutenant. This needs to go in the place where it'll act the quickest."

"What?" asked Burner uncertainly.

Without ceremony, Hendrix stepped closer and jabbed the needle through the flexible combat suit and into Burner's neck. The injector hissed as it forced its contents into his body, though the sound of it was mostly hidden by the stream of expletives pouring from his mouth.

"Damn that hurt."

"You get used to it, Lieutenant," said Recker, patting him on the shoulder.

In about thirty seconds, you're going to feel like you can punch a Daklan body builder clean through a two-metre plate of warship armour, Lieutenant," said Hendrix, giving Burner the new recruit lecture.

"Yeah, don't go running off ahead," said Aston, grinning.

Burner rolled his shoulders. "You're talking like this is my first time."

Recker was impatient to be off and he gave Sergeant Vance the nod. A couple of soldiers scouted the staircase again. Raimi came back to declare the room below clear of hostiles.

"Montero's watching from the bottom in case anymore of the enemy show," he said.

The squad descended in stages. Having survived this long, Vance was unwilling to see the soldiers wiped out by a surprise shoulder launcher attack - the blast from which might be enough to kill anything caught in the stairwell.

Recker and Aston were best equipped to fly one of the two shuttles, so they stayed close to the back in order to avoid a potential instant kill surprise attack from the Daklan. Everything in the stairwell was a mess of char, melted alloy and carbonised body parts. The intense heat should have burned away the worst of the stench, yet somehow it lingered, bitter and acrid, redolent of once-living creatures.

As he stepped into the lower room, Recker felt enormous relief to be out of the stairwell's confines. He'd seen death before, but the moment it stopped affecting him was the moment he'd have drifted too far from his humanity.

The carnage continued in the lower quadrant room and Recker guessed that fifteen or twenty Daklan had perished, though many of the bodies were fused together making it difficult to obtain an accurate headcount. Recker didn't even try.

Meanwhile, Private Enfield reminded everyone of his heroic charge during a lull in the fighting, in which he'd dropped one of his larger explosives before escaping back upstairs in order to detonate it remotely.

"Must've taken out all these poor bastards in one big boom," he said, nudging a corpse unsympathetically with his foot.

The mood of the other soldiers was grim, despite their

victory, and they didn't say much. This battle had been won by everyone, not just the man who happened to be carrying the explosives.

Sergeant Vance took himself off, along with Corporal Givens, to scout the shaft leading the deployment craft's original docking place. He returned shortly and Recker could read the outcome in the other man's face.

"No Daklan, no shuttle," he announced. "They must have had enough when their battleship came down and they decided to fly elsewhere."

"Same as the those on the other shuttle which left," said Recker. "Sergeant, take us to door for the second shaft."

The access door wasn't in this quadrant and the squad gathered at the entrance to the adjacent area. Sergeant Vance remained cautious and sent in three of the squad to search for Daklan.

As he waited in the first room, Recker couldn't help but stare at the particle beam hole in the wall and the extensive damage to the surrounding hardware caused by the missile from the Daklan shuttle. The opening itself was a stark reminder that the species which attacked this cylinder had plenty of firepower at their disposal, and if the original attack had indeed occurred eighty years ago, they'd had time to make their weapons bigger and better.

"See the flex in the walls?" said Aston, tracing an imaginary line with her finger.

Recker had missed it until it was pointed out to him. With his attention drawn to the area, he could see how the ceiling was fractionally lower at one side and the walls were slightly bowed.

"We're clear in here, sir," said Private Steigers. "Zero Daklan."

The squad hurried through and Sergeant Vance strode for the door leading to the second shuttle access shaft. Once again, he took it steady and the soldiers aimed their guns towards the entrance from positions of cover. Recker watched approvingly – he'd seen plenty of soldiers lose their lives because they let down their guard when they thought the fighting was done.

Once Drawl and Montero had scouted ahead, Vance declared it was time to move. The squad entered the shaft and started the descent. When it was his turn, Recker noted how the docking clamps had been damaged, resulting in a half-metre gap between the shuttle and the shaft.

The gap presented only a minor challenge and soon Recker was inside the alien vessel, along with everyone else except for Private Rick Joiner who'd been killed by the Daklan missile.

Getting so far was a victory itself, but Recker wasn't ready to settle. Now they had to escape from the cylinder and that job fell to him.

CHAPTER TWENTY-SIX

THE INTERIOR of the shuttle had been in a vacuum until the last man closed the upper hatch. Now, it was slowly filling with breathable air, though the process would take several minutes to complete.

Aside from that, it was cold, cramped and lit by a single glowing orb embedded in the ceiling. Recker guessed this shuttle had never been intended to carry significant numbers of passengers, a view reinforced by the lack of seats. The sound of the propulsion carried through the solid floor, given a muffled edge by the thin atmosphere.

This small bay at the bottom of the entrance shaft had a ceiling only just high enough for an average human to stand upright and with space to accommodate twenty in total at a push. A monitoring panel was bolted to the left-hand wall and, aside from the light orb, was the only visible sign of technology.

Recker knew where he was going – a short, narrow

passage led directly towards a sealed door. He activated the security panel, hoping the atmosphere was stable enough that the fail-safes wouldn't trigger. The door opened with a swish and he stepped into the cockpit, with Aston, Burner and Eastwood crowding behind.

"Two seats," he observed, taking the closest.

"Looks basic," said Aston. She dropped into the second seat and cast her gaze over the panel which ran full width across the front of the cockpit. Behind, Eastwood and Burner shuffled along the rear bulkhead, so they were nearby in case they were needed. The cockpit was cramped for two and four occupants made it far worse.

"Basic or not, everything's online," said Recker, calling up the software. "That's the important part."

Recker had learned much from the more sophisticated consoles on the levels above and he was already confident he could fly this shuttle. Manual control was handled by a pair of stubby control sticks, with a backup pair in front of the second seat.

"Activating sensors," he said. "Let's see what damage that battleship caused." Recker's voice was calm, but this was the moment of truth. The annihilator might have crushed the cylinder so badly that the exit holes were squashed closed or made too small for the shuttle to fly through.

Recker fleetingly thought that if the exits were blocked that meant the Daklan transport was also trapped in the cylinder. The enemy shuttles were fitted with weapons and Recker was sure the one he was piloting had none. An engagement would be one-sided and short-lived.

The sensor feeds appeared on a two-by-three arrangement of screens which lit up on the sloped forward bulk-head. Recker stared, trying to comprehend the magnitude of the destruction.

"Messy," said Aston.

Where before, the cylinder's interior had been damaged, it had still been possible to see how it was originally constructed. Now, the immense space was changed beyond recognition. The upper curve of the shell had been pushed in by the impact of the battleship, so that it formed a slanted wall beginning a few hundred metres from where the shuttle was docked.

In the intervening area, snapped and bent spokes were crushed and flattened, twisted together or jutting at different angles. The main pillar – or what part of it was in the visual arc of the sensors - was broken into jagged pieces that were scattered everywhere. When he looked at the debris, Recker wasn't sure if the pillar had even been made from metal, since the way it had broken made him think of an enormous piece of stone shattered by a heavy blow.

A dark grey lump of immeasurable weight lay in the centre of it all, pieces of wreckage protruding from beneath the half-disintegrated ternium of the Daklan battleship's propulsion system. The irregular block threw out enough particles to kill a health and safety officer at a million klicks.

"No sign of a way out," he said. "And no sign of that Daklan shuttle."

"I can disengage the clamps," said Aston.

"Do it."

The gravity clamps were damaged and Recker

prepared himself for a hardware failure. Instead, a green light appeared and the shuttle dropped free of its docking place. The autopilot kicked in, but Recker cancelled it at once and fed in enough power to keep the vessel stationary in the air.

Rotating the shuttle slowly allowed a better view of the crushed interior and Recker watched carefully for a place he might use as an exit. For a time, he found nothing and began to think the Daklan had escaped just before the battleship crashed.

"There," said Aston. "Beneath that overhang on the left."

"Let's take a look," said Recker.

The alien shuttle was easy to fly, and he piloted it towards the place Aston had indicated. With so many jutting pieces of debris, he was required to take great care. His patience was wearing thin and the slow approach was frustrating.

"A way out," said Aston. "Looks tight."

"I reckon this shuttle is little more than engines and plating, Commander," he said, sizing up the opening. It looked like one of the original missile breaches had been crushed into a longer, narrower shape than before. "If necessary, we'll use it as a battering ram and smash our way through."

Like Aston said, it was tight, but Recker got the shuttle through without striking the sides or having to resort to more drastic means. The cylinder's armour was thick, and it required some careful positioning before the spaceship finally emerged on the far side – out into the thin air of Oldis.

"Watch for that Daklan shuttle," he said, unwilling to drop his guard for a moment.

"No sign of anything nearby, sir. Our arrays aren't the best."

"Do what you can."

Recker didn't hang about and he tapped into the shuttle's propulsion, uncertain what it was capable of. A few gauges and electronic needles jumped, and the vessel accelerated vertically at a more impressive rate than he'd expected.

"I don't know about everyone else, but I've had enough of Oldis," he said with feeling.

"I've seen a few crap-holes, and this is another one on the list," said Eastwood.

The shuttle climbed higher, revealing more of the destruction below. Pieces of the annihilator were strewn across a huge area and where the two largest sections had crashed down, countless fissures snaked away across the rock, many of them in excess of a hundred metres wide.

The cylinder itself was likely damaged beyond repair – certainly beyond the expertise of the HPA, though it might yet contain some recoverable tech. Recker felt sure that a salvage operation wasn't going to happen. The Daklan would be here in days, while the HPA military high command timidly scoured through deep space data looking for a dead cert win that was never going to materialise. Not against the Daklan.

"Where's the hole our depletion burst made?" asked Burner once the shuttle had gained enough altitude for the sensors to detect the pocked area of the surface.

It didn't matter and Recker wasn't interested in

finding out. Nor were the others, judging by the lack of response to Burner's question.

"Exiting the upper atmosphere," said Aston. She offered her middle finger to the sensor feed and grinned like the gesture gave her enormous satisfaction.

"Let's find out how fast this shuttle will go," said Recker, pushing the engines to maximum.

While the propulsion grumbled, Aston came out with the question he'd been waiting for.

"I take you're not planning to park us in empty space and wait for Admiral Telar to send a rescue party?"

"We're going to Tanril."

"The crashed ship?" said Eastwood.

"You have a better plan, Lieutenant?"

"No, sir."

"Tanril is 120 million klicks," Burner observed. "Maybe a little more."

Recker glanced at the velocity gauge. The language module attempted to work out how fast the shuttle was travelling and failed. Using the sensors, Recker located Tanril – a tiny speck from this range - and obtained an estimate of the distance, which, combined with the rate at which that distance was falling, allowed him to come up with an approximate time to arrival.

"Six-and-a-half days," he said. "Give or take."

"I guess I should be thankful this shuttle is faster than it looks," Burner muttered.

"Better get used to standing," said Aston with another grin. "You've got a lot of it coming up."

"Along with suit energy shots," said Eastwood.

A combat suit could keep its occupant alive for several

weeks, even in complete isolation. It wasn't much of an existence, but it was better than dying.

Recker gave Vance the bad news and was impressed when the other man accepted it without complaint. A few of the soldiers weren't so restrained and their language was colourful.

The journey was more physically demanding than most Recker could remember from his long career. Exploration of the hardware revealed no surprises and the vessel wasn't equipped with an FTL comms unit. Recker found nothing to counter his first impression that this spaceship's single intended purpose was lugging around huge weights during the initial construction of the tenixite converter.

It was hard to sleep in the two flat-backed seats, while the floorspace was hard and impossible to get comfortable on. Recker held off the booster drugs as long as he could, but by the end of day four he was so tired that he gave himself a shot. It felt like an admission of weakness, though it was preferable to the alternative of making an error that resulted in everyone onboard being killed.

"What do you think will happen at Tanril, sir?" said Aston.

"We'll find that crashed spaceship." Recker shrugged.

"And fly it back home."

"It's something the Daklan don't know about, Commander. We've got a chance to salvage useful tech."

"Hey, I'm still happy to be alive," said Burner. "Anything on top of that is going to be a bonus."

The elation of escape had long since faded and now all that Recker could think about was what lay ahead on

Tanril. He knew he shouldn't make his life so hard, but it was impossible for him to stop pushing.

The final two days dragged more than he could have thought possible and he felt the creeping tiredness that the drugs failed to mask. Subsequent uses of the booster drugs became less effective - they could keep a soldier awake for a couple of weeks if necessary, though at the cost of debilitating exhaustion once they were stopped.

Tanril itself was nothing remarkable - a cold sphere orbiting a sun. Aston and Burner did what they could to extract some extra performance out of the shuttle's sensors. Unfortunately, the tech wasn't playing ball and they weren't able to gather anything better than scant details. Burner had downloaded the coordinates of the crashed spaceship from the tenixite converter's databanks, so although the destination was known, it would have been useful to see what they were approaching.

At last, the shuttle came within half a million kilometres of Tanril and the sensor feed became useful. Much of the planet was crusted in ice and its atmosphere was both thin and toxic. Other than that, Recker gave the plains of stone, the chasms and the mountain ranges little attention. He accepted the possibility that the Daklan might arrive, so he didn't accept a reduction in vigilance, however, he felt with utmost certainty that a prize awaited – a prize of far-reaching significance and consequence.

"The planet's rotation means our target is currently blindside," said Burner, standing between the two seats and leaning eagerly forwards.

Having slowed the shuttle to a safe approach velocity, Recker guided it along a new trajectory at an altitude of a hundred kilometres, which would circle the planet and eventually take them to the waiting spaceship.

These final few minutes at the end of such a long flight seemed to last forever. Recker tried not to imagine that the culmination of this journey might be no more than a billion tons of scrap, destroyed by the tenixite converter, or a vessel so badly damaged by its impact with the surface that it would offer the HPA nothing worth the effort of recovery.

"It should be coming into view any time now," said Aston.

The first sign was a deep, thirty-kilometre-long furrow, created by a heavy object striking the surface at an oblique.

"The furrow continues beyond this mountain range, sir," said Aston.

The peaks followed a north-south path across Tanril. They were low and unremarkable, and the impacting spaceship had skipped over the entire range without a collision. From there, the furrow resumed and this time it was sixty kilometres in length, followed by another gap and then a third furrow, this one much shallower than the others.

At last, the target came into sight and when Recker saw it, his heart jumped with an excitement like he hadn't experienced for many years.

A spaceship had come to a halt right-side up, allowing Recker a good view of it. At 1200 metres in length, it was nothing remarkable in size. The vessel's overall shape was that of a V, with a squared-off stern and a blunt nose. At its widest point, the sensors estimated the spaceship was 800 metres, narrowing to 400, and Recker guessed its mass at two billion tons or maybe more, depending on the materials of its construction.

It looked every inch a warship, with angled plates of scarred dark grey and surface imperfections that could be nothing other than concealed weapons launchers.

"That's not Daklan," said Burner.

"No shit?"

Aston enhanced the feed and the damage to the spaceship's plating became more apparent. It had been subject to concentrated fire from multiple sources of high-calibre rapid-fire weaponry, of the kind which had no hope of bringing down the warship but left it with the appearance of a veteran of many conflicts. Elsewhere, the plating was darkened in irregular patches as a result of intense heat.

"Sergeant Vance, come and take a look at this," said Recker, figuring that the man deserved to see what his hard work killing Daklan had earned.

"Sir?" asked Vance, appearing in the doorway, his expression a mixture of drug-wired interest and exhaustion.

"There's our prize, Sergeant. *Everyone's* prize. We've earned this."

"An alien warship," said Vance slowly. "Where did it come from?"

"Elsewhere. From a distant sun," said Recker, the words coming out of nowhere. He shivered.

Vance stared for long moments. "Looks like a mean son-of-a-bitch, sir."

"That it does."

"And ancient."

"That too."

"Will it take us home?"

"We're going to find out, Sergeant."

With that, Recker piloted the shuttle towards the crashed vessel.

END

The underside hatches for the spaceship were inaccessible, which forced Recker to land on the upper plating. The larger craft was at an angle and getting the stolen shuttle into a stable place required a few minutes of careful positioning.

Exiting the shuttle was a relief and for a few seconds, Recker stood, stretching out the knots in his muscles while the sub-zero planetary winds buffeted him.

He located the entry hatch and noted that the access panel was unlit, suggesting the warship was offline. A recessed lever moved smoothly when he pulled it outwards and the hatch slid open with hardly a sound.

The interior was cold, cramped and unlit. Recker, his crew and the soldiers hurried through the tight, cold passages, the beams of their flashlights dancing across featureless walls. They encountered no signs of life and the internal defences were all offline.

They arrived at a square door, larger than the others

and at the top of some steps. This - the bridge door - could also be operated mechanically, again by means of a single lever. Feeling many different emotions, Recker hauled on the lever and the door rumbled to one side.

The bridge was V-shaped like the hull, and no more than five metres front to back. Two consoles were fitted to the forward bulkhead, with a row of three others directly behind. Recker paused on the threshold, directing the beam of his helmet light into every corner.

Then, he entered, made his way directly to the front and chose the left-hand console. The curved seat was designed for a species about the same size as a human and, when Recker sat, he found it far more comfortable than the equivalent on the shuttle.

With the other members of his crew gathered around, Recker stared at the console. It was different enough to the hardware on the cylinder for him to believe its history was not the same. The faintest of humming sounds indicated that the console was powered up, though only one of its many screens displayed any data. His language module recognized the words, though with a delay in processing.

Core override. Backup restore complete. Partial failure 242X-1302G.

Retry?

Recker entered a response.

>Ignore. Set online status to 1.

Every console on the bridge suddenly illuminated, and orbs in the ceiling glowed with a cold blue light. Recker watched and waited, giving the hardware time to come online. The bridge was in hush and even the squad comms was quiet.

A new prompt appeared.

Security restore failure. Commence biometric re-scan?

Hardly daring to breathe, Recker typed in his answer.

>Yes.

The process completed without Recker having to touch a fingerprint scanner or take any other action.

Biometric re-scan complete. Primary systems accessible.

Recker typed again.

>Set active status to 1.

The engines fired up immediately, with an abrasive growl that made Recker think of countless wild animals, desperate to be freed from captivity. For ten or fifteen seconds, the sound continued and then settled to a volume which made speech possible.

New text appeared.

Vengeance: Active status 1.

When he saw the warship's name, Recker felt a fleeting giddiness at what it implied – forgotten wars and extinction. It was something for later. He directed his crew to their seats and then turned his attention to the console in front of him.

Thirty minutes later, the alien warship *Vengeance*, climbed away from the surface of Tanril and ten minutes after that, it entered lightspeed, carrying the occupants towards a faraway HPA world.

———

Follow Anthony James on Facebook at
facebook.com/AnthonyJamesAuthor

ALSO BY ANTHONY JAMES

1. Augmented

2. Fleet Vanguard

3. Far Strike

4. Galaxy Bomb

5. Void Blade

6. Monolith

7. Mission: Destructor

———

The Fire and Rust series

1. Iron Dogs

2. Alien Firestorm

3. Havoc Squad

4. Death Skies

5. Refuge 9

6. Nullifier

7. Scum of the Universe

———

The Anomalies series

1. Planet Wreckers

2. Assault Amplified

———

The Savage Stars series

1. War From a Distant Sun